hard to CHOOS

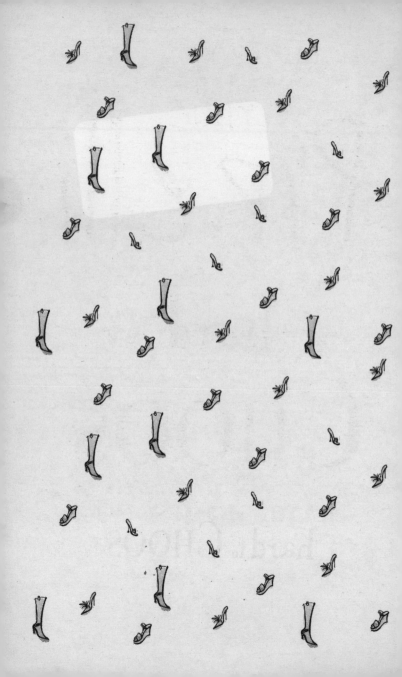

Pixie Pirelli

hard to CHOOS

a KATE THOMPSON *novel*

Pixie Pirelli

Copyright © 2006 Kate Thompson

Hard to Choos
First published 2006
by New Island
2 Brookside
Dundrum Road
Dublin 14

www.newisland.ie

The moral right of the author has been asserted.

ISBN 1 905494 07 6

Permission to use the extract from Anaïs Nin's *Little Birds* was granted by
Barbara W. Stuhlmann, Author's Representative. All rights reserved.

British Library Cataloguing in Publication Data.
A CIP catalogue record for this book is available
from the British Library.

Typeset by New Island
Cover design by New Island
Printed in the UK by Cox & Wyman, Reading, Berks.

10 9 8 7 6 5 4 3 2 1

For Cathy Kelly and Marian Keyes

To find out more about Pixie Pirelli, *Sex, Lies & Fairytales* – a novel by Kate Thompson – is pretty essential reading. Pixie's website is www.pixiepirelli.com

Enjoy!

Pixie

xxx

Acknowledgments

On mature reflection, exactly *who* should I acknowledge? It's very hard to choose ...

Should I thank all those in Princessa Publishing, or all those in New Island? Should I thank Pixie's editor, Deborah Millen? Or do I thank Tana Eilís French? Should thanks go to Pixie's mum and dad, who live in Gloucestershire, or to my family in Dublin? Should I thank Pixie's friends Mariella and Dilys, or my great mates Hilly and Amelia? Should I pay tribute to Lorraine Lavelle or Deirdre Purcell; Rufus or Malcolm; Camilla, or Joe and Tom and Gráinne? It's a Chinese box, but it's been *enormous* fun!

Pixie and I have lots in common, but there is one mutual friendship that stands out. That is the friendship we share with gals called Marian and Cathy, to whom this book is dedicated.

one

Charlotte never quite understood why she entered the competition to win a holiday for two in Paris. She supposed it was just because she knew the answer to the question read out by Patrick Proctor on his morning radio show. She reached out an automatic hand for the phone and gave her personal details to the electronic voice that responded.

'Charlotte Cholewczyk,' she said. 'That's C-H-O-L-E-W-C-Z-Y-K. And the answer to the question is the Moulin Rouge.'

The following Friday, as she was having lunch with two of her best girlfriends, Charlotte's phone rang.

'I'm going to be rude and take this,' she announced, getting up from the table and shimmying towards the door of the café. 'I'm expecting a call from Patrick Proctor.'

She'd said it as a joke, but when she pressed the green key, a voice said, 'It's Felicity Wynne-Jones here, from *The Patrick Proctor Show*. I'm Patrick's PA. Is that Charlotte Cholewczyk?'

The pronunciation of her surname was so mangled she barely recognised it. 'Ho-lev-chick,' she corrected.

'Well, congratulations, Charlotte! You've been selected to take part in our fun "Easter in Paris" quiz!'

'Oh, God.'

'Yes! You lucky person! There were *thousands* of entries, and just three came out of the hat. You must be *thrilled*!'

Charlotte registered the italics and the exclamation marks in Felicity Wynne-Jones's voice, and amended her own reply: 'Oh – *God*!!! How wonderful!'

'The first thing I have to establish,' resumed Felicity in her upbeat voice, 'is whether you are free to go to Paris over the Easter weekend.'

'Um. Ye-es.'

'Good!' Charlotte heard the click of a mouse, and then, 'Springtime in Paris! No better time to go. If you win, you'll be flying out with the lucky travelling companion of your choice on Good Friday. You can check out all the details on our website.'

'Er – what happens next?'

'I phone you on Monday after the nine o'clock news, and you'll go on air to take some questions from Patrick, along with two other contestants.'

Charlotte gulped. 'You mean I'll be asked questions *live* on radio?'

'No worries. Patrick will put you at your ease. He's a consummate pro.'

'Oh, I'm sure I'll have no problems with Patrick. But will the questions be, well, tough?' Charlotte had no intention of setting herself up as a target for public ridicule. Her friend Vivien had once gone on *Who Wants to be a Millionaire?* and pronounced the French place name 'Ypres' as 'Wipers'. After the event, she had been barraged by piss-takers, with puns that ranged from 'windscreen wipers' to 'Why've Saint Laurent'.

There was a reassuring smile in Felicity's voice. 'They'll be a mixed bag, Charlotte. But they'll all be connected with the city of your dreams – Paris! Now, just let me take down some details for Patrick. What's your occupation?'

'I'm a copywriter in an advertising agency.' Charlotte never used the more accurate 'junior copywriter' unless her boss was around.

'Are you married or single?'

'Single.'

'And your age bracket is? You don't have to be specific.'

'I'm in my late twenties.'

'Any children?'

'No.'

'And, going by your land-line number, you live in North London?'

'That is correct.' Sheesh! She'd slipped into quiz-speak mode already!

'Well, I'd say that's enough info for Patrick to go on. I'll talk to you on Monday, Charlotte! Be sure to be on stand-by on your land line from nine o'clock. And you will try to ensure that the line's clear, won't you?'

Nine o'clock? Yikes. That would make her late for work: she usually left her apartment before half past eight. She supposed she could ask Felicity to call her on her mobile number, but she really didn't relish the notion of fielding questions from Patrick Proctor while negotiating the halls of Hades that was the London Underground. 'No worries, Felicity. I'll make sure the line's free. Thanks very much.'

'Enjoy your weekend!'

'You too!'

Charlotte negotiated her way around the café tables back to where Anna and Vivien were poring over the property section of the paper, laughing like drains.

'A *mere* million and a half!' chortled Anna.

'Yeah – and look at this *mother* of a bargain at nine hundred and fifty grand. It boasts a *shower rrroom!*' When Vivien got animated, her Scottish burr became even more pronounced.

'No bath?'

'No bath! Ha ha ha!'

'Pah!' said Anna, sending the paper skidding across the table top. 'When are we ever going to get even our baby pinkies on the property ladder? Life sucks.'

'Yeah,' said Charlotte, resuming her seat opposite them. 'It really does.'

'What's wrong now? Another narky marketing manager on the phone?'

'No. That really *was* Patrick Proctor calling – or, rather, his PA. I'm in the quiz to win Easter in Paris. The woman sounded so delighted when she broke the news to me that I just couldn't say no. I've to go on the radio on Monday morning.'

'Hey! That's brilliant!' said Anna and Vivien in unison. They looked at each other, then turned back to Charlotte.

'Oh. We forgot,' said Anna.

'You hate Paris,' said Vivien.

It was true. The last words that Charlotte had uttered on French soil had been 'I am *never* coming *back* here in my *life*!' She would have loved to raise a fist to the sky, the way Scarlett O'Hara does in the film when she declares that as God is her witness she will *never* be hungry *again*, but she knew that if she'd pulled that stunt she would have provoked yet more circumflex eyebrows and curled lips. Yeuch! How she hated the Parisians! She hated their snooty *vendeuses*, she hated their officious officials, and she especially hated their oh-so-superior waitresses. She had dined in the restaurant at the top of the Pompidou Centre once, and had been waited upon by serving staff who behaved as if they were strutting their stuff down a catwalk, carrying their haute-cuisine tableware like sceptres – or, at the very least, Birkin bags.

'Why don't you just not pick up the phone to Patrick Proctor on Monday?' suggested Vivien.

'Would any woman in her right mind not pick up the phone to Patrick Proctor?' said Anna. 'He is a dude.'

'You have a point there,' conceded Vivien. 'Maybe you should just deliberately get all the questions wrong and allow someone else to win.'

'What? And run the risk of having egg all over my face, like you did when you made your "wipers" gaffe?'

Charlotte and Anna shared a complicit look and sniggered, while Vivien ignored them with *hauteur*. 'Don't worry,' she said. 'Maybe you'll lose by a hair's breadth. Then your self-esteem will still be intact and you won't have to go to Paris.'

Charlotte considered. 'I guess that's the optimum scenario.'

'How insane *are* you?' said Anna. 'I'd *love* to win a trip to Paris. That weekend I spent there with Finn was the most romantic of my life.'

'It rained the entire time I was there,' said Charlotte.

'I cemented my first publishing deal there,' said Vivien, with a nostalgic expression. 'In that *preposterously* chic restaurant at the top of the Pompidou Centre.'

'*Georges?*' squawked Charlotte. 'I *hated* that place! The staff made me feel like the Cookie Monster.'

'Didn't you at least get the chance to see some great art while you were there?' Anna was still wearing her incredulous expression. 'Surely *that* would have made your trip worthwhile.'

'I didn't see a thing,' said Charlotte. 'Most of the museums were on strike. And when I trailed down about seven million boulevards to the only one that was open, the queue was so long that I ran all the way back to the hotel in the rain. Duncan said I reminded him of the geezer in the Munch painting.'

'Why didn't you take the Metro?'

'The trains were on strike too.'

'I bought this bag in Paris,' remarked Vivien, fishing her ringing mobile out of her posh designer bag and checking the display. 'Actually, I stole it. Excuse me while I take this.' She got to her feet and headed for the café door.

'Bloody Vivien and her kleptomania,' said Charlotte, shaking her head. 'She's going to land herself in very deep doo-doo someday.'

'It's not, strictly speaking, kleptomania,' remarked Anna. 'You know she only does it for ethical reasons. And sometimes I think she's right. When you think how much those poor Asian sweatshop kids earn sewing on zips for designer labels! The mark-up's obscene.'

'I did *try* to buy a bag in Paris,' volunteered Charlotte.

'What do you mean, "try"?'

'I was perfectly prepared to part with a stupid amount of euros for it, but when I saw the way the salesgirl was looking at my fake Jimmy Choos, I teetered out of the shop like a geisha on speed.'

'Poor Charlotte! You really *did* have a crap time there, didn't you?'

'Oh, yeah.'

Charlotte tried hard to sound careless, but the fact was that neither Vivien nor Anna knew the real extent of the wretchedness she'd suffered in the French capital. It was there she'd discovered that Duncan – the boyfriend who had whisked her off on a 'romantic' break – had been two-timing her. She had found out when she'd woken early from an afternoon siesta, only to come across him writing a postcard on the terrace of their hotel. Charlotte had sneaked up on him from behind, intending to surprise him with a butterfly kiss on the nape of his neck, but as soon as he'd become aware of her presence, Duncan had turned the postcard over. The picture on the front had been the famous Cartier-Bresson photograph of the couple kissing in front of the Hôtel de Ville. But Duncan hadn't turned the postcard over quickly enough, and Charlotte had plainly seen what he'd written on the back: 'Darling Phoebe. Wish you were here. This will be *us* soon – I promise. Love you.'

'I would *kill* to go to back there,' said Anna now, taking a bite of wholegrain-sprout bread and making a face. 'Think of all those fabulous *pâtisseries*. Imagine sitting at a table in that café where Picasso and his cronies used to hang out – what was it called?'

'The Café de Flore?'

'Yeah. That joint.' Behind her glasses, Anna's swimming-pool-blue eyes went all dreamy, and she started playing with a strand of her hair. 'You could be reading a book over a *café au lait* – *Madame Bovary*, say, or some existentialist stuff by Camus to make you look intellectual – and you could glance up from it occasionally to bestow your mysterious gaze upon the dark-haired, black-eyed dude opposite who's going to offer to buy you a pastis—'

'You've been reading too much chick lit, Anna.'

'But seriously, Charlotte. Don't you think you should give it a second chance?'

'*Never*! Now, if it had been a trip to Rome, I would have jumped at it. I'd be spending the weekend swotting on the internet. I *love* that city.'

'Who did you go to Rome with? Duncan?'

'No. I went with Alex, that time he went to interview the bloke who directed *Life is Beautiful*.'

'Alex speaks Italian, doesn't he?'

'Yep.'

'Wow! The sexiest language in the world,' said Anna.

'And Alex is fluent. He could even wise-crack with the waiters.'

Alex was a mutual friend who worked for a prestigious broadsheet. He had risen through the ranks to become a highly respected journo, which Charlotte found hard to take seriously, since she'd known Alex from way back, when he'd sported scabs on his knees from climbing trees and playing footie with her. The five of them – Charlotte, Vivien, Alex, Anna and her boyfriend Finn – all hung out together, and liked to think that they got on nearly as well as the friends in the sadly deceased television series. There had even been six of them, until Duncan had done the dirty on Charlotte and had been summarily ejected from the cosy coterie. Vivien worked in publishing, Anna was a mostly resting actress, and Finn was a hot-shot barrister – which was just as well, because it meant that he could afford to support his beautiful, scatty girlfriend.

'Oh, shite,' said Charlotte, checking out the display on her purring mobile.

'Narky marketing?'

'Yeah. Gotta take it. Mr Kemp! How can I help you? … Mm-hmm … Mm-hmm … Yes. That's certainly a big improvement on my suggestion.' She took a pen from her bag and started making notes on her paper napkin. '"Specially selected and packaged *with care*." Yes, I shall certainly incorporate that … Well-being? You got it … Harmonising body and spirit? Check … Yes. Yes. Yes. Will do, Mr Kemp. Enjoy your weekend!' She pressed 'End call' with an emphatic thumb before adding, 'You great big imaginatively challenged bastard.'

'But I'm sure Mr Kemp knows best!' said Anna with exaggerated jauntiness.

'Pah, Anna. Does he really believe that women are still falling for cliché after cliché when it comes to shampoos? When was the last time you had an orgasm when you washed your hair?'

'Just last night, actually. But I wasn't washing my hair. Finn was.'

'Smug bitch,' said Charlotte, getting to her feet. 'Time to make like a wage slave and work on some words. "Our seaweed shampoo will make Johnny Depp fall in love with you. It guarantees you the most beautiful hair in the world. You will get a glamorous job as a shampoo model and earn shed-loads of cash for swinging your hair in front of a camera."'

'I'd buy that brand,' said Anna.

'But you don't need Johnny Depp,' said Charlotte. 'You've got Finn.'

* * *

'Now, Charlotte. Patrick will ask each of the contestants three questions. In the event of a tie, there will be a sudden-death round. Whoever ends up with the most correct answers wins the trip. The next voice you hear will be Patrick's. Are you ready?'

'Yes,' lied Charlotte. She was pacing her sitting room, picking at a cuticle, certain that her Wipers moment was imminent. In an attempt to centre herself, she stopped pacing and stood in front of the mirror with one leg twisted around the other.

Her reflection looked back at her, a little forlornly. Charlotte was always reading in romantic novels about heroines whose eyes were 'rather too far apart' or whose mouths were 'rather too large'. Pah! You couldn't have *too*-far-apart eyes – that was what made Kate Moss so sexy, for heaven's sake – and every doxy in the land was injecting gallons of collagen into her lips to make them 'too' big.

Charlotte's eyes were placed in the normal place in her face, her eyebrows were straight and her mouth – when she wasn't smiling – was a rosebud. She didn't have Vivien's killer cheekbones, angular jaw and lean-limbed loucheness, and she didn't have Anna's Nigella-Lawson-esque sensuality. Her tawny hair was so thick and 'rebellious' (if you were to believe the ads) that she'd taken to straightening it, and *then* – because she hated the stripy, straight-haired look – she had to tie it in a knot while it was still a little damp, in order to give it movement. She'd done that last night before she'd gone to bed, so that it would look good and swingy for Patrick Proctor on the radio, even though he couldn't see her. She was also wearing one of her favourite outfits for him: a floaty, floral-printed dress from Biba that she'd found in a vintage shop. It was a quintessentially girly dress, and Charlotte thanked her lucky stars that her job as a 'creative' meant she didn't have to wear a uniform or a suit to work. The only suit she owned was a winceyette sleep-suit that she wore when she was feeling fragile, which wasn't that often. Charlotte was soft, pretty and feminine-looking, but she liked to think that she was tougher than she appeared.

She could hear Patrick introducing the contestants down the phone line. One was a fashion student whose most passionate dream was to visit the Musée de la Mode in Paris, where all the hautest of haute couture was displayed. One was a commis chef whose most passionate dream was to dine at the Paris Ritz. And then there was—

'Charlotte! I understand you work in advertising?'

'That's right, Patrick.'

'Have you ever been to Paris, Charlotte?'

'Yes. It's a fabulous city!' Thank goodness her job meant that she was more adept at lying than most people.

'So you'd be glad of an opportunity to go back there?'

Patrick's chocolatey voice was intimate in her ear. Maybe Paris wouldn't be so bad if you had a man like Patrick Proctor to take you there, she speculated. Patrick Proctor looked a bit like the actor the agency had hired recently for an ad for trendy sofas, but she hazarded a guess that, when it came to IQ, Patrick Proctor had to be aeons ahead of the actor, who had announced in all seriousness that he needed to know his motivation for sitting on the sofa.

'Absolutely, Patrick! I'd love to go back. I threw all my loose change in that fountain in order to make sure of it!'

'Which fountain?'

Oh, shit. She'd been thinking about the Trevi, in Rome. Her Wipers moment loomed large. 'Um. The fountain outside my hotel,' she improvised lamely.

'Well, here's hoping you get your wish, Charlotte! Now. Maud, Jasper – are you ready?'

'Ready, Patrick!' enthused the other contestants.

'Maud. Which famous couturier has headquarters in the Avenue Montaigne?'

Charlotte thanked God she hadn't been asked this one. What was this? A 'fun' quiz, or *University* bloody *Challenge*?

'Coco Chanel,' came the prompt response. Well, being a fashion student, of *course* this Maud would know that! It wasn't fair. Charlotte caught a glance of her outraged face in the mirror and realised that she was almost fulminating. Oo-er. Was she entering into the spirit of the quiz despite herself?

'Coco Chanel is correct! Jasper, here is your question. In which famous hotel did Princess Diana enjoy her last meal?'

Doh! Was this quiz rigged or something? Jasper had told Patrick at the top of the competition that the Ritz in Paris was where he dreamed of dining!

'It was the Paris Ritz, Patrick.'

'Correct! Charlotte. The Café de Flore in Paris was the haunt of which famous French artist?'

Yay! 'It was Picasso,' said Charlotte.

'Correct!'

Thank goodness! Her Wipers moment had been deflected, leaving her feeling oddly smug. She was reminded of English class in school, where she'd spent one year as teacher's pet. The next year, the teacher had gone on to a new girl called Bobby Pinn. Funny how stuff like that stayed with you, and important stuff like French literature and art didn't.

'Maud,' said Patrick in his attractively authoritarian voice. 'Which famous Parisian museum features in Dan Brown's *The Da Vinci Code*?'

Hello? What kind of a no-brainer question was *that*?

'The Louvre,' said Maud obediently.

'Correct! Jasper. What is the name of the famous steel tower that was constructed in Paris in the nineteenth century?'

'Was that the Eiffel Tower, Patrick?'

'Correct! Charlotte. In the film *Gentlemen Prefer Blondes*, Marilyn Monroe and Jane Russell wind up in Paris. Which famous American author wrote the book on which the film was based?'

Easy-peasy! 'It was Dorothy Parker, Patrick.'

'I'm sorry. That's the wrong answer. It was Anita Loos.'

Oh, *shit*! Of *course* it was Anita Loos! Hadn't Charlotte, only last month, used a quote from Loos's *Kiss Hollywood Goodbye* for a marketing campaign? If she'd been wearing her killer steel-tipped stilettos, she would have kicked herself.

'Maud. What is the name of the capital's most famous thoroughfare?'

'Um ... the Boulevard Saint-Germain?'

'Wrong!'

Ha, ha, thought Charlotte.

'It's the Champs-Elysées! Jasper. In what building in Paris is the Museum of Modern Art housed?'

'Er ... pass.'

'Charlotte. What name does the palace of the Sun King go by?'

'Versailles.'

'Correct! Maud ...'

And so it went, on and on, and one person got it right and another person got it wrong, and things were ping-ponging along until Charlotte realised she was going to be so stonkingly late for work that she'd be bawled out by the senior copywriter – and for what? For a trip to Paris that she didn't even want to win. She was just about to speedily make her excuses and abandon ship when Patrick said,

'If you answer this question correctly, Charlotte, *you* will be our winner!' He allowed a dramatic pause to fall, leaving Charlotte several more moments late for work. 'Tell me. Who took the famous photograph of a couple kissing on a Paris street?'

She knew this. Of course she knew this. 'It was Henri Cartier-Bresson, Patrick.'

She heard the sound of a donging bell, followed by Patrick Proctor's fulsome tones as he announced, 'Congratulations, Charlotte! You are the lucky winner of our trip for two to Paris!'

'Thanks, Patrick!' said Charlotte, trying to sound enthusiastic. Then – *Oh, shit*! she thought, as a new dilemma struck her. If she did pluck up the courage to visit Paris again, Vivien and Anna would most certainly expect her to take one or the other of them with her. The burning question was – and it was many degrees more burning than any of the questions Patrick had just asked her – which one?

* * *

It was Freshers' week at London University, and Charlotte had spent the past five days partying and joining societies and choosing her friends with care. She'd been warned that you spend the first year at college trying to get rid of the friends made in the first week, and she wanted to avoid making that mistake. She'd taken particular care to avoid the scary girl with the Scottish accent who looked like Erin O'Connor. The über arrogant-looking supermodel had just appeared on the scene, and Charlotte wished that she had an ounce of her cool. Some chance! To paraphrase the bard, some are born cool, some achieve cool, and some have coolness thrust upon them. Charlotte knew that she would never even have coolness thrust upon her. When she had enthusiastically announced her intention to run for class rep, she had been completely floored by the beyond-disdainful expression the cool Scottish girl had turned on her. So Charlotte had curbed her enthusiasm and tried to choose her friends prudently.

And yet, the very first friend she'd made seemed gorgeous. Her name was Anna, and she was fun and friendly and didn't seem to have agendas or ulterior motives or chips on her shoulders. She, like Charlotte, was studying French and English, but she was completely upfront about the fact that she was only doing the course to have something to fall back on if her acting ambitions came to nothing. Anna wanted nothing more in life than to be a jobbing repertory actress, and – she'd told Charlotte – if that didn't happen, she was perfectly happy to settle down and make babies with a gorgeous bloke. In the meantime, studying French and English seemed like a good way of passing the time until the casting people or the right man discovered her.

Charlotte and Anna had arranged to meet for lunch on this, the last Friday of the first week of term, in a cheap and cheerful café on Gower Street. Charlotte had nipped to the loo to do girl stuff, only to realise that was she out of tampons. She appeared to be out of change for the machine as well, and there was no one in the ladies' to beg, borrow or steal from. She was rummaging in her bag for any maverick coins when, in the mirror, she saw the door open, and *that* girl – the scary Erin O'Connor clone – walked through. There was no way Charlotte was going to approach *her* for change!

The girl hadn't seen her – the machine was in a kind of annex. Charlotte shut her bag and was just about to discreetly exit the loo when she saw that the other girl had leaned towards the mirror and was dabbing at her eyes with a tissue. It was only then that Charlotte realised the scary girl was crying.

Charlotte stepped out of the annex. 'Can I help?' she asked.

The girl turned, clearly mortified to have been caught. 'No!' she said. And then, to Charlotte's horror, the girl's face crumpled, and she doubled over the basin and started crying buckets more.

'What is it?' Charlotte asked, moving towards her and laying a hand on her arm.

'I canna tell ye,' sobbed the girl. 'Ye'll only think I'm stupid.'

'I won't think you're stupid. Why should I?'

'Because I *am* stupid. I made a big mistake.'

'What mistake?'

The girl sniffed, straightened up and looked at Charlotte with huge, miserable eyes. 'I'm in my first year at university here,' she said.

'I know. I've seen you.'

'Do you think I'm a loser?'

'No. Are you mad? I think you look like the kind of gal who takes no prisoners.'

'Ha! That's a joke. D'ye ken – I was so scared about coming to London that I decided to pretend I couldn't care less whether

I made friends or not. And I've spent the past week acting snooty, and now everybody hates me and I'm *sooo* lonely!'

'How – how do you know everybody hates you?' asked Charlotte, feeling guilty that, while she hadn't *hated* this girl, she certainly hadn't warmed to her.

'I can tell. I can see it in their faces. And now I'm scared that I'll spend the next three years here having a completely *hellish* time.'

'No. No, you won't have a hellish time.'

'I will so! And it's all my own fault. Oh, oh, *oh!*' And the girl started dabbing at her eyes again with her screwed-up tissue.

'Listen,' said Charlotte impulsively, 'why don't you come and have lunch with me and my friend Anna? She's upstairs in the café.'

'No! I couldna do that.'

'Please do.'

The girl shook her head.

'I wouldn't ask you if I didn't mean it,' coaxed Charlotte.

There was a pause. 'Are you sure?' the girl said, looking at her doubtfully. 'I wouldna want to intrude.'

'You wouldn't be intruding, honestly. Anna's the sort of person who loves to make new friends.'

'Well, that's bloody good of you.' The girl blew her nose. 'The name's Vivien, by the way.'

'And I'm Charlotte. Um … you wouldn't happen to have a spare tampon on you, would you?'

'Sure.' Vivien fished in her bag for a Tampax, then peered at her reflection in the mirror. 'Jeez. I look like shite.'

'Here,' said Charlotte, unzipping her make-up bag and handing Vivien a pack of *papier poudré*. 'This stuff's great for shiny noses.'

'You're a pal,' said Vivien.

* * *

And that was no word of a lie. Since that day, Vivien, Anna and Charlotte had been pals – virtually inseparable ones, at that. They had Interrailed together, partied together, shared secrets, laughed and cried together, and – most importantly – they had supported one another. Anna and Vivien had taken turns to sleep in Charlotte's bed and hold her hand during the long, dark nights when her father was dying; Charlotte and Anna had understood Vivien's grief when her cat was run over and everybody else thought she was overreacting (it was only a *cat*, after all). And Vivien and Charlotte had listened for hours and hours and *hours* to Anna when she first started going out with Finn and he was the only subject in her world worth talking about. The three of them had that special kind of love for one another that only very lucky women find.

And now Charlotte had to choose between them. She couldn't do it.

* * *

In their favourite tapas bar later on that day, the way Vivien and Anna were looking at her reminded Charlotte of Donkey in *Shrek*. Their expressions were eloquent, and they both said, 'Choose me!'

'I've put a lot of thought into this,' said Charlotte, 'and I've decided that I'm not going on the holiday.'

'What?' said Anna with a theatrical gasp. 'You *can't* not go! You'd be insane to turn down a prize like that.'

'I'm not turning it down.'

'But you've just said that you don't want to go.'

'*I* don't want to go,' said Charlotte. 'But you two do – and go you shall! *Ping!*'

She waved an imaginary magic wand, and Vivien looked at her as if she was barking. 'Are you serious?'

'Absolutely.'

'*No*, Charlotte!' said Anna. 'You *can't* be serious.'

'Damn right I'm serious. You two can kiss Paris's ass for me.'

'Oh! Oh – you complete angel!' Anna dropped her olive and flung her arms around her friend, making little whimpering sounds of gratitude. 'Are you *absolutely* sure?' she added when she'd recovered her equilibrium and was sitting back in her chair, gazing at Charlotte as if she were Derren Brown.

'I'm sure,' said Charlotte. 'But there is one condition.'

'Name it.'

'You bring me back a pair of *genuine* Jimmy Choos.'

'Done deal!' said Anna.

'Can we steal them?' asked Vivien. 'Or do we have to buy them?'

'You cate*gorically* have to buy them,' said Charlotte.

'How will we know which ones to get?' asked Vivien.

'Well, that's easy,' said Charlotte.

'They'll tell us themselves?' hazarded Anna.

Charlotte smiled. 'Of course they will,' she said.

two

'Y*es*?' Charlotte barked into her phone, without bothering to check the display.

It was Friday evening and she'd been kept late at work, tweaking the script for a demo radio commercial. The agency was pitching for a new account, and at times like this tempers got frayed and stress levels rose like mercury.

'Ooh, darling, you sound stressed!' The dulcet tones on the line belonged to Anna.

'That's because I am. *Extremely* stressed. Sorry for picking up like the famous grouse, but you're actually lucky you didn't get an earful of expletives. That travel company I was telling you about have brought their dates forward, and we're having to pitch a week earlier than we expected.'

Anna made a suitably sympathetic cooing sound. 'In that case, you deserve a reward. Good food, good company and poker. Our place at eight.'

'That sounds like the best invite in the world.' Charlotte glanced at her computer screen: the time was half past six. 'But there's no way I'll make it. I've still a stack of work to do, and then I'd have to get home and shower and change and—'

'What are you wearing?'

'My new Monsoon dress.'

'Phooey. Then you don't have to bother about changing. Just come straight from work. You know we don't do pomp, and there'll be no one you need to impress with your wit and erudition.'

'So egg-head Thea's not going to be there?'

'No. Thea's off on location in the Caribbean, acting her socks off.'

'Except Thea wouldn't be seen dead in socks.'

'What does Alex *see* in her?' they said in unison – and not for the first time.

The easy-going vibe that existed among Charlotte and Co. had been compromised recently, since Alex had acquired a stunning new girlfriend called Thea. Charlotte always felt like a jackass in her presence.

'So you can relax and be uncomplicated and drink lots of wine,' continued Anna. 'Especially the latter.'

'You obviously want my poker face to slip.'

'Of course I do. If you get rat-arsed, I might stand a chance of winning for once, especially since I won't be drinking.'

'Why not?'

'The doctor's issued me with a repeat prescription for that kidney infection.'

'Oh, poor you. How are you feeling?'

'Running to the loo a lot. But otherwise, I'm fine.'

Charlotte debated. The prospect of good wine, good food, good company, a poker session and *no Thea* was extremely enticing. But she still had her copy to write, and it could take her another hour at least ...

'Hell, I'd love to come,' she said. 'But I won't get to your gaff until nearly nine o'clock at this rate.'

'That's cool. I'll delay serving the food until then.'

'Are you sure, Anna?'

'Absolutely, absolutely, absolutely. Now, I'd

better dash and sling supper together. See you later – and bring loads of loose change!'

'Will do. Bye, sweet pea.'

Charlotte put the phone down, feeling marginally less stressed. Dinner and poker *chez* Anna and Finn was like entering a comfort zone: they were part of the SHEF (Stay Home and Entertain Friends) brigade. Anna had a regular habit of staging impromptu soirées in their tiny flat, somehow managing to squeeze eight people round the table, because Anna was one of those enviable people who had *the knack*. She had the knack of conjuring virtual feasts from store-cupboard ingredients, she had the knack of transforming her living space into something Lawrence Llewellyn Bowen might envy, and she had the knack of growing exotica from seed. Her bonsais were topiary in miniature, her pot plants were so glossy they looked artificial, and the herbs she kept on her kitchen windowsill were so exuberant with good health that it was borderline slaughter every time she took her scissors to the basil.

Charlotte went back to her copy. Ironically, the travel agents they were pitching to specialised in city breaks, and one of their top destinations was Paris. The marketing idea

Charlotte had come up with invited a series of comparisons. 'If Paris were a woman, she'd be Audrey Hepburn … If Paris were a motorcar, she'd be a Bugatti … If Paris were a stimulant, she'd be a double espresso.' That kind of thing. Charlotte was tempted to cross it all out and start again. 'If Paris were a woman, she'd be Cruella de Vil … If Paris were a car, she'd be a road hog … If Paris were a stimulant, she'd be a cattle prod.'

Seeking more inspiration, Charlotte went online and searched for 'Paris – images'. And, of course, one of the first images to confront her was that of the most famous Paris of them all. Ms Hilton.

* * *

At ten to nine, Charlotte was buzzed up to Anna's apartment. Finn opened the door to her. Finn always reminded Charlotte of an aristocratic gypsy, and this evening the gypsy in him was uppermost. He was barefoot, he had swapped the smart threads he wore to the office for jeans and a T-shirt, and his earring, a chip of jet obsidian, had been reinstated. The film-star smile he greeted her with was worthy of a young Brad Pitt – and it was a smile full of genuine warmth.

Finn was so ridiculously good-looking that Charlotte often wondered how she'd never harboured a secret lust for him. But how could you fancy your best friend? After Anna and Vivien, Finn came next in Charlotte's affections. If the girls weren't around, it was Finn she'd phone to gossip to, Finn she'd phone to gripe to, Finn she'd phone to confide in.

'Hey, you,' he said, giving her a peck on the cheek, then another one for good measure. 'Come on in.' A babble of voices was coming from the sitting room, and someone was laughing a little riotously. Finn took one look at Charlotte's drawn face and said, 'I sense refreshment is needed before you switch into sociable mode. Let's dive into the kitchen. Red?'

'Please,' said Charlotte, following him into the tiny space and leaning against the fridge door.

'Tough day in the office?' said Finn, sloshing Bordeaux into a long-stemmed goblet.

'Damn right. It's difficult to wax panegyric about a product you hate. It makes me feel like the barrister who defends the bad guy. No offence.'

'What's the product?'

'Paris.'

Finn laughed. 'Anna and Vivien haven't shut up talking about all the shopping they're planning to do while they're over there. Damn your eyes, Charlotte, for making it possible for my inamorata to bankrupt me. I may end up cheating tonight.'

'Cheating?'

'At stud.'

Finn handed her the wine glass, and Charlotte was so relieved that she gulped as thirstily as a warthog at a watering hole, not caring if she looked like a lush.

'They're in there now, arguing over whether they should take a train south or fly,' he told her.

'South?' Charlotte knew she sounded like an aurally challenged parrot, but she was so brain-dead she didn't care.

'Yes. Didn't they tell you?'

'Tell me what?'

'They've decided to extend their holiday and spend some time in Cap Ferrat. Vivien's overdue holiday time, and Anna doesn't have so much as an audition to look forward to, so there's nothing to stop her from staying there as long as she likes. They're planning on spending a fortnight in Claudia's villa.'

Claudia was Anna's stepmother. She'd

recently acquired property in the south of France, and Anna had shown Charlotte pictures of the fabulous pink-stuccoed villa on the coast at Cap Ferrat. It looked like something from *Homes & Gardens*, with a pool and a hot tub and a yoga pavilion, and it was festooned with bougainvillea. It was the kind of joint you fantasised about staying in.

Charlotte took another swig, then set her glass down with such force that wine swilled over the rim. 'Well, isn't that fucking swell for *them*!' she said.

There was a hiatus. 'Ah,' hazarded Finn. 'I can tell that you're not overjoyed by the bulletin.'

'Shit!' Charlotte covered her eyes with her palms, sucked in a breath and held it for many moments, swelling with self-loathing. Finally she exhaled in a rush and removed her hands from her face. 'I'm sorry, Finn. I must seem like a complete bitch in a manger. It's just that I had such a shite day today that the notion of my playmates shimmying down to the Riviera and having fun in the sun without me does nothing to bring out my inner Mother Theresa.'

'It's OK,' said Finn, giving her shoulder an awkward pat of reassurance. 'It's kinda understandable. You're probably wishing now that you'd never offered them Paris.'

'*Au contraire.* They're welcome to *that*. But I've wanted to visit the south of France ever since I read Scott Fitzgerald's *Tender is the Night.*'

'There, there,' said Finn. This time he rubbed her shoulder. Physical contact was not Finn's strong suit. The way he was rubbing made her feel like Aladdin's lamp. 'Poor Charlotte. But hey, you mustn't fret too much. The weather can be bloody miserable on the Riviera at this time of year.'

'I'm not such an embittered bitch that I'd wish bad weather on them. And it's OK, Finn. You can stop rubbing me now.'

He withdrew his hand and looked relieved. 'Why don't you join them there? You could forgo Paris and liaise in Cap Ferrat.'

'I can't. I've got this poxy presentation coming up. I'll be lucky if they don't lock me in the office over the Easter weekend.' It wasn't too much of an exaggeration. The creative director of the agency had once bullied an unfortunate junior in the art department into working until midnight on New Year's Eve. 'Oh, Finn. I know being unemployed isn't a bed of roses, but sometimes

I envy Anna being able to just take off whenever she likes. How has Vivien been able to wangle a fortnight off work, incidentally? Sorry – I know you said something about it, but after the words "Cap Ferrat" I stopped listening.'

'She's overdue holiday time.'

'Sheesh. I'm overdue a *holiday*, full stop. Preferably somewhere like the Caribbean. I hear Thea's gone off to shoot a movie there.'

'Yeah. Aruba.'

The divine Thea had appeared on the scene after Anna had met her at an audition. For some reason they'd got on quite well – most unusually, for actresses in competition for the same part – and big-hearted Anna had ended up inviting Thea to one of her at-homes. It was then that their mate Alex had fallen for Thea's not inconsiderable physical charms, and it was only then that Anna and the rest of them had realised – too late – that Thea was a complete bitch. Thea had more faces than the Hydra, she was catty enough to have her own pedigree and she was vainer than Snow White's stepmother. That was why Charlotte had initially had reservations about showing up at Finn and Anna's this evening. When you were feeling shite, Thea had an unerring ability to make you feel shiter.

'What does Alex *see* in her?' Charlotte asked Finn. But Finn just looked inscrutable, and Charlotte shrugged and said, 'Sorry. I forgot that even men as clued-in as Alex make mistakes when their dicks are doing the thinking for them.'

There came another loud laugh from the sitting room, and Finn gave her a look of enquiry. 'Feel ready to face them?'

'Yes. Thanks, by the way, for letting me know in advance about Cap Ferrat. I'm not sure how graciously I'd have welcomed the news if I hadn't been forewarned.'

She leaned forward to kiss his cheek, and he gathered her to him and said, 'Hush, hush, sweet Charlotte.'

Charlotte gave a little laugh. 'You've probably been looking for an opportunity to say that for ages,' she told him. Finn was something of a film buff.

'You're right,' he confessed. 'I have.'

'Hello, chumlets,' came a silky voice from the door. 'Might we persuade you to join the company?'

Alex was leaning against the jamb, nursing a bottle of Budvar. A lock of dirty blond hair had fallen over his eyes, and he pushed it back to reveal his green gaze.

'Oh, hi, Alex,' said Charlotte, looking round. 'I'm ready to join in the fun now.'

She picked up her wine glass and, followed by Alex and Finn, traversed the metre-long hall.

'Hi!'

'Hi!'

'Hi, darling!'

Anna waltzed up and gave her a kiss, Vivien blew her a lazy kiss from a fingertip and Charlotte looked round at all the smiling faces.

'Hi!' she said back.

Sitting at the table were an actor friend of Anna's, nicknamed (for some reason nobody had ever found out) 'Toad'; Russ, the gay architect from down the hall; and Angus, who was a scenic artist. Everyone was smiling and telling her how generous she was on account of the Paris thing, and Russ patted the seat beside him inviting her to take it. Suddenly Charlotte felt suffused with gladness to have such good friends, and not a little guilty that she'd begrudged the happiness of two of the best of them earlier. She found herself smiling too as she sat down between Russ and Finn and raised her glass.

'Here's the soppy bit,' she said. 'To Anna and Vivien. Here's hoping that springtime in Paris does exactly what it says in the song.'

'What does it say in the song?'

'Something about loving Paris even when it drizzles.'

'Well, rain won't stop *me* playing,' announced Anna.

'Planning any day trips?' asked Charlotte.

'Day trips?' said Vivien, as incredulously as if Charlotte had asked her bra size. 'To where?'

'I dunno. Somewhere picturesque. Like Wipers.'

'I never took you for a dimwit, Charlotte! It's pronounced Ypres,' said Russ, elongating the 'Y' into an 'ee'.

'Aha!' said Anna. 'You, Russ, have clearly not heard the Vivien *Millionaire* story.' She filled him in with glee. 'It was the worst moment of your life, Vivien, wasn't it?' she finished happily.

'Well, since you derive such perverse enjoyment from recounting the story, I guess it must have been,' drawled Vivien.

'I enjoy it because it's the only uncool thing you've ever done.'

'Are you telling me,' said a scandalised Russ, 'that you studied French at university level, Vivien Mackenzie, and you couldn't even pronounce Ypres properly?'

Vivien raised her shoulders in a very Gallic shrug. 'That's what made it doubly *excruciating*,' she said, rolling the 'r'. 'My nerves got the better of me. Everyone who appears on *Who Wants to be a Millionaire?* admits that they could do with a transfusion of *sang froid*.'

'Hello?' said Russ. 'Isn't appearing on *Millionaire* a pretty uncool thing to do in the first place?'

'When you're an impoverished student, money is more important than street cred, believe me. That thirty-two thousand got me through my final year of uni in style. And it afforded me the exquisite pleasure of dissing the accounts tyrant in that fast-food joint where I was slaving.'

'How did you diss her?'

'I told her to get her enormous fat arse up the stairs and sort my money ASAP. Ha! You should have seen the expression on her mealy-mouthed face. To paraphrase Byron, "Sweet is revenge – especially to wage-slaves."'

'It must have been the pits, working in that joint,' said Anna with a shudder. 'Have you seen how they make those chicken nuggets? Don't you feel guilty for having doled out tons of mashed-up beaks and claws to an unsuspecting future generation?'

'Someone has to do it. And at least I didn't stoop so low as to do page three of *The Sun*.' Vivien slid an oblique look at Anna, and all eyes went immediately to the glorious cleavage she was displaying.

'Darling!' said Anna. 'If *you* appeared on page three, readers would ask for their money back.' She turned on her heel and stalked into the kitchen.

'Cat-fight!' said Toad. 'Whoa. I'd love to be a fly on the wall in your hotel room in Paris.'

'Don't worry,' said Charlotte. 'They'll kiss and make up. Won't you, Viv?'

Vivien's shrug was even more Gallic.

'The best thing about our kind of friendship,' resumed Charlotte, 'is that we can insult each other with impunity.'

'Vivien!' called Anna, putting her head around the door of the sitting room. 'Would you mind lending me a hand in the kitchen? The surfaces could do with a good wipe, and you're one of the best wipers I know.'

With a world-weary sigh, Vivien got to her feet and strolled to the door. 'See you, hen?' she said. 'You have to be the most jejune person I know. And, because I could hazard a safe guess that you haven't a clue what the word "jejune" means, I suggest you look it up in the dictionary. If you own one.' And then Vivien took Anna's face between her elegant hands and gave her a languorous kiss, full on the mouth.

'Wow!' breathed Toad, all agog. 'When you said they'd kiss and make up, I didn't think you meant it literally, Charlotte. Now I wish even harder that I could be a fly on the wall in your hotel room. Do you wear night-dresses or pyjamas to bed, girlies?'

'Pyjamas, of course,' said Vivien, heading for the kitchen to wipe surfaces.

'Victoria's Secret? Ann Summers?'

Vivien's backward look was scathing. 'Nothing as tacky as Ann Summers,' she said. 'The pyjamas *we* gals wear are the cat's.'

* * *

'I'll see you.'

'House of spades.'

'Bastard. It's all yours.'

Dinner (garlicky pasta with asparagus and cream, green salad, crusty bread, an apricot tart) was over, Louis Armstrong was oozing over the speakers and the poker game was under way.

Vivien raked in the cards and shuffled them with panache. 'Dealer's choice,' she announced. 'Draw. One-eyed jacks are wild.'

Poker sessions at Anna's were conducted in a seriously frivolous fashion – in fact, poker faces were frowned upon, and Botox faces completely banned. There was much shouting and laughing, great quantities of wine were consumed and Alex had once improvised a mock commentary through the entire game – much to the disgust of a card-sharp mate of Finn's, who had ended up storming out of the flat during a particularly juvenile game of Muzzy Face. The sessions were really just excuses to get together and have fun. They'd evolved when a consensus had been reached that going out to socialise was just too much hassle: clubs were no longer their *raison d'être*, restaurants were expensive and there was more fun to be had at Anna and Finn's than anywhere else. Oh – and the food was generally better, too.

On Charlotte's left, Russ, who had sat out

the last round because it had been his deal, was intriguing her with details of his sexual peccadilloes; on her right, Finn was filling Alex in on his plans for the Easter weekend. 'Cholyngham,' heard Charlotte, and even though Russ was describing a particularly weird fetish-y thing he was into, her right ear went into elastic-band mode.

'Oh, man, how fantastic,' said Alex. 'I'd love to get down there with you, but the joint's bound to be booked out.'

'Funnily enough, it's not,' said Finn. 'A party cancelled at the last minute and it looks like my mother could be seriously out of pocket.'

'Why's that? I thought guests who cancelled without giving notice still had to pay the going rate.'

'Not this time. The cancellation was due to a family bereavement, and Mum felt it was only decent to refund the deposit. There are rooms going begging, and she's working down the waiting list.'

'Is my name on it?'

'Sure. If you've no other plans.'

'I had until Thea got the news about that Caribbean movie. It's a toss-up between Cholyngham or Babestation on 172, and even *I* can't handle a bank holiday weekend of wall-to-wall masturbation. I'm coming with you, man.'

Cholyngham was a country house hotel that belonged to Finn's mother and father, Lavinia and Colin. It had established itself as one of the most popular places to stay in the Home Counties, and was a perennial favourite of American tourists, who found the eccentricity of its owners 'quaint'. In fact, Lavinia and Colin were neither eccentric nor quaint. They were extremely savvy business-people who knew how to keep their customers happy, and if keeping their customers happy meant behaving like scatty aristocrats, then that was a small price to pay for the custom of the hordes of Yanks who kept coming back year after year to 'that crazy Cholyngham'.

The house had been built in 1871 by some ancestor of Finn's – a wealthy Mancunian industrialist – as a wedding present for his wife. Death duties had taken their toll, and the stately pile had languished for years until the early 60s, when Finn's grandmother had rescued it from decrepitude, sensitively re-stored it and turned it into a hotel. Charlotte loved it. Any time she visited, she pretended she lived there, and wafted from room to room trying to decide which was her favourite. The reception rooms had all been furnished in the Victorian style, but the emphasis was on comfort rather than stern sit-up-straight furniture, and the bedrooms were retreats from real life. The time Charlotte had gone down there with her then boyfriend, Duncan, they'd had such a fantastic weekend that Charlotte remembered it as one of the most perfect of her life – in spite of the fact that that duplicitous bastard had been part of the equation.

'Can you open?' Vivien directed the question to Angus, who was on her left.

'No,' said Angus.

'Are you guys talking about Cholyngham?' Anna asked, adding a bright 'I'll open!' as she tossed a pound coin into the centre of the table.

'Yes,' said Finn, selecting a coin from his stash. 'Mum said to tell you she'll miss you this Easter.'

'That's only because I helped out in the model farm last year. Hey, I've got a great idea!' Anna said as coins rained onto the middle of the table. 'Why don't you go down, Charlotte?'

'To Cholyngham?'

'Yes. If I knew you were taking things easy there, I wouldn't feel half so guilty about me and Viv swanning off to Paris.'

'Well ... I'd love to, of course, but the presentation's—'

'Oh, fuck the presentation!' said Vivien, dealing Toad the three cards he'd asked for. 'You're entitled to a bit of R&R on the Easter bank holiday. Go tell your creative director to eat his Y-fronts. I certainly would, if I had the opportunity to spend a long weekend lolling around Cholyngham.'

'She's right,' said Anna. 'You'd reserve a room for Lottie, wouldn't you, darling?' Anna was a devotee of diminutives. The only person she hadn't found a diminutive for was Finn. She'd tried calling him 'Fin-fin' once, but he'd become most uncharacteristically aggressive.

'Sure. I'd have to check it out with Lavinia, of course,' replied Finn.

'Hang on, Viv – did you say that *all* jacks are wild?' said Anna, peering at her new cards.

'No, lame-brain. Only one-eyed ones.'

'Crap. I'll phone your mother now, Finn,' announced Anna, producing her phone from her highly impractical baby-blue suede handbag, 'and ask her if there's room for Lottie.'

'Don't you think we should draw the line at making phone calls in the middle of our poker sessions, beloved?' said Finn.

'The rule is that you're allowed to use the phone if you fold. And that's exactly what I'm doing. I thought I had two queens, but my cards are actually rubbish. I think you deal me crap cards on purpose, Viv.' Anna shot the dealer an aggrieved look before slinging her cards onto the table and pressing 'Call'.

'Tell the world, why don't you, and spoil the game,' said Vivien. 'Strictly speaking, you should be fined for opening in the first place, and I should redeal.'

'Redeal!' commanded Angus.

'Couldn't be arsed, hen.'

'That's all right. I'm cleaned out anyway.' Angus helped himself to more wine.

'Lavinia!' purred Anna into her phone. 'Hello – it's me.'

'Raise you one.' A chink as a coin was added to the pile that was amassing on the table.

'I know, I know.' Anna's tones contrived to combine apology and regret with an effortless sweetness. Charlotte made a mental note to ask her friend for some telephone-manner tips, and found herself thinking how strange it was that Anna didn't get more work as an actress. 'I'm sorry I won't be there, La-la, but a girl can hardly turn down a trip to Paris.'

'See you,' said Toad. Chink!

'Yes. She won it on Patrick Proctor's radio show. Wasn't it sweet of her?'

'Raise you two quid.'

'Finn says there are vacancies next weekend.'

'I'll see you, too.' With feigned non-chalance, Charlotte dropped two pound coins onto the table. Because she held four aces, she could have raised the stakes a lot higher, but if she did that, the other players might guess that she was holding a one-eyed jack. Unless they figured she was bluffing, of course … *as if*! Everyone around this table knew that bluffing had never been Charlotte's strong suit. She snuck another look at Finn, trying to see past his poker face. Beside him, Alex was looking at her strangely. She dropped her eyes immediately and resumed what she trusted was a mask-like countenance. The cards she was holding made her want to grin like a fool.

'Do you think you might manage to fit Charlotte in, La-la?' cajoled Anna.

'Do take your time, Russ,' said Vivien waspishly.

'Alex is going down as well!' Anna made it sound like the most exciting pronouncement since Chantelle won *Celebrity Big Brother*. 'Finn told him it would be *fine*.'

'Piss-pots. I'm folding,' said Russ. 'Give us a look at your cards, Charlotte.'

'No!' Charlotte pressed her hand against her chest so that Russ couldn't sneak a peek. 'I'm not revealing my strategy.'

'I didn't know there *was* a strategy for consistently losing at poker,' said Vivien, raising an eyebrow. 'Toad?'

'I'm folding,' said Toad after a moment's deliberation.

Anna put her hand over the mouthpiece of her phone. 'La-la's checking reservations,' she said.

'I'll see you,' Alex told Finn, tossing coins into the pot.

'Charlotte?' said Vivien.

'I'll raise you five, Finn.'

'If Charlotte's raising the stakes, then she's gotta be onto something good. I'm gone.' Alex laid his cards on the table. He was still looking at her weirdly, through narrowed eyes. But then, Alex often looked at her weirdly, as if he couldn't understand how the rather ditzy person he'd known since childhood had actually made it into adulthood. As for him – the gangly brat Charlotte had played footie with – he'd cleaned up quite well. Well enough for a glamour-puss like Thea to find him alluring, anyway.

'With five,' said Finn.

'And another five.' Charlotte slid a tenner from her wallet with studied carelessness, then gave Finn a look of enquiry. He continued to gaze imperviously at his hand.

'Coming right back at you with five,' he said, tossing two fivers onto the spreading carpet of cash.

Charlotte's hands started to sweat, as they always did when the stakes got this high. 'Ten,' she said.

'With ten.' This time he peeled off a twenty.

'And another – er – five.' Twenty-five more quid? Sheesh! This was categorically the most reckless poker game Charlotte had ever played. She stood to win a pile, but if she lost, she could wave goodbye to the little ostrich-skin bag she coveted, the one that said a cheeky 'Hello! Wanna buy me?' from the window of the boutique she passed on her way to work every morning.

The Satchmo CD that had been playing came to an abrupt end. For a moment or two there was silence, then came Anna's song of praise: 'Yay! You're a star! Thanks, La-la. Now I won't feel so bad about abandoning your boy. Byee!' She stuck her phone back in her bag. 'You're in luck, Charlotte,' she said, sending her friend a radiant smile. 'The Boudoir is all yours!'

Charlotte returned the smile and mouthed, 'Thanks, Anna.'

'Isn't that the room that has the four-poster?' asked Russ.

'Yep,' said Alex. 'I spent a *most* illuminating night there with Thea once.'

'Honestly, Alex, what you get up to with Thea is—'

'Cut it out, Russ,' came the authoritative voice of the dealer. 'We have reached a moment of tension nearly as high as the stakes.'

'Oops! Sorry, Viv.'

Finn was still studying his cards with deliberation. Finally he raised his eyes and regarded his opponent with a challenging expression. Charlotte lifted her chin and looked back at him unflinchingly. Finn's eyes were gleaming. He raised an amused eyebrow at her. *Oh, shit.* Did this mean he was onto a sure thing? She had thought her four aces – well, three plus a one-eyed jack – were as good as it got. Covered in confusion, she looked down at her hand.

'I'll see you,' Finn said, with a meaningful smile.

'Four aces.' Charlotte fanned out her three aces and her one-eyed jack on the table, then dared to look back at Finn.

Finn shrugged his shoulders, conceding defeat. 'Flush,' he said.

And flush is exactly what Charlotte, suffused with success, did. As she raked in the pot, all eyes were upon her pink face. One pair of eyes, however, gleamed green with suspicion.

three

Late on Good Friday afternoon, on their way to Cholyngham, Finn, Charlotte and Alex dropped Anna and Vivien off at the airport. Their plan was to splash out on the executive lounge and pretend that they were rich.

'We'll send photographs!' Anna called as Finn put the car into gear.

Charlotte stuck her head through the open window of the passenger seat. 'Promise to send me a pic of the shoes!' she commanded as the car pulled away from the drop-off point. 'Bye! Have a great time!'

'What was that guff about shoes?' asked Alex from the back of the car.

'They promised to buy me a pair of Jimmy Choo heels in return for my magnanimity.'

Finn looked at her blankly. 'What *is* it about girls and their shoes?' he said.

'Do you really want to know? It's pretty arcane stuff.'

'Enlighten us simple men on the mystery of the female psyche, we importune you, oh fair one,' Alex said in a supplicant drone.

'Well,' began Charlotte, 'it's not just shoes. It's handbags too, and sometimes sunglasses – but never hats. They talk to you.'

'Hats *talk*?' Finn gave her a look of pure incomprehension.

'No. Hats *never* talk. But all the other stuff does.'

'In what language? Klingon?' asked Alex.

'No. Girl talk, of course.'

'I see.' Finn put on his indulgent-uncle voice. 'Give us an example of the kind of thing they say.'

'Well, the last time I was in Harvey Nicks, I kind of saw this pink thing waving at me, trying to get my attention.'

'Pink thing,' repeated Alex, deadpan. 'I thought copywriters were meant to be word-savvy. Can't you be more specific?'

'Think Barbie meets bubble gum.'

'Well, that's taken care of the pink,' said Finn. 'Now define "thing".'

'It was a handbag.'

'A handbag waved at you in Harvey Nicks?' said Alex. 'Cool. Tell me what you were on, so I can get some of that gear for myself.'

'It didn't just wave. It cooeed.'

'Ah. And did you cooee back?' asked Alex.

'Are you mad? You don't talk to the bag in the shop. You wait until you get it home.'

'Of course you do. How stupid of me. So what did you do when it cooeed?'

'I tried hard not to meet its eye, but once I did, I was hooked.'

'This bag had eyes?'

'Oh, yes. Big pleading ones.'

'Like a puppy dog in the pound?' hazarded Finn.

'*Exactly* like a puppy dog in the pound. *Now* you're talking the talk.'

'Good. I'll be able to girl-talk with Anna if we keep this up. Tell me – once you were hooked, what did you do?'

'I kind of sidled over to it.'

'Why "sidled"?'

'Well, you never approach the bag directly. You can't let it know that it's the Favoured

One. So you approach it in a roundabout way, picking up loads of its rivals on the way and admiring them, so that the Favoured One gets jealous. And then eventually you get to the Favoured One and you pick it up.'

'Reverently?'

'No. You can't allow the bag to see how badly you're smitten. You have to look un-interested. It's a bit like playing poker, really.'

'That's amazing! The very first thing that came into my head when you mentioned a pink bag was poker.'

Charlotte shot Finn a snooty look. 'And after you've given the outside of the bag the once-over, you open it and navigate all its inner workings. All its cunning little pockets and compartments and its zips and clasps and tasselly bits.'

'Couldn't you get arrested for that?' asked Alex.

'No. It's not serious harassment. It's flirting, really.'

'Let's try another analogy. Speed dating?'

'Absolutely not. There's nothing speedy about it at all. It can take hours, days – sometimes even weeks. And then you realise that you've left it too late, and you race back to the shop in a panic because some savvy bitch might have gone off with *your bag*, and once you see that it's still there, you grab it with a sweaty hand and dash to the till and pass the salesgirl your card before you can change your mind. And you *never* look at the amount on the credit slip.'

'What's the most you've ever paid for a bag?' asked Finn.

'I'm not telling you.'

'Go on!'

'No. It's too embarrassing.'

'A hundred?'

'I'm not saying.'

'More than a hundred?'

Charlotte didn't quite succeed in suppressing a snort.

'You snorted, so it *must* be more than a hundred,' said Alex.

'I never snort. It's common knowledge that girls who buy pink handbags never snort.'

'Two hundred?'

Charlotte looked out the window.

'*More* than two hundred?'

Charlotte started humming.

'Look – she's going all red! Jesus – who in their right mind would pay more than two hundred pounds for a handbag?'

'But she wasn't in her right mind,' said Finn.

'Oh, yeah. I'd forgotten that she was strung out on class junk, talking gobbledygook girl talk with some day-glo bag.'

'I *told* you I don't talk to them until I get them home. Anyway, how much did you pay to see Arsenal lose?' returned Charlotte.

Alex's voice was scathing. 'But that's *football!*'

'I rest my case.'

There was silence for some minutes as the men digested their lesson on the female psyche. Then Alex said, 'What does underwear say to you? Or is it a bit like hats?'

'What do you mean?'

'Well, you said hats can't talk.'

'Hmm. I've never really thought about underwear.'

'Think about it now,' urged Alex. 'What do girls really, really like to wear under their, erm, outer things? I've often wanted to buy Thea underwear, but I read in *The Guardian* that women don't like men buying them lingerie.'

'That's a complete lie!' said Charlotte indignantly.

'Oh? What kind of, er, stuff should I be thinking about, then?'

'Well, I can tell you what you *shouldn't* be thinking about. Never crotchless, and never red.'

'Oh, Christ. Don't you hate it when someone tells you not to think about something?' groaned Alex.

'What do you mean?'

'Well, what exactly do you think I'm thinking about right now?'

'Red crotchless panties,' said Finn.

'Got it in one.'

'What colour *should* they be, then, Charlotte?' asked Finn tentatively. 'If you can't have red?'

Charlotte considered. 'Well, black, obviously, or white. Champagne is good, and pale pink, and hot pink. And baby blue. And green and turquoise can work to great effect, especially on a redhead. Polka dots are sweet, but zebra- and leopard-skin prints can be problematic.'

'OK. So basically, any colour except red.'

'No. Purple is dodgy, and brown would be bad too.'

Both men made 'yeuch' noises. 'Brown underwear would be *gross*,' said Alex.

'Erm, what about … what do you call that stuff that they sew on for decoration?' asked Finn.

'Trimmings?'

'I guess.'

'Well, a little frothy lace can be lovely. And marabou is gorgeous, but usually only on negligees.'

'What's the received wisdom on stockings versus tights?' asked Finn.

'You mean you don't *know*? Tch, tch, Finn.'

'Well, I have a pretty good idea, but it would be nice to have it confirmed from the horse's mouth.'

'There's a joke there, somewhere,' observed Alex, but Charlotte ignored him.

'The answer to your question, Finn, is stockings,' she said. 'Definitely stockings. Or stay-ups, preferably lace-topped. Wolford do the best, but they're expensive.'

'Wolford, hmm? I must remember that.' From his tone, it was clear that Alex was warming to the subject. 'What about thongs?'

Charlotte shuddered. 'Never! I would rather go without than wear a thong.'

'I rather think we've exhausted all the permutations,' said Finn categorically.

'No, we haven't,' contradicted Alex. 'Tell us where to go to buy this stuff.'

'In London? Agent Provocateur, of course,' said Charlotte with authority. 'And

Rigby and Peller. And Coco de Mer in Covent Garden.'

'Is that anywhere near the Disney Store?' asked Alex.

'The *Disney* Store?' repeated Charlotte, investing her voice with a measure of scorn. 'I wouldn't know.'

'The Disney Store's great,' said Alex happily. 'I get all my nephews' and nieces' presents there.'

'I got some fantastic stuff for Anna there,' said Finn meditatively.

'In the Disney Store?'

'No. In Coco de Mer.'

Well, how lucky was Anna? Charlotte found herself thinking as they turned in through the main gates of Cholyngham. She realised that she was feeling a tad sorry for herself. It was, after all, an awfully long time since a man had bought underwear for her.

* * *

Cholyngham always surprised her. One minute you were bowling along a tree-lined, serpentine driveway; the next you were rounding a bend and beholding the stately granite pile reflected in the lake in front of it. The house (it was more of a castle, really) had been constructed in the neo-Gothic style, all turrets and battlements and slit-windowed towers. It looked just like a castle in a fairytale, the kind you'd expect to find princesses languishing in.

On the left-hand side of the driveway, a herd of goats was cavorting in a coppice.

'Yo!' said Charlotte. 'The Gruff Gang!'

The Gruff Gang was the name that had been given to a bunch of maverick goats that roamed the estate like horned hoodlums, terrorising the more elderly of the hotel residents and having al fresco sex all over the place like, well, goats. A pair had escaped from the Cholyngham model farm some years ago; Finn's parents had tried to round them up, without success, and now the goats and their numerous offspring had become part of the Cholyngham legend. Postcards of them were available at the gift shop.

The car pulled up by the steps that led to the front door, and a porter stepped up to take their luggage. "'Ello, 'ello, 'ello!' said the porter when he saw Finn emerge from the car. 'Yer mum told me to expect you. How was your drive?'

'Very educational, thanks,' said Finn. 'Where is she?'

'Yer mum? She's down the kitchen.'

'Would you show Ms Cholewczyk to her room, Roger?' asked Finn, hefting Charlotte's bag out of the boot. 'She's in the Boudoir.'

'Wiv pleasure.' The porter turned to Charlotte. 'Please follow me, madam.'

It didn't happen often that Charlotte was addressed as 'madam', but any time she was, she hated it. It made her feel like an impostor. She would also have preferred to carry her own bag, but she couldn't remember exactly where the Boudoir was, and it was easy to get lost in Cholyngham.

Roger started clambering up the steps, Charlotte's suiter over his shoulder.

'Come down for a drink when you've freshened up,' Finn called after her. 'We'll be in the drawing room.'

'Cholewczyk?' said Roger as he held the front door open for her. 'Your father's Polish?'

'My grandfather was.'

'Like Lech Walesa, friend of the people, Gawd bless him. How long are you wiv us?'

'Until Monday evening.'

'Time enough to relax and unwind. You've been here before, of course.' He gave her an appreciative wink. 'I never forget a pretty face.'

'This is my fourth time.'

'So you know the place well.'

She did. But that didn't stop Roger from giving her a history lesson as he trundled across the polished oak parquetry of the lobby, up several flights of stairs and along labyrinthine corridors. There were, he told her, over seventy rooms in the building. Each bedroom had been individually named, and the Boudoir had been the private quarters of the lucky bride for whom the castle had been built. As they navigated the bewildering geography of the building, Roger pointed out objects of historical importance and portraits of Finn's gloomy-looking ancestors. Each portrait had some romantic or blood-curdling story attached to it, but in fact Charlotte knew that the portraits were all fakes that had been painted by an artist who specialised in forgery. He'd been commissioned by Finn's grandmother during her restoration project, because all the original portraits had been sold off to pay death duties. However, smooth-tongued Roger was so well versed in the bogus exploits of Finn's 'ancestors' that Charlotte was almost inclined to believe him.

'But the current crowd's not just a bunch of old fogies, I'll have you know,' he told her with pride as they climbed what Charlotte sincerely hoped was the last flight of stairs to her room. 'We've all mod cons here, too. Even I've learned to speak the old Techno-jargon in the last six months. The Web and the Internet are all available to guests. If you need to go Online, we've a Wi-Fi connection in the library.' The capital letters were clear in his voice, and Charlotte tried to look suitably impressed.

* * *

The Boudoir was exquisite. It was quintessentially feminine, carpeted in white, with lace curtains lifting in the light wind that wafted through the open bay window. The four-poster bed was draped in powder-blue cretonne and piled with pillows, and a single white rose had been left on the turned-down sheet. Opposite the bed was a fireplace surmounted by a shelf upon which stood a pretty ormolu clock. The shelf was supported by two voluptuous caryatids of carved white marble, and a scroll-shaped frieze on the chimney-breast depicted canoodling cherubs. Charlotte found a DVD player discreetly tucked away in a white-painted French *armoire.*

There was more white marble in the bathroom, on the floor and walls. The bath was easily big enough for two (sob!), and candles had been placed at intervals along its length. There were piles of fluffy white bath towels, a complimentary robe and slippers, and a basket full of the kind of products you love to steal: mending kits (she still had the one she'd stolen the last time she'd been here), shoe-shiners, bath-caps and – best of all – Molton Brown products. Yay!

Charlotte stripped off and dived into the shower. She washed her hair, then cursed her lack of forethought in not packing her GHD. She'd shaved her armpits the night before and done her toenails, but the make-up she'd applied that morning needed retouching. She selected a CD and hummed along to Ella Fitzgerald as she tussled with her rebellious hair, and then she spritzed herself with Jo Malone and surveyed the contents of her suiter.

Cholyngham's dress code was smart-casual, and Charlotte had packed accordingly. She decided on a demure white linen dress and a white shrug cardigan that she'd bought in Next. The finishing touches were a pair of plain white pumps and a couple of strings of pearls from Claire's Accessories. Unfortunately, her hair looked mad – she resembled a pre-Raphaelite model wired up to the mains – so she just twisted it up on the top of her head and secured it with a jaws clip. As a finishing touch, she tucked the white rose into her improvised coiffure.

Before she left the Boudoir, she studied her reflection in the cheval glass that stood beside the fireplace. What a shame she had no boyfriend to tell her that she didn't look fat in white linen. What a shame she had no boyfriend to tell her she was the most beautiful girl in the world. What a shame she had no boyfriend, full stop. Sometimes, on the tube on her way to work, she'd close her eyes and lose herself in the rhythm of the train as it rumbled along the tracks, dreaming of dancing in someone's arms while he murmured sweet nothings in her ear. She closed her eyes now and hugged herself, allowing herself to dream a little.

When she opened her eyes, her reflection was regarding her with a rather piteous expression. *Oh, stop feeling so sorry for yourself, girl*! she told herself. And then she turned abruptly away from the mirror, grabbed her bag and marched out of the room.

She wandered upstairs and down and took numerous wrong turns before she hit on the right way to the drawing room. She'd never been able to figure out the layout of Cholyngham; she always felt like Alice trying to get to the house in *Through the Looking Glass*. In the drawing room there were several groups of people nursing G&Ts and murmuring decorously, and Finn was leaning up against the mantelpiece (no, no! she must remember to call it a *mantelshelf*, the way Finn's mother did), talking to Alex. One of the Cholyngham dogs was lying at Finn's feet with its nose on its paws, gazing up at him rapturously.

'Hey, Charlotte,' said Alex when he saw her come in, and Finn turned to greet her. The look on his face when he clocked her could only be described as 'taken aback'. He took a step forward as if to kiss her on the cheek, then stopped, as though he'd thought better of it.

'Charlotte. Hi. You look – yes. Lovely.'

'Thanks,' said Charlotte. 'You look pretty good, too.'

It was true. Finn was wearing a white shirt open at the neck, white jeans and white trainers.

'Jeez,' said Alex, whose concession to 'smart casual' was a fresh T-shirt, 'you both look as if you've been *styled*. What's with the white vibe?'

'If I'd known, I'd have worn something else,' said Finn apologetically. 'Sorry.'

Alex started laughing. 'The pair of you could have walked out of the pages of a Sunday fucking supplement,' he said. 'Do you mind if I have dinner at a separate table? I find the idea of dining with Mr and Mrs Beckham a tad intimidating.'

'I don't look anything like Victoria Beckham,' protested Charlotte. 'But I wish I did.'

'I don't,' said Finn gallantly. 'You're much more beautiful. Shall we go in? Or do you want a drink first?'

'No, thanks. I'm starving.'

'Good. There's a new chef on, and I'd be glad to know what you think.'

As Finn started to move towards the dining room, Charlotte saw Alex give her the kind of look he used to give her when they were children and he'd caught her cheating at Cluedo. What was with him?

'Finn's right,' he said, *sotto voce*. 'You look fantastic. But I'd wipe that bit of snot off your nose before you sit down to dinner, if I were you. It rather spoils the effect.'

'Oh!' said Charlotte, whipping a tissue from her bag. 'You're a pain in the arse, Alex Thornton. Trust you to notice something like that.'

'Would you have preferred it if I had said nothing and allowed you to sit snottily at the table and put us off our gourmet cuisine?'

Charlotte took a hand mirror from her bag, inspected her face, then blew her nose.

'That's better,' said Alex. 'But tell me this – what's with the sexy dress, Cholewczyk?'

'There's absolutely nothing sexy about this.'

'Oh, yes, there is. It goes completely transparent when you stand against the light. I suggest you wear a slip underneath next time, unless you're intent on giving some geriatric a cardiac arrest. That old geezer's eyes have been out on stalks since you walked into the room.'

* * *

There were two factors that looked set to spoil dinner. The first was a particularly obnoxious girl child who was sitting at the table next to them. She whined and whinged her way through her hors d'oeuvres, describing the food as 'gross' and complaining over and over that she wanted McDonald's.

'Tomorrow, Charmelle,' her harassed mother kept telling her. 'I promise we'll find a McDonald's tomorrow.'

The second factor was Alex, who was continuing to send Charlotte suspicious looks. Because he was clearly in a black mood about something (probably the fact that he hadn't had sex since Thea had gone to the Caribbean), she decided to teach him a lesson by making him feel like Norman No-Friends, and concentrated all her attention on Finn, who was in great form. Finn was always gorgeous, but he was somehow even more irresistible when he was at Cholyngham.

As they waited for their starters (Charlotte had ordered asparagus with Hollandaise sauce), she asked him to tell her the story of his and Anna's first date. She'd heard it before, but it was so romantic that it never failed to make her go all glowy, as if she'd feasted on Ready Brek.

It went like this: four years ago, Vivien, who had met Finn at a fund-raising gig for cancer research, had set up Anna and Finn on a blind date. She'd arranged for them to meet on the terrace of a restaurant in Covent Garden, but, because Anna had been too vain to wear her glasses, she hadn't recognised Finn from his description and had ended up sitting at a table all by herself. The beauty of the story was that Finn had sat there fancying the arse off the person who happened to be Anna, and hoping that his blind date (whom Vivien had described simply as 'very, very pretty, with glasses') wouldn't show up. They had finally got together after a pair of jokers had run across the terrace, randomly spraying mustard from a squeezy bottle at the al fresco diners. Anna had been one of those hit, and Finn had immediately come to her rescue. He'd tenderly wiped mustard off her poor surprised face, and when she saw him close up, Anna had realised who he must be and had fallen in love at first sight.

As Charlotte listened to the story, she realised that a solitary diner at a table across the room was watching her. She slid a glance in his direction. Tall? Check. Dark? Check. Handsome? Double check. As she returned her attention to Finn, her smiles became a little more expansive, her laughs a little more flagrant, her body language a little more eloquent. *Yay*! It was working. Tall, Dark and Handsome was clearly finding her mesmerising. She picked up an asparagus spear, dipped it in Hollandaise and daintily nibbled the tip. Result! There was a lot to be said for anonymous flirting.

'Thank you!' she said to the waiter who arrived with her main course, and who, sadly, obscured the view while he arranged dishes and poured water and refilled her wine glass.

'*Bon appetit*!' said the waiter, backing away. As he did so, she saw that TD&H had been joined by a lady friend, who was clasping his hand across the table and gushing apologies for being late.

No! Charlotte looked down at her plate. She'd ordered fresh turbot with dill sauce, and now she wished she hadn't because the turbot's head was still on. Registering the reproachful way its eye gazed up at her, she knew instantly that she had lost her appetite. *Damn and blast TD&H's lady friend*, she thought, taking a big swig of wine. She'd made Charlotte look like a complete tool.

'*Bon appetit*!' said Finn, laying into his venison with gusto.

'*Bon appetit*!' said Alex, laying into his T-bone like a savage.

'*Bon appetit*!' said Charlotte, poking the turbot gingerly with her fish fork.

'What do you think?' asked Finn.

'Ace,' said Alex.

'Lovely!' said Charlotte, who was trying hard to avoid the accusatory eye glaring up at her. 'Absolutely lovely!'

She spent the next ten minutes toying with the turbot and was relieved when Finn excused himself from the table to go to the jakes, because it meant that she could wrap the fish up in tissues and stow it in her handbag. She hadn't wanted to do it in front of him in case he thought it an insult to the new Cholyngham chef, who had apparently been awarded many Michelin stars.

'What the *fuck* are you playing at, Charlotte?' Alex hissed at her the moment Finn disappeared through the door of the dining room.

'I don't want the chef to take offence when he sees how little I've eaten,' she explained, sliding the turbot into the tissue-paper nest she'd concocted. Charmelle at the next table was looking on with undisguised fascination. 'Especially since he's only new. I do this all the time in restaurants where the staff are lovely. They always take it so personally if you leave loads of food on your plate.'

'That's not what I'm talking about.'

Charlotte gave him a wide-eyed look of incomprehension. 'What *are* you talking about, then?' she asked.

'I *know* you, remember? Are you stirring things up?'

'What do you mean?'

'There's this weird fucking vibe hanging between you and Finn. What's going on?'

'Vibe? What vibe?'

'I don't know, but it ain't pretty. It ain't pretty at all. I think it's called doing the dirty on your best friend.'

'Ex*cuse* me?' Charlotte was outraged. 'What are you suggesting?'

'I'm suggesting that you're out to seduce your best friend's boyfriend.'

Charlotte felt her face flare up. 'How *dare* you, Alex! There's *nothing* like that going on. You're imagining things. You've probably had too much to drink.'

'Oh, and you *haven't*, Ms Goody Teetotal Two Shoes?' He leaned back in his chair and gave her a look of appraisal that made her face go redder with indignation. 'You know what they say about alcohol fuelling desire? I wouldn't have any more wine if I were you. Things have the potential to get incendiary here, Flirtypants.'

'Well, sod you!' said Charlotte, draining her glass to spite him and lunging for the wine bottle. 'I shall drink as much as I damn well please.'

Before she could pour, the sommelier came hurtling over, consternation scrawled large on his face. 'Madam! Allow me.'

'Sorry.'

Charlotte and Alex sat there, looking mulishly away from one another, while the sommelier replenished their glasses. The sommelier was followed by the busboy, who came to take away their plates and brush crumbs off the table. And the busboy was followed by the waiter, whose pleasure it was to present them with the dessert menu. As soon as it was safe to talk, they launched into each other again.

'How do you think Anna would feel if she knew you were sitting here in Cholyngham making snake eyes at her man, when she's been decent enough to organise a room for you? Were you planning this even as she was on the phone to Finn's mother the other night, when you were eyeing him up? And don't think I didn't see that tender embrace in the kitchen.'

'That "tender embrace" was Finn trying to comfort me,' Charlotte told him indignantly. 'And I was *never* "eyeing him up"!'

'So what was with all the little coy sideways smiles that were going on around the table?'

'It's called playing poker, Alex.'

'I've never seen you simper and flirt and blush when you've played poker in the past.'

'That's because I've never held a winning hand in the past. If I blushed, that's because I was flushed with success for once, loser.'

'That doesn't go any way towards explaining your vampy behaviour this evening.'

'Oh, please don't be ridiculous, Alex,' she said scornfully. '*Vampy* behaviour? You're making me sound like some seductress in a bad B movie.'

'Well, based on the evidence I've seen this evening, I'd say that's a pretty accurate character assessment.'

'Oh, for Christ's sake, Alex! You're behaving like some hen's-ass older brother.'

'Darling, you seem to forget that I'm the older brother you never had. Which makes it even more difficult for me to sit here and watch you exude sexual vibes left, right and centre like – like *ectoplasm*!'

'What's going on?'

Finn was standing at the table, looking down at them with a puzzled expression.

'Nothing,' said Alex and Charlotte simultaneously.

'What's all this about sexual vibes?'

'Oh, I accused Charlotte of fancying one of the waiters.'

'Really?' said Finn, resuming his seat and giving Charlotte a curious look. 'Which one?'

'That one,' said Alex, pointing randomly across the room.

Simultaneously their gaze lit upon a waiter who bore an uncanny resemblance to Worzel Gummidge.

'Really, Charlotte?' said Finn, sounding unconvinced. 'What's there to fancy about him?'

Alex answered for her. 'She says he exudes animal magnetism.'

'I did *not* say that!'

'Yes, you did,' said Alex in a maddeningly unruffled fashion. 'You said that a man didn't have to be good-looking to be attractive. You said that the way he looked at you when he put the fish in front of you made you want to grab his face and kiss it off.'

Charlotte was so gobsmacked that she couldn't think of a thing to say except 'Liar, liar, pants on fire', which was one of the more intelligent insults she and Alex had traded as kids.

Finn was looking even more confused. 'Would you like me to, you know, put a word in with him for you? He's worked here for years, so I know him quite well.'

'*No!*'

'Charlotte plans a rather more subtle seduction technique,' said Alex. 'She's going to ask for room service later, and she's going to be *very* specific about the waiter who's to provide it.'

'Jesus, Charlotte. I'm not sure my mother would approve of you having sex with a member of staff.'

'Alex is *joking*, Finn! Can't you see that? He's always winding me up. Ha ha ha.' She shot Alex a steely look across the table. 'Now the joke's over. OK? It's starting to wear a little thin.'

'Well. I must say it's interesting to know what type of man floats your boat, Charlotte,' remarked Finn, looking at Worzel Gummidge. 'Sexual magnetism, eh?'

Alex got to his feet, took his phone out of his pocket and switched it on. 'Excuse me,' he said. 'I need to make a call. I told Thea I'd phone at four o'clock Caribbean time. Don't you want to phone Anna, Finn?'

'I already did,' said Finn. 'That's why I was away from the table for so long.'

'See you later, then.' Alex narrowed his eyes meaningfully at Charlotte before turning and ambling from the room.

'How is Anna?'

'She's fine.' Finn was still looking a little perplexed. 'So – do you or do you not fancy that waiter, Charlotte?'

'No,' she told him firmly. 'That was just Alex playing silly buggers.'

'I see. So, er, why were you talking about sexual vibes?'

'I can't remember,' said Charlotte, looking down at the napkin on her lap and wanting to pleat it. But pleating a napkin said too much. It said: *I'm uncomfortable, I'm unsettled, I want to get out of here.*

She was racking her brain for something to say when: 'Darling! Sorry for not being able to join you sooner. The kitchen was chaos. Charlotte, how lovely to see you!'

'Likewise!' said Charlotte, stapling on a big smile and rising to air-kiss Finn's mother, who was wearing a frilly pink bath cap.

'Hey, Lavinia!' a big American sitting at a table opposite called over in a matey way. 'You sure are zany. Didn't you know you were still wearing your bath cap?'

'Am I?' said Lavinia, sitting down in Alex's chair. 'Goodness gracious! How silly of me.' She reached up and took the offending item off.

'Ha ha ha,' went the American. 'Cholyngham sure is run by the quaintest folk. Ha ha ha!'

'Ha ha ha,' Lavinia said back, before returning her attention to Finn and Charlotte. 'Dear God,' she resumed, under her breath. 'It really is quite exhausting pretending to be eccentric. Sometimes I wish I hadn't started.'

'How many times have you pulled that bath-cap stunt?' asked Finn.

'Too often. I'll have to ring the changes and start wearing my solar topi instead.'

'Are you still coming down to breakfast in your tiara?'

'Afraid so. I've even taken to wearing it at a rakish angle for maximum effect.' She leaned back in her chair and surveyed her son. 'Well,' she said. 'It's lovely to see you, darling. I'm sorry that Anna couldn't come, but I'm sure she's having a fabulous time in

Paris. How sweet of you, Charlotte, to offer up your prize to your friends!'

'It was no sacrifice, really. I'd much rather be here in Cholyngham than in Paris.'

'What a kind thing to say!' Lavinia returned her attention to Finn. 'How's Anna's morning sickness?' she asked.

'Oh God, Mother.' Finn's tone was leaden; he looked stricken. 'That was meant to be a secret.'

'Oh, Lord! I am sorry, darling. I completely forgot that you haven't told anybody yet. Pretend you didn't hear that, Charlotte.'

'Please do.' Finn shot his mother a look of mega-reproach.

'Now, let's organise puddings and coffee.' Lavinia let her gaze wander round the dining room in an attempt to locate a waiter.

Pretend you didn't hear that? That was on a par with ignoring the remark Alex had made earlier that day about red crotchless panties. Charlotte *couldn't* pretend that she hadn't heard. She looked at Finn with a kind of agonised enquiry. Were he and Anna having a baby? Why hadn't Anna told her? They *never* kept secrets from each other! 'We. Need. To. Talk,' she mouthed at him.

But Finn failed to register the pantomime.

He was distracted by the return of Alex, who had come back into the dining room and was pulling up another chair to the table.

Charlotte immediately clamped her mouth shut and swivelled her eyes away from Finn, but she knew Alex had seen.

'Alex!' said Lavinia, presenting her face for a kiss. 'It is, as always, a real pleasure to see you.'

'The pleasure's all mine, ma'am,' said Alex, kissing Lavinia first on her left cheek, then on her right. As he did so, he raised a saturnine eyebrow at Charlotte. She stuck her tongue out at him and gave him a murderous look in return.

'How is your beautiful girlfriend?' Lavinia asked as Alex resumed his seat.

'Thea? She's off shooting a movie in the Caribbean.'

'How glamorous!' said Lavinia, with a sigh. 'What wouldn't I give to be in the Caribbean right now? It couldn't be any hotter than that kitchen, that's for sure.' She slid a cigarette from the pack that she had set on the table in front of her, and Finn shot her a reproachful look.

'I thought you were going to give up, Mum,' he said. 'How are you going to cope when the new smoking regulations come in?'

'Oh, we shall manage somehow. If they can do it in Ireland and Italy, we can jolly well do it here.'

'Allow me,' Alex said, picking up the matchbook with the Cholyngham logo that nestled between the cruets. He struck a match, lit the cigarette, then blew it out, looking thoughtful. 'Let's order flaming sambucas,' he said.

'Flaming sambucas?' said Lavinia. 'Wouldn't you prefer brandy?'

'I know Charlotte wouldn't.'

'What? What are you on about?' asked Charlotte.

'Why, a flaming sambuca will give you the opportunity to indulge in your favourite game, Ms Cholewczyk.'

Why did Alex have to be so insufferably cryptic? 'My favourite game? And what might that be?' she asked, with an attempt at hauteur.

Alex shot her a satanic smile. 'Playing with fire,' he said, sliding the matchbook into his pocket and returning the beam of his attention to Lavinia.

Finn poured wine all round and took a

hefty swig from his glass; Charlotte, likewise, took one from hers. And then, utterly unaware of what she was doing, she reached for the napkin she'd discarded on the table and began mechanically to pleat it.

four

They took their coffee into the library, where Lavinia quizzed them about the new chef. Was he not a genius? Was he not a *maître*? Oh, yes, indeed! Charlotte was singing his praises and waxing lyrical about the turbot when Finn interrupted her. 'How sweet!' he said. 'Grishkin's taken a real shine to you, Charlotte. She's normally very snooty around strangers.'

Charlotte looked down at Grishkin, the Cholyngham cat, who was practically sitting on her feet, rubbing her face against Charlotte's handbag and purring profusely.

'Oh, shit!' said Charlotte. She grabbed the bag and set it on her lap.

'I thought you loved cats,' said Finn.

'She does,' said Alex, joining them. 'She adores them. I remember when she was a little girl, one of her kittens died. She dug up its grave every night so that she could sleep with it, until her mum rumbled her.'

Grishkin was looking up at her with hungry eyes, calculating the distance between the floor and Charlotte's knee. Before Charlotte could do anything to discourage her, the cat leapt onto her lap in a fluid movement. She then proceeded to sniff rapturously at the bag, kneading Charlotte's thighs through the white linen of her dress as she did so.

'Get off, you!' said Charlotte in a panicky voice. She swept the cat violently off her lap onto the floor, where it landed in an ungainly fashion, then leapt to her feet, holding her handbag aloft. Grishkin eyed her with an expression that contrived to be both injured and rapacious.

'Goodness, Charlotte,' said Lavinia, giving her a surprised look. 'There's no need to be quite so rough with the poor cat.'

'You really must love that bag,' said Alex in an overly concerned voice, 'if you'd inflict injury on an innocent little pussycat in order to protect it.'

'I – I *used* to love cats,' improvised Charlotte, 'until I, um, until …'

'Until you developed a dreadful allergy to them,' supplied Alex.

'Yes. That's right.'

'They make you sneeze something dreadful, don't they?'

'They do?'

'Yes. They do.' Alex was categorical. 'That explains why your nose was so runny earlier.'

'I gue-ess …' she said, wishing she had a stun gun handy to blast the irritating smile off Alex's face. He raised an eyebrow at her, and: 'Ah-*choo!*' she went obligingly. Then: 'Excuse me. I'd better run to the loo.' 'Run' being the operative word. She needed to get rid of the offending contents of her bag at the earliest opportunity.

'I'll come with you,' said the mistress of the house, rising to her feet and setting off across the room. As she went, Lavinia executed little dance steps and clicked her fingers, and all the guests in the library applauded. It had become part of the Cholyngham myth that she had been one of the more obscure members of Pan's People on

Top of the Pops way back in the early 70s, and Lavinia felt it incumbent upon her to deliver the goods. It was amazing, thought Charlotte as she followed Lavinia, how gullible people were, how they chose to believe what they were told to believe.

'Hey, Lavinia!' boomed an elderly German as she click-clicked past him. 'Dig zat crrrazy beat! Maybe we could hef a danz togezzer later?'

'Yeah! Rock on,' said Lavinia, sending him a bright smile. But Charlotte heard her add, under her breath, 'In your dreams, buster.'

Charlotte was feeling rather crestfallen. Her plan had been to flush the fish down the loo, but it wouldn't be quite so easy to dispose of it with Lavinia powdering her nose in the next cubicle. Out through the library door they went, into the parquet-floored lobby, and then Charlotte became aware of the *scritch-scritch-scritch* of clawed feet skittering along beside her. Looking down, she realised that she was being pursued with relentless intent by Grishkin, who was glaring up at her with obdurate eyes. She tried to outstrip the cat, but her progress was hampered by the funky little twirls that Lavinia was performing for the American couple who were making enquiries at reception as to the whereabouts of the nearest McDonald's. Whiney Charmelle was selecting postcards, complaining that there were none of Prince William. Charlotte stumbled as Grishkin started weaving between her legs, and she had a sudden vision of herself toppling to the parquet, her bag bursting open and its fishy contents being disgorged all over the Cholyngham lobby. She gave the cat a shove with her foot, whereupon Grishkin gave an aggrieved meow and Charmelle's voice behind her said, 'Mom! That lady kicked the poor cat.'

Lavinia shot her a curious look over her shoulder and said, 'Your allergy must be seriously bad, Charlotte, if you have to resort to physical violence.'

'Yes, it is,' concurred Charlotte earnestly. 'I'm sorry to have to use brute force on the animal, but if her fur comes into contact with my skin, I'll erupt in the most awful rash.'

'Poor you,' said Lavinia. 'I have some antihistamine cream if you need it.'

'Thanks,' said Charlotte, adding a theatrical 'Aaahchoo!' for good measure.

At last, at *last* they reached the sanctuary of the loo. Charlotte dived through the door and shut it firmly in Grishkin's furry face.

'You wouldn't happen to have any *papier poudré*, Charlotte, would you?' asked Lavinia, peering in the mirror. 'My cheeks have gone very shiny. You wouldn't believe the heat of that kitchen.'

'No,' lied Charlotte. She actually had a brand new packet of *papier poudré* in her bag, but there was no way she was going to go rooting around for it, in case the smell of fish came wafting out.

'Oh, well,' said Lavinia. 'I'll just have to make do with repairing my hair and lippy.' And she set about titivating herself, smoothing her Louise Brooks bob. 'I'd love to be able to grow it long like yours,' she told Charlotte. 'That chignon's so quintessentially romantic. But the chef doesn't approve of Rapunzel tresses in the kitchen.'

Charlotte snuck a look at herself. In fact, her chignon was starting to look a bit dishevelled, but she decided that now was no time for titivation. The sooner she got rid of the chef's special, the better.

In the cubicle, she extracted the parcel of tissue paper that contained the turbot and essayed a rather unconvincing 'Ahchoo!' to camouflage the splash as she dropped it into the loo. *Yay!* she thought, reaching for the porcelain handle of the lavatory chain. Success was hers!

She yanked on the chain, but nothing happened. She yanked again, more vigorously. Still no result. And again. *Nada*. Oh, Christ. She was reminded of something Samuel Beckett had once said about trying and failing, and failing better. She, Charlotte Ahchoo Cholewczyk, was failing quite spectacularly.

'Is that loo not flushing?' came Lavinia's voice over the cubicle door. 'It's rather temperamental, that one. I'll get the janitor to have a look at it.'

'Oh. OK.'

There was obviously nothing else for it. The unfortunate janitor would be the one obliged to execute the denouement of this particular fishy tale. Charlotte tried one last half-hearted flush before emerging from the cubicle and joining Lavinia at the mirror. She had just taken her flacon of scent out of her bag when the door of the ladies' opened and Charmelle, the miniature animal-rights protester, darted through and made directly for the loo that Charlotte had just vacated. Charlotte was just about to shout 'Not that one!' when the child emitted a yowl of disgust.

'Ew! Someone's varminted into the john!'

'What?' said a startled Lavinia.

'There's varmint in the john!' squealed Charmelle, reeling out of the cubicle like one of the actors confronted with the creature popping out of John Hurt's chest in *Alien*.

Lavinia turned uncomprehending eyes on Charlotte.

'It wasn't me,' said Charlotte. 'Well, actually, it *was* me,' she added, as second-thought syndrome kicked in. Who in her right mind, when you analysed it, would elect to use a loo in which somebody else had upchucked? The culprit *had* to have been Charlotte.

'Oh, Charlotte, I'm so sorry,' said Lavinia, sounding genuinely horrified. 'What did you have to eat at dinner?'

Oh, no! Now she would have to point the finger of suspicion at the hapless Michelin chef whose professional pride she had gone to such convoluted lengths to protect.

'It wasn't the dinner,' she said hastily, clocking the stricken look on Lavinia's face. 'It definitely wasn't the dinner. It was the – the cat.'

'Oh, my God! Your allergy to cats is that extreme? How shocking. Should I call a doctor?'

'No, no,' said Charlotte hastily. 'I'll be fine now that I've, you know, chucked up.'

'Ew!' said Charmelle, backing out through the door of the varmint-infested ladies. 'That is *so* gross.'

'What shall we do with you, Charlotte dear?' asked Lavinia, full of concern. 'Let's see … Let me think … I know! Brandy and port. That's the very thing for queasy stomachs. Actors swear by it, apparently.'

And if actors swore by it, Charlotte mused as she followed Lavinia back to the library, it probably *was* the very thing. After all, her acting skills that evening could have won her an Oscar nomination.

In the library, Finn and Alex were talking boy talk to each other in low voices and eyeing the arse of a quite famous singer who was posing by the French windows with her glamorous motor-racing boyfriend. Grishkin was sitting up very straight in the armchair that had been Charlotte's. The cat gave Charlotte a baleful look as she approached, and Lavinia said, 'Quick, Finn! Get rid of Grishkin at once. She's made poor Charlotte frightfully ill.'

'Really?' said Finn, abstractedly. He was clearly reluctant to drag his eyes away from the singer's bootyliciousness.

'Yes. She threw up her dinner in the lavatory. I'm going to fetch some brandy and port,' added Lavinia, bustling off in the direction of the honesty bar. 'And you lock Grishkin in the stable, Finn. We don't want her to be responsible for ruining Charlotte's weekend.'

'Sure.' Finn scooped the cat off the arm-chair, and as he moved past her with Grishkin in his arms, he gave Charlotte a smile of concern. Charlotte took care not to return the smile. She didn't want Alex levelling any more accusations at her.

She went to resume her seat. 'I'd brush the cat hairs off before you sit down,' advised Alex, who was still ogling the singer's arse. 'They obviously have an extremely emetic effect on you. You'll be coughing up fur-balls next if you're not careful.'

'Ha ha, Alex,' she said, with a distinct dearth of amusement. 'This is all your fault, you know.'

'My fault? *My* fault? Who, pray, was responsible for saving your face when that cat was doing its damnedest to expose the fact that your precious handbag was full to the brim with Michelin-starred fish? How would you have explained your way out of that?'

'Don't you see that it's an indication of my sensitivity,' said Charlotte, 'that I should choose to run the risk of inflicting damage on my handbag by filling it with fish rather than risk offending a new chef's sensibilities?'

'His wrath, more like,' said Alex. 'You were probably just scared that he'd come blazing out of the kitchen at you with a meat cleaver like Marco Pierre White. What did the handbag say, incidentally, when you filled it with fish? Was it indignant?'

'Not at all. *She* understood my predicament.'

'You are *so* weird, lady.' Charmelle, who had been sitting at a table behind them playing samples of ring-tones, had climbed up onto her seat and was looking at Charlotte over the back of her chair as if she were Linda Blair in *The Exorcist*. 'Not only do you kick cats and varmint in the restrooms, you carry fish around in your purse. People like you shouldn't be legal.'

'That's enough, you little shit,' said Charlotte, giving the child a steely look. 'And don't you dare tell your mother I called you a little shit, because if you do, I shall invoke the headless Cholyngham ghost and command it to visit you in your bedroom this evening. Now bugger off.'

'Huh,' said the unimpressed child. 'I don't believe in ghosts.'

'Don't you?' said Alex. 'Then you're even stupider than you look. There's one out there on the lawn.'

One of the Cholyngham goats was cutting capers in a rose bed.

'That's not a ghost, loser. That's a *goat*.'

'That's what you think, farm girl. That goat is the ghost of a disciple of Old Nick.'

'Old who?'

'Old Nick. The devil himself, with his cloven hoofs and his horns and his pointy beard. Here.' Alex reached for a book from one of the library shelves. It was Dennis Wheatley's *The Devil Rides Out*. 'You can read all about him in this.'

Charmelle took the book from Alex and studied the image on the jacket. It depicted a goat's skull that sported lethal-looking curved horns. Yellow eyes with pupils narrow as arrows gleamed in the sockets, and clouds of brimstoney smoke were puffing out of its fleshless nostrils. The girl looked at Alex, and then she looked out through the window, where the goat was now standing stock-still, staring right back at her.

'Dare you to go out there,' said Alex.

'No.'

'Then bugger off, like the lady said, and enjoy your bedtime reading. And don't forget what she said about the headless ghost.'

Charmelle sank back down in her armchair with a face that would have been as white as the Cholyngham ghost's – if it had had a face, and if it had actually existed.

'Finn suggested a picnic tomorrow,' said Alex, resuming his scrutiny of the singer's arse. 'If the weather's halfway good.'

Charlotte brightened. 'Oh? Good idea.'

'If you've recovered sufficiently from the attack of nausea brought on by that hapless cat, that is. Just think of the poor little beastie, shivering in the stable all night instead of in its comfy basket, just because you have a deluded aversion to it.'

Charlotte didn't bother telling him to shut up.

On the other side of the room, the posey singer turned her head slowly and caught Alex's eye, which had finally moved from her arse to her face. She returned his interested look, her mouth curving in one of those sexy 'if only I were single' smiles.

'Get you, Alex,' said Charlotte crossly. 'What a hypocrite you are to give me grief about some non-existent sexual attraction between me and Finn, while you're busy ravishing that girl with your eyes. If you're not careful I'll take a picture of that stupid expression on your face and send it to Thea, to let her know what you're up to.'

'Fire ahead, sweetheart,' said Alex. 'Thea is so solipsistic she'll automatically assume from the lustful expression that I'm thinking about her.'

Charlotte didn't want to let him know that despite her degree in English and her job as a copywriter, she hadn't a clue what 'solipsistic' meant, so she just kept schtum. Luckily, Lavinia chose that moment to roll up with Charlotte's brandy and port. 'Sorry for the delay,' she said. 'We were clean out of Remy Martin, so I had to nip down to the cellar for it.' She handed Charlotte the brandy balloon and said with a meaningful look, 'You know, Charlotte: the *cellar*.'

'Oh, yes! The *cellar*!' said Charlotte, picking up on her cue and pitching her voice so that the Americans sitting by the fireplace would hear her. 'Jeepers, Lavinia, I don't know *how* you have the *nerve* to go down there.'

'What's that?' said one of the tartan-trousered Yanks. 'Is there something in the cellar that you don't want us to know about?'

'The Cholyngham ghost,' began Lavinia in lugubrious tones. 'The story goes ...'

Charlotte didn't listen. She'd heard the story before. Instead, she allowed her gaze to wander round the room, taking in the relaxed ambience of Cholyngham after dinner – the blazing fire, the golden lamp light, the hazy blue hue of the sky beyond the French windows. There was Finn now, out on the lawn, talking to one of the prettier Cholyngham chambermaids. She wished Alex wasn't acting like such a nanny around her and Finn. She really *did* want to talk to him, she'd love to know more about the baby.

Charlotte drew her legs up under her and hugged herself. On her left, Alex was texting with dexterous thumbs; on her right Charmelle, bored with Lavinia's ghost story, was playing a game on her phone. She glanced up, caught Charlotte's eye, then nodded towards the window.

'Your boyfriend's flir-ting with another gi-irl,' she said in a sing-songy aside.

'He's not my boyfriend,' Charlotte snapped back.

'Then why are you staring at him with that sappy look on your face?'

'I'm not staring at him with a sappy look!' Charlotte turned away so that Charmelle could no longer see her expression.

A moment later her text alert sounded. She took her phone from her bag and read: *Liar liar pants on fire. A.*

* * *

Later, around midnight, Charlotte hung up her white linen dress in the wardrobe of the Boudoir and performed bedtime ablutions, wondering all the while about Finn and Anna and the baby. A baby! Her best friends were going to have a baby. Joy! But as she spritzed her face with toner, it occurred to her that perhaps there were problems. Lavinia had asked Finn about Anna's morning sickness, so the pregnancy couldn't be very far advanced. Maybe it was too early to celebrate? Maybe Finn really, really *didn't* want to talk about it just yet. And since Anna had said nothing, it might be as well to stay schtum for now. She would respect her friends' privacy, Charlotte decided, and not raise the subject of the baby until – and, indeed, unless – they did.

Charlotte slathered on some Vitamin E cream, then set the alarm on her phone. She wanted to get up early, so as to make the most of her time at Cholyngham. She set the phone down on her white-painted bedside locker and slipped naked between nubbly linen sheets. How lovely it would be to have someone with whom she could share the bed, so quintessentially romantic was it! How lovely to dress up in a negligee of silk chiffon or charmeuse, underpinned by pretty, frothy, scanty things. How glorious to quaff champagne in bed and feast on fruit and chocolate ... It had been so long since Charlotte had made love that she wondered if she'd remember how to do it – *if* an opportunity ever came her way again. She'd been single for nearly a year, she realised. The last time she'd slept with anyone had been with Duncan in Paris, and while Duncan had turned out to be a complete shit, he *had* been a fantastic lover.

She thought of Vivien and Anna and wondered if they were asleep in their Paris hotel room, or if they were strolling along boulevards, perversely revelling in the atmosphere of the vile French capital in the springtime. And then she thought of how

Anna had told her about Finn washing her hair in the bath, and she thought, *Oh, how lovely, how lovely* – to have a man's strong, shapely fingers massaging her skull, then maybe trailing down her cheek, lingering on her lower lip, sliding past her collarbone, cupping a breast while he dropped kisses on the nape of her neck, and then perhaps caressing the incline of her rib cage and the swell of her tummy and beyond … and beyond …

Charlotte fell asleep hoping that she'd dream about Johnny Depp.

She didn't. When she woke in the morning, she knew she'd dreamt about somebody with very kind eyes. But it hadn't been Johnny Depp. It had been Worzel Gummidge.

five

The picnic the Michelin chef (or, more likely, one of his minions) prepared for them was a virtual feast. The three of them – Finn, Charlotte and Alex – cycled down to a forest that adjoined the Cholyngham estate to enjoy it, because the day was one of those blue-sky, blindingly hot days that Easter sometimes delivers like a present. Whitethorn blossom was dripping from branches, the drive was confettied with pink petals from cherry trees and the green velvet of the verges was polka-dotted yellow and white with buttercups and daisies. The day had been gift-wrapped by Mother Nature, and the score that accompanied it was pretty special, too. The birdsong bouncing from tree to tree was ebullient.

They spread a rug under the branches of a chestnut and plundered the contents of their rucksacks. They gorged on new potato salad, crudités with a blue-cheese dip, a selection of salamis, a gloriously runny Brie, home-baked tomato-and-fennel bread and gingered peaches. There was lots of fresh fruit, too, but Charlotte steered clear of the figs, because figs had the same effect on her as baked beans did on other people. There were also a couple of bottles of very good chilled Sancerre.

Charlotte was lying on her tummy on the rug, with her bare feet in the air. Having listened to the forecast the day before they'd travelled down from London, she had had the foresight to pack a sundress and a sunhat. The sunhat was a straw affair trimmed with tiny silk rosebuds that she fancied made her look like a character from a Merchant Ivory film, and the dress was of feather-light cheesecloth that had kept fluttering up over her thighs as they cycled, but that was OK, because she'd also had the foresight to St Tropez herself on Thursday night. She'd painted her toenails as well in a rather fetching shade of peony-pink.

'Why do women paint their toenails?' asked Alex, taking a photograph of her with his phone.

'I don't know,' confessed Charlotte. 'I suppose to disguise them. Toenails are disgusting.'

Finn stretched out his legs and scrutinised his bare feet. 'I guess feet in general are disgusting. Mine in particular. Look at them! They're weird.'

Actually, Charlotte thought, Finn had rather elegant feet. Alex's, on the other hand, were too big. They had to be at least a size twelve.

'I bet Jennifer Lopez's feet aren't disgusting,' said Alex. 'I wouldn't mind sucking *her* toes.'

'That's because she can afford to have a pedicure every day if she wants,' said Charlotte.

'Anna'll need a pedicure when she gets back from Paris, Finn,' said Alex. 'After all that trotting around shopping. Especially if she's wearing shoes as silly as Charlotte's.'

'They're not silly. They're perfect for a day like this.' Charlotte's footwear today was a pair of flat leather sandals, with long straps that crisscrossed Grecian style.

'I suppose a pedicure's not a bad idea,' said Finn. 'Maybe I'll book one as a present for Anna. Who would you recommend, Charlotte?'

'I've never had one, believe it or not – and I doubt I ever will. The pedicure scene in *Desperate Housewives* put me off the idea forever.'

'What happened?'

'One of the housewives gave the Filipina woman who was doing her feet a kick in the face, and the viewers were expected to find it funny.'

'I'm glad to know you have a social conscience after all, even if you fork out a small fortune for a bag that was probably constructed by the same Filipina's six-year-old daughter,' said Alex.

Charlotte gave a sigh of ennui. 'You're never going to let me forget that, are you?'

'No, ma'am.' Alex flashed her a narrow-eyed smile and lay back on the grass.

There was a kind of lazy silence for a while. Even the birds had shut up in the heat. Charlotte thought she might drift off to sleep, but Finn broke the silence by saying,

'It's weird to think that I'll be dressed in a fucking suit again next week.'

'Why do legal eagles have to wear suits?' asked Charlotte.

'Because nobody would employ a barrister who wore jeans.'

'I would,' said Alex.

'You're not a nobody,' Finn reminded him. 'You're a celebrity.'

'Cut the crap, man.'

Alex had had his fifteen minutes of fame when he had talked a potential suicide down from a crane. He had happened to be in the crowd, taking notes for the broadsheet he worked for, and as a qualified Emergency First Responder, he'd volunteered his services and climbed up to spend six hours with his legs dangling at sixty feet. The guy on the crane had ended up being reconciled with his estranged wife and family after Alex's intervention, and he had given Alex all the credit for it. Alex had been on television, he had been interviewed by *Today* and his picture had even appeared in *Hello!* magazine, which was a source of no little embarrassment to him. Charlotte kept the cutting in her wallet and derived great pleasure from flashing it around at parties just to annoy him.

Finn reached out an arm for the wine bottle. 'Shit,' he said. 'It's nearly all gone. Charlotte? Can I interest you in a refill?'

'No. You and Alex share the last of it. I'll stick with water.' The wine had made her very thirsty. 'There's not much of that left, either,' she observed, unscrewing the cap.

'Finish it,' said Finn. 'We can refill the bottle from the spring on the way back.'

Lavinia had recently started bottling the Cholyngham water and selling it for a tidy profit in the shop attached to the hotel. The shop also stocked Cholyngham jams and chutneys and soups and shortbread and tea towels and gardening tools and hot-water bottles and besoms and … well, you name it, it had 'Cholyngham' stamped on it. They had even started a mean line in string puppets of the Cholyngham goats. Little wonder the place was thriving. And it was all down to the marketing savvy of Finn's supposedly eccentric parents.

Finn poured the last of the Sancerre into paper cups and glanced at his watch. 'I guess we'd better make tracks,' he said, 'if we're going to fit in our swim.'

'A swim? At this time of the year? Are you barking fucking mad?' said Alex.

Finn looked sanguine. 'I always have my first swim at Easter.'

'But the water'll be freezing, man! It was scrotum-tightening when we last did it, and that was at the height of summer.'

Two summers before, Finn and Anna and Alex and Vivien and Charlotte and duplicitous Duncan had all swum to the island in the middle of the Cholyngham lake. The island had been Finn's playground as a child: there was a hut on it, and a swing, and a canoe that could no longer be used because the bottom had rotted away. That was when the tradition of swimming to the island had been initiated.

'I am not going back to London,' said Finn, 'without having had a swim in the Cholyngham lake.'

'I'd actually love a swim,' said Charlotte. 'It's a bitch of an uphill climb back to the hotel, and it's still very hot. I'd be glad of a chance to cool down.'

'I bet you would.' Alex shot her a look, which she ignored.

'We'll pack up, then,' said Finn, draining his wine and lobbing the cup into the rubbish bag. 'But I'd better have a pee before I go.'

'You should save it for the swim,' said Alex. 'It might warm the water up a bit.'

'Alex! You are so gross,' Charlotte told him.

'Not as gross as some people. Did you know that scuba divers often pee in their wetsuits for warmth when they get into the water?'

'No!' exclaimed Charlotte, giving him a lash with the straps of her sandals. 'Gross, gross, *gross*!'

'Girl,' returned Alex.

'I couldn't save it for the lake even if I wanted to,' said Finn. 'A man's gotta go when a man's gotta go.' And he headed off in the direction of a bosky bit of forest.

Alex was looking at Charlotte suspiciously. 'What do you think you're going to swim in?' he asked when Finn was out of earshot. 'Your pelt?'

'No. My underwear, of course,' she said, a tad indignantly.

'Is it sexy?'

'You tell me, pal.' She flashed her knickers at him.

'It's sexy. You're to keep your bra on, OK?'

'I didn't last time.'

'That was because there were other girlies present last time. Under no circumstances are you going to swim topless on your own with two men, young lady. You have a reputation to think about.'

'*Two* men? I thought you weren't going to swim?'

'There is no way,' Alex told her, 'that I am going to allow you to flutter-kick off to Love Island on your own with Finn. You need a chaperone, my girl.'

'Oh, for God's sake, Alex,' she said crossly. 'You're behaving just like Mammy out of *Gone with the Wind*.'

'That's not a bad analogy. Because I've every intention of making sure, Charlotte Cholewczyk, that *you* don't get the opportunity to start behaving like Scarlett.'

* * *

Even with her bra on, even with the Dutch courage instilled in her by the Sancerre, Charlotte couldn't help feeling a little vulnerable as she stripped off her dress and sandals by the lakeshore. She folded the dress and weighed it down with a stone to prevent it being blown away by the wind, and did the same with her hat.

'Last one in's a lingam,' shouted Finn, racing down the shore and wading into the water. Charlotte followed him, looking over her shoulder to where Alex brought up the rear.

She stuck her tongue out at him. 'Looks like you're the lingam, loser,' she said, and the next thing she said was 'Aaaaaiiieeee!' as the water made contact with her foot.

'Oh, yeah?' said Alex, curling his lip at her as he strolled past. Once the water had reached his hips, he dove straight in, leaving Charlotte standing up to her ankles in the water.

She dithered and dithered. Finn was halfway to the island now, and Alex was drawing level with him. She couldn't wimp out – she just couldn't. Alex would sneer at her and call her a girl, and she wanted to prove her mettle. She took a deep breath and started to move forward until she'd reached a depth where she could dive.

Sweet Jehovah! The initial shock took her breath away, and once she'd got it back she started to gibber to herself like somebody suffering from Tourette's syndrome. The water felt like silk that had been left in the fridge. Charlotte knew that when she got to the island her skin would be so pimply with goosebumps that even her Aveda scrub might not be able to shift them – if she'd had the nous to bring it with her.

It wasn't that far to swim, just about a hundred yards, but it took her quite a long time to get there because the chill factor cramped her style – quite literally. Charlotte prided herself on being a strong, elegant swimmer – she had been on the team at school – but today she was reduced to a clumsy dog-paddle in an effort to keep as much of her upper body out of the water as she feasibly could.

Alex and Finn had made the shore, and were standing on an embankment with their hands shading their eyes from the sun, watching her progress.

'Shit,' gasped Charlotte as she finally stumbled onto dry land. 'That was an act of lunacy.'

'Welcome to shore, little mermaid,' said Finn as he reached out a hand to help haul her onto the grassy bank.

'Welcome to shore, little lingam,' said Alex, doing likewise.

Charlotte stood there with one leg wound around the other, dripping all over the grass, hugging herself for warmth and shivering. 'What is a lingam, anyway?' she asked.

'A lingam,' said Finn, 'is a phallus symbolising the male principle of the universe.'

'I'd be interested to know how polar bears procreate,' said Alex. 'My own personal lingam could best be described as a shrunken head after that dip in melted ice.' But when Charlotte found herself looking, she decided that that couldn't possibly be true.

'My advice to you is to run around the island two or three times, sweetie-pie,' Finn advised her. 'It's the best way of getting the circulation kick-started.'

'OK,' said Charlotte. She knew she was going to look like a tool, but she was so cold at this stage that she didn't care.

'I wish I'd been able to bring my phone,' Alex called after her as she jiggled off. 'I could blackmail you forever if I got a shot of you trotting round an island in your scanties like Rebecca Loos.'

'Ha ha, Alex. Apply for a job as Cholyngham court jester, why don't you?' she returned.

It took her two minutes to circum-jog the island. When she reached the spot where she'd left the boys, the pair of them were doubled up with laughter.

'It's not *that* bloody funny,' said Charlotte.

'That's what you think,' managed Alex, when he'd finally stopped laughing. 'Take a look over there.'

'Where?'

'There,' said Finn, pointing towards the shore, still weak with laughter.

On the edge of the lake, the Gruff Gang had assembled like the Jets in *West Side Story*. They were dancing and capering on the foreshore, urging on two of their number who were engaged in a game of tug-of-war. But the tug-of-war wasn't over a rope. It was over Charlotte's cheesecloth dress.

'Oh! Oh! Oh!' squealed Charlotte, somehow managing to jump up and down with rage and stamp her bare foot at the same time. 'Oh, you – you *beastly* goats. Oh, no – no! Not my shoes as well! Not my *hat*!'

Two of the billy goats were chewing Charlotte's pretty sandals, while another had lit with glee upon her rose-trimmed sunhat. He impaled it with one of his horns and proceeded to strut up and down the foreshore like Naomi Campbell modelling Philip Treacy.

'Gather ye rosebuds while ye may,' said Alex. And he and Finn doubled up with renewed mirth.

Charlotte turned on them. 'You *bastards*!' she said with feeling, and then she ran down to the water's edge and dived straight in. She barely felt the cold at all this time, so intent was she on getting her clothes back. She swam as fast as she ever had at a school gala, and her exertion was such that she could feel her panties – which had not been designed with such strenuous activity in mind – begin to slip down her legs. She emerged staggering from the water, clutching her knicks and trying to pull them up as she made her way over the stones to where the goats were still partying.

They literally toppled over themselves to welcome her to their crib. One of them butted her ass, causing Charlotte to fall to her knees; another took the lacy trim of her bra strap between rubber lips and proceeded to chew it; another tried to mount her with alarming enthusiasm. One of them breathed goat-breath in her face, and another stuck his nose in her cleavage. A big, bearded bruiser had dragged the picnic rug from a rucksack and was lolling on it, inviting her to join him with lascivious yellow eyes. Charlotte quickly decided hot-footing it back to the lake was preferable to joining in the Gruff Gang's orgy. She hurled herself into the icy embrace of the water once more, praying that none of the goats was into synchronised swimming.

She trod water, watching helplessly as hoots of laughter floated over the water from the island and Naomi Campbell flounced around on the foreshore. The winner of the tug-of-war was calmly enjoying the spoils, chewing implacably on the remains of Charlotte's frock. Once he'd swallowed the last mouthful, he licked his lips the way a gourmet might after sampling the Cholyngham chef's special. Then he got to his feet and helped himself to the picnic rug. It dragged after him like a chieftain's cloak as he moved majestically away, followed by his henchmen, all yodelling goat rap and break-dancing and exchanging high-hooves.

Finn and Alex had swum up behind Charlotte. They were still spluttering with laughter.

'It's just as well that there was nobody around with a videocam,' said Alex. 'On the internet, that footage could have made some lucky sod more money than Paris Hilton ever grossed.'

They made their way back to shore, and Charlotte bent down to pick up one of the little pink rosebuds that had fallen off her hat. She was still holding on to her panties with her other hand.

'The one thing I really, really want to know,' she said, tucking the rosebud into her wet hair, 'is this. How on earth did they suss I was a Capricorn?'

* * *

Getting Charlotte back to the hotel took some doing. Alex lent her his T-shirt, but even though it covered her waterlogged panties, she still had to hang on to them in case they ended up round her ankles. Because none of them at this stage conformed to the Cholyngham dress code of smart-casual (the Gruff Gang had made off with one of Finn's shoes), they decided against cycling up the main approach and abandoned the bikes by the lakeshore. Finn suggested that they access the rear entrance via a roundabout route, and they proceeded by stealth, like guerrillas, diving from sally bush to rhododendron to hydrangea.

They had reached the last sally bush before the final stretch and were lurking under it, trying to decipher how clear the coast was, when the branches parted and Charmelle appeared like Chucky in the horror film.

'I know what you've been up to. You've been having sex in the bushes, haven't you? I know all about that. I read about it in one of my dad's magazines. It's called a menagerie at Troy.'

'Go play with the goats, farm girl,' said Alex.

'Watch it, buster,' said Charmelle. She aimed her phone at them as if it were a gun. 'Unless you want this to go on the Web. I could do it riiiight now.'

Before they could do anything to stop her, Charmelle was running in the direction of the French windows that led into the library, where the Cholyngham guests had access to the internet.

Six

The next day, Sunday, there was to have been an Easter-egg hunt in the Cholyngham grounds. But as luck would have it, Nature, who had been in such a benign mood the day before, decided on this occasion to be spiteful, and they woke up to torrential rain. Finn's parents had to put their contingency plan into action: indoor treasure trails. One trail was arranged specially for the children in the morning, while the adults were to be treated to a more challenging one in the afternoon.

Charlotte spent most of the morning reading her book in the conservatory, while

Alex and Finn played pool in the Billiard Room. Charlotte wasn't enjoying the book much. It was a must-read, according to the literary pages of the broadsheets, and destined for the Man Booker, but Charlotte would have preferred to relax with something a little more escapist and a lot more fun. However, she didn't want to run the risk of Alex crowing if he discovered her with her nose stuck in a volume of chick-lit. He'd already scoffed at her today when she'd voiced her anxiety about Chucky uploading that compromising photograph of them in the sally bush, with her clutching at her knickers.

'So what's the problem if it goes out on the Net?' he'd said. 'The likelihood of anyone who knows us seeing it is about one in a zillion, lame-brain. And at least Chucky didn't get a pic of you with the goats. Now *that* would have been a scoop worthy of a paparazzo.'

After lunch (there was no sign of Chucky in the dining room: her mom must have kept her promise and located a McDonald's outlet), Alex and Charlotte joined the other guests in the library of the hotel, to be filled in on the rules of the Easter-egg hunt. The egg

– a work of art created by the Cholyngham chef – was displayed on a plinth that usually held the bust of one of Finn's 'ancestors'. It was a sphere of scrummy-looking rich dark chocolate emblazoned with edible gold leaf, and it was so elaborately decorated that it could have been designed by Fabergé.

Lavinia was standing next to the plinth, holding an old-fashioned megaphone. 'The Easter-egg hunt starts here!' she announced from under the brim of a bonnet bedecked with spring flowers. 'The prize is this magnificent egg, and the winner will be the first person to successfully complete the treasure trail. My son, Finn, will now take the egg and conceal it in its hiding place.'

Finn lifted the egg reverently between white-cotton-gloved hands and left the room with it.

Alex smirked. 'Well, that's put paid to any romantic notions you might have had about skipping around Cholyngham searching out the treasure trove with the son and heir at your side,' he said.

Charlotte ignored him and started humming 'Easter Parade', which Lavinia had been playing on the grand piano in the drawing room earlier in the day.

'There are six clues in all!' boomed Lavinia through the megaphone. 'And this is Clue Number One!

'This creature has a synonym

That is pronounced Houyhnhnm.

Find his image made of stone

To have the second clue made known.'

'What in hell's name,' said Charlotte, 'is that supposed to mean?'

'Hmm,' said Alex. 'You know what a Houyhnhnm is?'

'Haven't an idea,' said Charlotte cheerfully.

'You're an illiterate savage, Cholewczyk,' said Alex. 'The Houyhnhnms were a race of beings that Gulliver met on his travels. They were impeccably noble creatures who were uncorrupted by lust, lying or cheating, and they were *never* led into temptation. Unlike the sex-mad Yahoos.'

Charlotte yawned theatrically. 'Get to the point, pal,' she said. But she couldn't help being impressed by his literary savvy. The only people she knew about that Gulliver had met on his travels were the Lilliputians.

'They were also horses,' Alex told her.

'Houyhnhnms were horses?'

'Yes, indeedy.'

'So we're meant to be looking for the image of a *horse*? Humph! This house is coming down with images of horses. Look – there's a portrait of one there, above the mantel ... *shelf*.'

Alex looked down at her with amusement. 'Ooh. Afraid we might make a social gaffe there, and betray our lack of breeding?'

'Piss off, Thornton.'

'Very eloquently put. Now. Think a little harder. What did Lavinia say the image was made of?'

'Um ... stone.'

'Very good! So we're not looking for a painting of a horse, we're looking for a statue.'

Charlotte had to hand it to him. For an annoying git, he was pretty clued-in.

'There are quite a few statues of horses around, too.'

'In that case, let's get cracking. And be surreptitious about it. We don't want other searchers copping that we're onto something.'

Alex led the way and they set off in different directions, hunting for Houyhnhnms. After covertly examining porcelain figurines and carved mahogany statuettes, Charlotte remembered that her brief was to find a horse made of stone. She was delighted when she came across a lovely little marble prancy one in the hall. Yes! There, tucked between its rearing front hooves, was a neatly folded piece of paper.

'Alex!' she hissed across the hallway. 'I've got it.'

'Show me.' Alex sidled over to her, and together they studied the clue that was written in Lavinia's elegant copperplate script.

'In the myth, goddesses grapple
For a very special apple.
She who won was a spellbinder,
And the study's where you'll find her.'

'I know! I know!' said Charlotte excitedly.

'You do?'

'Yes! In the Greek myth, three goddesses compete for the prize of the Golden Apple. Paris awards it to Aphrodite. There's a painting of her in the study, being ravished by some dude.'

'Well,' said Alex. 'Maybe you're not such a lame-brain after all.'

They slid the clue back between the horse's hooves for the next person to find, then legged it into the study, where, tucked behind the ornate gilt frame of the painting of Aphrodite being ravished (and quite clearly enjoying the experience, to judge by the expression on her face), was another folded slip of paper.

Charlotte reached up and tweaked it from its hiding place, and together they read:

'Romeo! Romeo! Wherefore art thou still?
Renowned words penned by one wily Will.
Two star-crossed lovers help to find clue three.
Try thinking hard – where might the couple be?'

'The library!' said Alex and Charlotte in unison, and together they raced back through the hall, where tartan-clad Americans were bumbling around looking mystified.

In the library, they scoured the shelves until they lit upon a massive, leather-bound edition of the complete works of Shakespeare. And there, between pages 752 and 753 (the balcony scene), was the third clue.

'Ancient Egypt did it best
When they laid their dead to rest.
This clue advises you to go
To the room where flowers grow.'

Charlotte shrugged. 'Well, it's obviously the conservatory, if it's the room where flowers grow. But what's that guff about the Egyptians and their dead supposed to mean?'

'I know what it's supposed to mean,' said Alex, leading the way to the conservatory.

'Something to do with the pyramids?' hazarded Charlotte.

'No. There's a model of a sarcophagus in the library.'

'What in hell's name is that?'

'Sarcophagi were like coffins, only beautifully decorated. Think Tutankhamun's mask.'

'Is there a sarcopha – copha—' She gave up. 'There's one in the conservatory?'

'Yeah, there's a papier-mâché model of the one that's meant to belong to Rameses the third, the last of the great Egyptian pharaohs.'

'Well,' said Charlotte, 'talk about learning something new every day. You could be a teacher, Alex.'

'No, I couldn't.'

'What makes you say that?'

'I've got a thing about school uniforms. They distract me.'

In the conservatory, the fifth clue was Blu-tacked to the base of the sarcophagus.

'Ephialtes, bound in chains,
Inhabited these dark domains.
You will find him if you zoom
Next door into the drawing room.'

'Ephialtes was a character in Dante's

Inferno,' said Charlotte, with fabulous authority. 'There's a cushion in the drawing room that has a picture of him on it, worked in tapestry.'

'Wow!' said Alex. 'Are you telling me you've read Dante's *Inferno*?'

'Yes,' she lied. She only knew about Ephialtes because he'd once been the answer to a question in a table quiz, but she had no intention of enlightening Alex as to how she was privy to the information.

In the drawing room, they found a cast-iron key under the cushion showing luckless Ephialtes all tied up.

'The poor bastard looks like a john in a dominatrix's boudoir,' observed Alex, unfastening the safety pin that attached the clue to the cushion. 'OK. Let's have a look at the final clue.'

'Congratulations! You have won!
We hope you had a lot of fun.
The trophy room contains your prize.
Unlock the door and feast your eyes.'

'Well, that's straightforward enough,' said Charlotte. 'The egg is in the trophy room, and this must be the key to the door.' She picked up the key, which boasted a silken tassel, and twirled it triumphantly.

'Whoooo!' A shriek worthy of the

Cholyngham ghost rang out, bouncing off the walls of the drawing room. Charlotte was momentarily spooked.

'That's never—' she began.

But she didn't get to finish the sentence, because Chucky had risen up from behind a couch like a vision rising from a grave in a nightmare. She vaulted over the back of the couch, raced past Charlotte and wrenched the key from her grasp. 'Yo, losers! Thanks for the info!' she called over her shoulder as she legged it out of the room and across the hall. She was surprisingly fleet of foot for a girl of such generous proportions.

'Hey, you! Farm girl!' yelled Alex.

Together Alex and Charlotte set off in hot pursuit, but it was too late. The door to the trophy room opened and shut, they heard the key turn in the lock, and they knew their prize was lost to them.

'The brat!' said Charlotte, incandescent with rage. 'The bloody little brat!'

'Calm down, Charlotte,' said Alex. 'And look at it this way. All the calories in that chocolate egg would have gone straight to your hips, and you'd have ended up on the treadmill in your gym like Brunetto Latini.'

'Who the hell's Brunetto Latini?'

'He was the bloke who was forced to run forever, as punishment for committing the sin of unnatural lust. I thought you'd read Dante's *Inferno*.'

'Oh, yeah. I'd forgotten about him,' said Charlotte, unconvincingly.

'Anyway, I have an idea for revenge.' Alex assumed a mysterious air and headed in the direction of the front door.

'Where are you going?' asked Charlotte.

'You'll find out in a minute.'

Charlotte stood in the middle of the Cholyngham hall, fulminating against Chucky. There was no way the child would have been able to work out all those clues for herself! Come to think about it, there was no way most of the other guests would, either. People were still meandering around looking helplessly in vases and under ornaments. It had been pretty fiendish of Lavinia to set such difficult clues. Maybe she had wanted to keep the egg for herself?

Charlotte wandered into the drawing room and sat down by the fire, where she could leaf through *Country Life* and keep an eye on the front door for Alex's return. Finally he appeared, wiping his feet on the Cholyngham welcome mat. He crossed the hall and joined her by the drawing-room fire. His hair was dripping, and his face was wet with rain.

'You got soaked!' she said.

'It was worth it,' he said, taking his phone from his jacket pocket. 'Take a look at this.'

There on the display was an image of Chucky sitting on the floor of the trophy room, holding the fabulous egg between her hands. She'd already demolished a sizable proportion of it. There was chocolate smeared on her face and hands, and traces of it in her hair. She looked like a human pig who'd been through a mud bath.

A broad smile spread across Charlotte's face. 'Well, there's one gal who's earned her nickname,' she said. 'She'll be chucking up like nobody's business for the rest of the day. How did you manage to get it?'

'I climbed up and took it through the window,' said Alex. 'And do you know something? It's going on the Web. We're gonna do it riiiight now.'

He stood up and reached down for her hand, and, flushed with the success of their Easter-egg hunt, Alex and Charlotte made straight for the Cholyngham library and the guest computer.

* * *

Easter Monday found Charlotte packing her suiter (making sure to include all the Molton Brown freebies) and saying goodbye to Lavinia, who gave her a puppet of one of the Cholyngham goats as a memento of her stay. It bore an uncanny resemblance to the goat who'd stuck his face in her cleavage, and Charlotte wasn't sure that she wanted to be reminded of that. Her cleavage felt itchy every time she thought about it.

The drive through Bank Holiday traffic was tedious, and was made more tedious still by Alex, who had perfected an uncannily accurate impersonation of Charlotte when she'd spotted the Gruff Gang disporting themselves with her clothes. 'Oh! Oh! Oh! Oh, you – you *beastly* goats. Oh, no – no! Not my shoes as well! Not my *hat*!'

Just before Finn dropped Charlotte off at her flat in Battersea, he got a phone call from Anna. The first thing he said to her was: 'I'm talking on the hands-free, and Alex and Charlotte are here with me, so don't say anything of an intimate nature, honey child.'

Oh! How Charlotte would have loved to have a man call her 'honey child'!

'*Salut*, Charlotte! *Salut*, Alex!' came Anna's voice down the speaker.

'*Salut*, Anna! How's it going?'

'Great!'

The four-way phone conversation was mostly idle chit-chat about Cholyngham, and about the fantastic time Anna and Vivien were having in Paris, and how they'd managed to get tickets for the latest Peter Brook production in the Bouffes du Nord, and how they'd visited the Musée Picasso and they'd decided against sending Charlotte a picture of the Jimmy Choos, because they wanted to see her face when they gave them to her. They were *beautiful* and easily the most expensive ones in the shop, and absolutely *made* for Charlotte.

Just as they were about to say their farewells, Anna said, 'Finn, I don't want you spending the entire weekend as a couch potato with a can of beer in one hand and the remote control in the other. You must take Charlotte out for dinner this weekend, somewhere posh. I feel guilty because Viv and I have just had the most extraordinary meal in a little brasserie off the Boulevard Saint-Germain. Promise?'

'Yeah, yeah. I promise. Anything to assuage your guilt, honey child. Talk to you soon.'

'*Au revoir*, Alex! *Au revoir*, Charlotte!'

'*Au revoir*, Anna!'

'Her wish is my command,' said Finn, turning off the phone. 'How about Friday evening, Charlotte?'

'Shit. I'd love to, Finn, but there's a birthday bash for one of my work colleagues on Friday.'

'Saturday, then?'

'No can do, I'm afraid, pal,' put in Alex. 'Charlotte's promised to spend Saturday with me.'

What? Charlotte turned round in the passenger seat and looked at Alex with blank astonishment.

'Don't you remember? You said the other night that you'd take me to that shop in Covent Garden that does the, erm, girly stuff and help me choose a birthday present for Thea. And I said I'd take you out to dinner afterwards as a reward.'

'I – I—'

'Aye, aye, as Captain Jack Sparrow might say,' said Alex, putting on a piratey voice. 'It's a done deal, me hearties. And here's where you get out.'

Finn had pulled up outside her flat. He swung out of the driver's seat and went to fetch her suiter from the boot. Charlotte felt a surge of pure rage rise in her. 'You are in-fucking-sufferable, Alex Thornton. What do you think you're doing, interfering in my private life?'

'While Anna's away, I am acting as your social secretary, you little lamia. And your diary does not include any windows of opportunity for getting up close and personal with Fin-Fin. Understood?'

Finn pulled open the passenger door for her. 'That's a shame about the weekend,' he said. 'But you can't tell Anna I didn't try.'

'No,' she said. 'I can't.'

'I'll meet you at five on Saturday,' said Alex. 'Outside that shop in Covent Garden. What did you say it was called again?'

'Coco de Mer,' said Charlotte automatically.

'Coco de Mer, here we come. At least, I personally am banking on it to help me do just that. Bye, sweetheart.'

'Bye, Charlotte. Don't forget your little goat.' Finn reached up, unhooked the Cholyngham puppet from where it had been hung as a mascot for the journey home, and passed it to her through the open window.

'Thanks. Bye.'

And the car pulled away from the kerb, with neither man giving her a backward look.

What a very strange weekend it had been, thought Charlotte as she climbed the stairs to her flat. She felt quite drained. *Spent*, that was the word – *le mot juste*. And she'd have to dream up a lot more *mots justes* when she was back at work tomorrow, racking her brains for nice things to say about Paris. The presentation to that travel company was imminent, and her creative director was confident that they could win the account. Pantoufle, the French word for 'slipper', was the name they'd dreamed up for the campaign, the rationale being that travelling with this company was as comfortable as wearing a pair of slippers. It didn't have the same ring in English, somehow.

She let herself into her flat and slung her suiter on the sofa before heading towards the kitchen and the makings of her *dîner-à-une*, feeling a bit sorry for herself. She preheated the oven for her rather elderly Marks & Sparks falafels, poured herself a glass of white wine, then went back into the sitting room to play all the messages that would have accumulated over the long weekend. There weren't any.

However, as she gazed at the unblinking red light, the phone rang. Alex's number appeared on the display. Well, fuck him! She wasn't going to bother taking a call from that meddling idiot. She'd let the machine pick up.

'Looking forward to our shopping spree on Saturday, sweetheart. And incidentally, have you checked out "lamia" in the dictionary yet?'

Lamia? What was he on about? And then Charlotte remembered that that was what he'd called her in the car, just before Finn had dropped her off. She set her wine glass down and wandered over to the bookshelf where she kept her lexicon of difficult words. Opening it at 'L', she ran her finger down 'lambast', 'lambent', and 'lamella' before hitting on 'lamia'. 'Lamia,' she read, '*n.* evil enchantress or female vampire, in Greek and Roman mythology, a blood-sucking serpent-witch.'

For heaven's sake! What was Alex *on*?

seven

Charlotte woke with a racking hangover on Saturday, after the birthday celebrations for her work colleague the night before. They had also been celebrating the fact that they'd won the travel agency account. 'Lucky girl!' the creative director had said to her. 'You'll be off to Paris for a weekend courtesy of Pantoufle!'

'What? Why?'

'To check out the hotel, of course. Tough work, but someone's got to do it!'

'Um, shouldn't Hilary be the one to go?'

Hilary was the senior copywriter, Charlotte's superior.

'She can't go. She's to be godmother at some christening. She's livid that she's missing out on Paris.'

She's welcome to it, thought Charlotte as she headed for the shower to wash away her hangover. What bloody awful irony that the place she hated most in the world kept being offered to her on a plate. She felt a bit like that character in the comic who keeps trying to spend millions only to have them coming right back at him.

As she soaped herself, she pondered what she might do with herself today. She'd get into her winceyette sleep-suit, she decided, and snuggle up on the sofa with a bowl of cheesy mashed potato, Clinique's Skin Calming Moisture Mask and a classic DVD – *Gone with the Wind*, her favourite. And then she remembered what Alex had said to her about behaving like Scarlett O'Hara, and then she remembered that … *Shit!* She was supposed to be meeting him today, to help him choose a present for bloody Thea. Well, he could go eat his socks. She wasn't going to make her hangover any worse by helping *him* out, especially since he had had the gall to call her a lamia.

And anyway, he had originally arranged

the shopping expedition as a device to prevent her meeting up with Finn. Did that mean that this was a completely bogus date? Maybe Thea's 'birthday' was a lie? If Charlotte went to all the trouble of going down to Covent Garden, would he even show up? She'd give him a ring to find out if this odious excursion was on or off. The last thing she felt like doing today was hanging around Coco de Mer looking as if she'd been stood up.

She wrapped herself in a towel, went into the sitting room and picked up the phone. 'It's Alex,' she heard as the call went straight to voicemail. 'It's also the weekend, so I'm not picking the phone up for anyone – not even for you, divine and beauteous Thea.' And then the phone went dead.

* * *

At five o'clock, Alex was standing outside Coco de Mer admiring the window display. Charlotte put on a grumpy face to let him know that the role of personal shopper was not one she felt any great inclination to play.

'Well,' he said as Charlotte drew alongside him. 'You *are* full of surprises. Fancy little Charlotte Cholewczyk, whom I used to know in bobby socks and pigtails, developing a penchant for fetishism.'

'Who said anything about fetishism?' said Charlotte. 'This place caters for all tastes. There's plenty of normal stuff in here, too.'

The first thing that confronted them when they went into the shop was the rear view of a statue of a naked woman bending over.

'Dead normal,' said Alex. 'My gran has a load of those in her garden since she got rid of her gnomes. Wow. This place is an Aladdin's cave. I think I've died and gone to heaven.'

'Stop ogling, Alex. This is serious business we're here on.'

'Serious?' Alex was examining a wisp of chiffon. 'How can you take clothing like this seriously?'

'Buying presents for a girlfriend is as serious as it gets, Thornton, believe me. I once ditched a boyfriend on account of the present he bought me.'

'What was it?'

'A pair of oven gloves.'

'Maybe it was a coded message. Maybe he was trying to tell you how hot you were.'

'I've no truck with that kind of symbolism.

It's too subtle for me. Now. What's first on your shopping list?'

'How about this?'

Alex unhooked a baby-blue bra from a hanger. Its scalloped cups were trimmed with layers and layers of ruffled lace, and there were ruffled panties to match.

'Hmm,' said Charlotte. 'What size is she?'

Alex looked down at Charlotte's chest. 'Well, I know she's taller than you, but she's around the same size as you in the bra department. I'd be able to hazard a more accurate guess if I had a feel.'

'Nice try, but no cigar. Listen up. The disadvantage of bras like this is that, while they are virtual works of art, they're impractical.'

'Why?'

'A gal can't wear them under anything close-fitting. They spoil the line. Imagine those ruffly cups covered by a layer of fine cashmere. Picture those panties under a tight stretch cotton skirt.'

Alex made a kind of groaning noise. 'Do I have to?'

'Yes. There's no way that can work, Alex. Bra-and-panty sets like this are designed to be worshipped. The only possible thing you could team them with is something like this.' Charlotte held aloft a wafty baby-doll nightie, trimmed with marabou feathers. 'And if you're to complete the look, you'll need heels. Like these. What size is she?'

'Um. About the same size as you?'

Charlotte kicked off the high-heeled slingback she was wearing and slid her right foot into a satin mule that boasted a marabou pompom. She looked down at her foot and arched the sole prettily. 'Oh, these are adorable!' she said. 'They're *so* Marilyn.'

'Who's Marilyn?'

'Monroe, moron. Think of her in *The Seven-Year Itch*.'

'Is that the one where her skirts blew up?'

'Go to the top of the class.' Charlotte reassumed her slingback and moved to a shelf that was stacked with books. 'Now,' she said in her best no-nonsense voice, 'to continue. What about some bedtime reading? I'm not talking *Winnie the Pooh*.'

'This looks good.' Alex helped himself to *The Encyclopaedia Anatomica* and started flicking through the pages.

'Alex, is this present for you or for Thea? She's not going to want to read that kind of stuff. Anaïs Nin is more her style. Or this.'

Charlotte picked up a copy of *The Story of O*.

'OK,' said Alex. 'Should I get the sequel, too?'

'The answer to that is a categorical "no". The sequel isn't half as good as the original.'

'You've read them both?'

'Of course,' Charlotte said with hauteur. 'Hmm. This could be helpful.' She took down a copy of *The Ultimate Guide to Cunnilingus – How to Go Down on a Woman and Give Her Exquisite Pleasure*.

'I'm not going to waste good money on that,' said Alex.

'Look on it as an investment in your relationship.'

'Luckily for Thea,' said Alex, 'it's an investment I don't need.'

Charlotte didn't say anything. Instead, she moved on to the next unit. The item on display here was a black leather chastity belt, with suspenders attached to black rubber stockings. Alex gave her a look of enquiry.

'Definitely not,' she said.

He redirected his gaze to a full-faced black leather mask with a hole for the mouth, then gave her an even more eloquent look of enquiry. Hmm. Charlotte was beginning to wonder if she shouldn't recommend something that Thea might really have an aversion to – but then what would that say about *her* sexual preferences?

'*Definitely* not,' she said, with authority.

'How about this?' he asked, picking up a blindfold. It was fashioned from soft gold leather and boasted plaited silken ties with gold leather tassels.

'Hmm.' Charlotte took the blindfold from him and examined it. 'It's very pretty. A definite possibility.'

Next up was a carved wooden device with feathers attached. 'I guess when Ken Dodd brandished his tickling stick he didn't quite have this in mind,' remarked Alex.

'I guess not.'

'What do you think?'

'Could provide hours of amusement.'

'I'll take two. What about whips?'

'Not the leather one. The horsehair might be worth a try.'

They'd reached a glass display case. 'Handcuffs?'

'Definitely. Those silver ones are *very* classy.'

'Anything else you see in there that I could add to my shopping trolley?'

'Oh, yes! What pretty dildos!'

'Purple, black or pink?'

'The pink one.'

'Why so?'

'It has the most beautiful shape.'

'Remind you of anyone?'

'Not telling.'

They studied the item in silence for a couple of moments, and then Alex said, 'Are we done?'

Charlotte did some mental arithmetic. She calculated that Alex had spent more than enough on that undeserving cow Thea. 'We're done,' she said.

'Thank God for that.'

'Was it such torment?'

'No. It was a pretty damn fine experience, and many thanks are due to you, Ms Cholewczyk, for your expert guidance. You may have noticed, however, that this shop is staffed exclusively by members of the unfairly fair sex, and the reasons for that are pretty plain.'

'They are?'

'There are too many distractions for a male employee. It would be like hooking him up to intravenous Viagra. I've been nursing an erection for quite some time now, and I'd rather like to get out of here.'

'Thank you for sharing that with me, Alex.' Charlotte didn't – *wouldn't* – look down. Instead she marched ahead of him with an uninterested expression firmly stapled to her face.

Their progress towards the till was held up when they came face to face with a display case that contained a ceramic object resembling an outsize baby's dummy. It had a fluffy pink tail attached. Alex and Charlotte looked at each other, then looked back at the offending item. '*Definitely not,*' they said in unison, before cracking up. Charlotte had a sudden graphic image of Thea capering round a bedroom with a furry tail sticking out from under her baby-blue baby-doll, and it was *so* un-Thea that she found herself on the verge of snorting with laughter. But then she reminded herself of what she'd once told Alex – that girls who buy pink handbags *never* snort – and she resisted.

As the girl behind the cash register wrapped each individual item in tissue paper, Alex became utterly engrossed in *How to Make Love like a Porn Star*. The girl slid a sideways glance at him as she detached the price tag from the pretty pink item, and then she looked at Charlotte and smiled. 'You're a very lucky girl,' she said in a low voice.

Charlotte was just about to say, 'Oh – they're not for me!' but she realised at once that it would look as if she was protesting too much, so she just smiled vaguely instead. Then, looking down at the little feathery objects, she found herself wondering where exactly Alex and Thea would be celebrating her birthday. And, to her surprise, she found herself blushing.

* * *

Her reward for being Alex's shopping consultant was dinner in Joe Allen's.

'Pretty, pretty, *pretty*,' said Alex, admiring the retreating rear of the greeter who saw them to their table. 'She's *definitely* not wearing ruffly knickers. See how much I've learned today? You make an excellent teacher, Ms Cholewczyk, even though you are rather strict.'

'What do you mean, strict?'

'Well, you didn't allow me to get away with any of my own little vagaries. Although I did manage to sneak one in without you seeing.'

'What did you sneak in?'

'The wooden ruler with "Teach Me A Lesson" written on it.'

'Sucker. You could have got one in a stationer's for half the price and written it on yourself.'

'I'm not sure Thea would find that quite as much of an incentive to don her "Little Miss Trouble" T-shirt.'

An Angelina Jolie lookalike came up and stood poised with her pen over her notebook. 'Can I bring you something to drink before you order?' she said, giving Alex the once-over with her heavily kohled bedroom eyes.

'Champagne?' Alex asked Charlotte.

'Yes, please.'

'Champagne for the lady. And I'll have a glass of Budvar.'

'Coming right up.' Angelina Jolie gave Alex another sideways look before turning and sashaying over to the counter.

Charlotte took up a menu and ran her eyes down it. Eggs Benedict or Eggs Joe Allen? Chicken or tuna? Vacillating over what to eat was one of the more pleasurable things in life, she decided as she reached down a surreptitious hand to scratch at an itch that had been bothering her.

'What's wrong with you?' asked Alex.

'What do you mean?'

'You keep wriggling. As if you have an itch somewhere.'

'That's because I do have an itch somewhere.' She cast a cautious eye right and left, to be certain that no one could hear her. 'I've a horrid feeling that I may have picked up a flea from one of the Cholyngham dogs.'

'Ah. When did the itching start?'

'Just today.'

'Then it can't be a flea. A flea would have made its presence felt way before now.'

'What makes you so knowledgeable about fleas?'

'My father was a vet, remember? He used to feed me all sorts of fascinating facts of the really gross variety that small boys love to hear.'

The way he was looking at her had an air of assessment about it that made her instantly suspicious. 'Why are you looking at me in that weird way, Alex?'

'We-ell,' said Alex. 'As I say, it's unlikely to be a flea. But it could be something else.'

Charlotte felt an awful wave of apprehension wash over her. 'What kind of something else?' she asked.

'It could be a tick.'

'A tick! A *tick*! Oh, Alex, gross! No, it *can't* be a tick. They're those awful things that embed themselves in your flesh and suck your blood, aren't they?'

"Fraid so. Lamias in miniature. The little beasties take their time getting to know you, but once they find a place where they feel at home, they dive right in and start feasting. They've got skin like an accordion, so they can expand as they suck.'

'Oh!'

'Some are so small they can't be detected, and the, er, host could end up with Lyme disease,' continued Alex remorselessly.

'*Oh*!'

'Why not pay a visit to the little girls' room and check it out?' he suggested with a smile Mephistopheles might have envied.

The thought that she might have a tick made Charlotte jump up and propel herself down the stairs and through the door of the ladies' faster than Road Runner.

In the cubicle, she lifted her skirt to examine the place that itched. There, on the inside of her left thigh, about two inches away from her pudenda, was a roundy dark lump the size of a dried pea. Yeuch, yeuch, yeuch! She had a tick! Oh, *gross*!

Back she raced to where Alex was calmly scanning the menu.

He looked at her over the edge. 'Well?'

Charlotte took a swig from the glass of champagne that was waiting for her. 'I think it *might* be a' – she could hardly bring herself to say the word – 'tick.'

'Oo-er,' said Alex. 'What does it look like?'

'It's – ew – dark brown. And it's about the size of a pea.'

'Wow! *That* bloated! It's clearly found your blood very, very tasty.'

'Ew ew ew! *How* could I have picked up a tick?'

'Well, after your close encounter with the Gruff Gang, it doesn't surprise me.' Alex laughed. 'Shit! You should see your face, Charlotte. It's gone as green as guacamole.'

'How can you laugh when I have a tick!'

'It's just a tick, Charlotte. Not a sexually transmitted disease.'

'Help me, Alex! How do I get rid of it?'

'Have you a pair of tweezers?'

She thought about it. 'Yes. There's a pair in my make-up bag.'

'That's how you do it. With tweezers. Except that, if you don't do it in one clean-cut action, all that happens is that the body comes off and leaves the head still embedded in the flesh.'

Charlotte covered her mouth with her hands. 'Oh, God. I really do think I'm going to get sick. I couldn't do that, Alex.'

He looked at her, deadpan. 'Are you asking me to do it for you?'

She thought about the intimate nature of the place where the tick was. Then she weighed the prospect of Alex coming into close contact with her inner thigh against the prospect of having a tick lodged there. Actually, there was no contest. The tick must die. She nodded.

'Where, um, *is* the tick?' he asked.

'On my thigh.' She didn't want to be more location-specific.

'Charlotte. You surely don't expect me to poke around with a pair of tweezers on your thigh in a public place, surrounded by a crowd of onlookers? That's kinkier than anything Coco de Mer could dream up.'

'We'll do it in the loo.'

'The ladies' loo?'

'Yes. Come on!'

'Hang on. Let me have a swig of my beer first. All that tick-talk has made me very thirsty.'

As soon as his glass was back on the table, Charlotte seized Alex by the hand and dragged him in the direction of the Joe Allen's ladies'.

'I hope no one witnessed the way you pulled me in here,' said Alex, when the doors closed behind them. 'Especially if they clocked the Coco de Mer carrier bags. They'll infer that you couldn't wait till we got home.'

'Shut up, Alex,' said Charlotte, extracting her tweezers from her make-up bag. 'Just do it. Do it quick!'

'Do you want to sit on the loo, or are you happy to lean up against the wall?'

'Up against the wall.'

'OK. Pull up your skirt for me, like a good girl.'

Charlotte pulled up the skirt of her dress until the hem was on a level with her pubic bone.

'It's a tight squeeze in here. You're going to have to angle your leg for me. Spread them a bit wider … No. That's not going to work. Why don't you put your foot up on the loo seat? Yeah. That's better.' Alex knelt down. 'Wow. He's a big bugger, isn't he? He's completely engorged.'

'Oh!'

'Did you know that ticks can increase their size up to a hundredfold?'

'*Oh!*'

'For God's sake stop squirming, Charlotte. I can't aim properly if you're wriggling around all over the place. Hold still until I've done.'

She did as he asked, averting her eyes and fixing her gaze on the ceiling as Alex got on with it.

'Yes!' he said at last. 'Do you want to see?'

'No! Flush it down the loo.'

'Whatever Charlotte wants, Charlotte gets,' he said, pressing the flush and handing her back her tweezers. 'I'll return to the table, shall I, and allow you time to compose yourself?'

Alex backed out of the cubicle with that devilish smile he did so well.

Charlotte rearranged herself, then went to wash her hands. She held the tweezers under the hot tap and scrubbed and scrubbed them, resolving to pour boiling water over them when she got home so as to remove any last trace of tick.

As she was stowing them back in her make-up bag, the door of one of the cubicles opened and the Angelina Jolie lookalike emerged. 'Well done, you,' she said, with an approving smile. 'Up against the wall in Joe Allen's loo is something every woman should do before she dies. And I have to say that if the dude in question was the one you came in with, then I can't blame you, darlin'.'

eight

Charlotte was having a very strange dream. She was standing in front of the cheval glass in the Boudoir in Cholyngham, regarding her reflection. She was wearing the cheesecloth sundress that had been chewed up by the goats, and it now exposed so much flesh it might have been designed by Julien Macdonald. She couldn't go down to a smart-casual dinner wearing this rag! She moved to the wardrobe to see what the alternatives were, but there was nothing in there apart from a bra-and-panties set in ruffled baby-blue silk, a baby-doll nightie in blue chiffon and a pair of high-heeled mules with marabou-feather pompoms. They'd

have to do. The ormolu clock on the mantelpiece – no, no! the mantel*shelf* – told her she
was running late. Quickly, she cast off the
offending goats' cheesecloth and got into the
lingerie before leaving the room and
navigating the maze of corridors that finally
brought her to the drawing room.

'Hey, Charlotte,' said Alex when he saw
her come in, and Finn turned to greet her.
The look on his face when he clocked her
could only be described as 'taken aback'. He
took a step forward as if to kiss her on the
cheek, then stopped, as though he'd thought
better of it.

'Charlotte. Hi. You look – yes. Lovely.'

'Thank you,' she said. But she wasn't
looking at him. She was looking at Alex.

He narrowed his green eyes at her. 'It's up
to you,' he said. 'You're the one who's in
charge of your own life. You've got to work
things out for yourself.'

'But I'm crap at working things out,' she
said.

'Pick up the phone,' Alex told her. 'Patrick
Proctor's on the other end. He'll be able to
advise you.'

She reached out a hand for the phone.
'Patrick?' she said.

'No,' said the voice on the other end. 'It's Finn. Who the hell's Patrick?'

Charlotte broke the surface of her dream.

'Oh, sorry, Finn. I was dreaming about Patrick Proctor.'

'The sexy chat-show host?'

'Yes.'

'In that case, I'm sorry to interrupt your lie-in, sweetheart. Shall I phone you back later?'

'No, no. I'm awake now.'

'Sure?'

'Sure, I'm sure. What can I do for you, Finn?'

'I was going to suggest that I call round with breakfast. To make up for the fact that I didn't get to buy you dinner.'

'Now?'

'If it suits.'

'It suits.'

'I'll be there in fifteen.'

'OK. See you then.'

Charlotte slid out from between the sheets. It was ironic, she thought, that only a couple of moments ago she had been sporting the kind of underwear favoured by screen goddesses. In her dreams! The reality was that Charlotte was wearing the winceyette sleep-suit that was as comforting as a teddy bear. She scooped her hair into a scrunchie, cleaned her teeth, then padded into the kitchen to switch on the kettle. While she waited for it to boil, she performed some stretching exercises. The mantra that ran through her head as she practised her rather lacklustre yoga went: *Do not ask Finn about the baby. Do not ask Finn about the baby. Do not ask Finn about the baby …*

The doorbell interrupted her profound meditations. 'Come on up,' she told Finn via the intercom.

A minute later, she heard him let himself into the flat. 'Hey,' he said, joining her in the kitchen.

'Good morning!' She finished spooning Illy into a cafetière, then filled it with hot water and turned to him. 'Oh, Finn! For me?'

'Yes,' he said, handing her a sheaf of purple and yellow irises.

'Thank you! There was no need, you know.'

'Ah, but I love walking down the street carrying a bunch of flowers. It's such a brave thing for a red-blooded male to be seen doing. You wouldn't credit the admiring looks I get from women.' Finn hefted carrier bags onto the kitchen table. 'There's champagne and orange juice for Buck's fizz.'

'Yay! What else?'

'Bagels and smoked salmon and cream cheese and *pains au chocolat.*'

'A feast! What fun. Better than dinner out. Will you set the table while I put these in water?'

Charlotte located a vase – yellow, to match the irises – then set about trimming the stalks so that the flowers would last longer.

'Where did Alex take you for dinner last night?' Finn asked.

'Joe Allen's.' Where she could never, ever show her face again. She carried on slicing stems, all the while thinking, *Do not ask Finn about the baby. Do not ask Finn about the baby. Do not ask Finn about the baby …*

'Um. About the baby, Charlotte,' he said.

Oh! Charlotte turned to face him. Finn was sitting at the table with an expression on his face that denoted, well, *significance.* The irises could wait. She drew out a chair and sat down beside him.

'You, um, didn't say anything to Alex about it, did you?' he asked her.

'Of course I didn't. You said it was meant to be a secret.'

'Thanks. You're a pal.'

'But *why* keep it secret, Finn?'

'Well, we didn't want anyone to know until we've got safely through the first trimester, just in case, you know, anything went wrong. The only people we've told so far are our parents.'

'Nothing will go wrong! Anna's as fit as anything.'

'I know. And she's looking after herself. That's why she spun that yarn about being on antibiotics – it was an excuse for not drinking. We hope to be able to announce the news after she comes back from France.'

'How pregnant is she?'

'The first trimester's just over. She was thrilled about the timing of your competition win, by the way. If it had been any earlier, she wouldn't have risked getting on a flight.'

'Well, this definitely calls for a celebration! Just as well you brought fizz,' said Charlotte, getting up and going to the cupboard to fetch champagne flutes.

'I guess. Although let's not propose a toast to the baby just yet. Anna's very superstitious about stuff like that.'

'What'll we toast to, then?'

'Um, have you heard about that new account yet?' asked Finn.

'The Pantoufle thing? Yeah. We won it.'

'Well, then. Let's toast to that,' he said, stripping foil off the bottle.

'But the bad news,' Charlotte told him, 'is that the senior copywriter isn't available to go to Paris to recce the hotel and schmooze with management and outline the Creative Rationale and all that jazz. So they want me to go instead.'

'No shit! Looks like that city's out to get you, Charlotte.'

The champagne popped and Finn poured. 'Here's to Pantoufle,' he said, raising his glass.

'And here's to smoked salmon and bagels for breakfast,' added Charlotte. 'Thank you for this. What a treat.'

She put her glass down and the pair of them set about organising breakfast, Charlotte peeling plastic off the fish, Finn buttering bagels. She was laying thin slices of smoked salmon on a plate when the phone rang.

'Could you get that, Finn?' she said. 'My hands are all fishy.'

'Sure.' Finn picked up the phone, glanced at the display and said, 'Hey, Alex. How's it going?' Several moments later he put the phone down and turned to Charlotte with a bemused expression. 'He says he'll be right round,' he told her. 'He sounded *weird*.'

'Weird? Like how?'

Finn thought about it. 'No,' he said. 'Strike weird. Make that *wired*.'

* * *

Twenty minutes later Alex was at the door. Charlotte buzzed him up, and the first thing he hissed at her when she opened the door was, 'Did you and Finn spend the night together?'

'No, we did not,' she told him indignantly. 'He only called round half an hour ago with breakfast.'

'You really expect me to believe that?'

'Look. I am *not* out to seduce Finn, Alex Thornton. Do you really think I'd be wearing this if I were?' She flapped the baggy bottom half of her winceyette sleep-suit at him.

Alex glared at her suspiciously for a moment, then relented. 'OK. Point taken. Even a man who hadn't had sex for a century couldn't find that get-up alluring.'

'Good. Does that mean you're going to stop looking daggers at me every time I ask Finn an innocent question?' she demanded, taking care to keep her voice down. 'Or are you going to invest every word I say to him with some weighty sexual innuendo? Does "Pass the butter, please, Finn" mean that I want to play Maria Schneider to his Marlon Brando?'

'OK, OK,' said Alex, spreading his hands in a gesture of conciliation. 'I stand corrected.' He tried out a smile on her.

In response, Charlotte gave him an unimpressed look and turned on her heel.

'I love the way you flick your ponytail when you're angry, Ms Cholewczyk.'

'Oh, shut up, Alex.'

In the kitchen, Finn was leafing through a Sunday colour supplement. 'Yo, Alex,' he said, 'there's an article about Thea in this.'

He set the magazine on the table, folded open at a photograph of Thea resplendent in a barely-there gold dress. She was glowering at the camera, one eye concealed by a waterfall of silky dark hair, the other saying, 'Wouldn't you just love to fuck me? (In your dreams, boys.)' The headline beneath the photograph trumpeted: 'Screen Goddess.' Pah! The whole package that was Thea in full come-on mode made Charlotte feel like a pyjama-ed pygmy in comparison.

Alex picked up the magazine and studied

the photograph with evident approval. 'That's my girl,' he said, before turning his attention to the copy. '"Thea de Havilland is set to be a rising star in the firmament of screen heaven,"' he read aloud. '"Her name derives from the Latin for 'goddess', and that couldn't be a more fitting epithet for an actress who is likely to get her fair share of fan worship when her new film, *Völuspa*, hits our multi-plexes next December. Thea lists the following among her many accomplishments: fencing, Thai-bo and riding" – all lies, incidentally,' remarked Alex. '"Her favourite place in the world is Cholyngham House, where she enjoys nothing so much as feeding the animals in the Cholyngham model farm. She deplores the fox-hunting ban, saying that riding to hounds with Lord and Lady Cholyngham was amongst the most uplifting and joyous experiences of her life – apart from being rogered by Alex Thornton."'

Charlotte looked at him, open-mouthed. 'Did she really say that?' she asked.

'Sadly, no. I made that bit up. But she *does* say that riding to hounds with your ma and pa was "uplifting and joyous", Finn.'

Finn looked puzzled. 'But Thea can't ride,' he said.

'She can't ride horses,' Alex corrected him.

'So why does she claim that she can?' asked Charlotte.

'It's an actor thing, isn't it? All actors claim to do things they can't. Do you really think that Tom Cruise performs all his own stunts?'

'He says he does.'

'Bollocks. Do you honestly think his production company could afford that kind of insurance?'

Finn took the magazine from Alex. 'What's with all the stuff about Cholyngham?'

'I'm ashamed to say,' said Alex, 'that Thea is a frightful snob. She'd like people to think that she moves in exalted circles.'

'My parents aren't exalted!' protested Finn.

'They're aristocrats.'

'Maybe. But *they* don't give a fuck about that.'

'Try telling that to Thea. Show her a blue-blooded arse and she'd be up it like a rabbit up a burrow.'

'Alex! That's a little too graphic for my tastes,' Charlotte told him.

'Sorry,' said Alex, sounding completely unrepentant. 'I forgot that *Watership Down* was your favourite bedtime book when you were little.'

Charlotte found herself glancing at the photograph of Thea and wondering how on earth Alex tolerated her bloody awful snobbishness.

'You're wondering why I tolerate her snobbishness, aren't you?' Alex asked Finn.

'No!' said Finn, too fast. 'We-ell … kind of.'

Alex took the magazine from Finn and held up the image of Thea magnificent in the gold lamé that barely concealed her assets. 'That's why I tolerate it.'

'OK. Understood,' said Finn.

'Jesus!' said Charlotte. 'You two are pathetic. How can I count amongst my circle of friends a pair of blokes who are living embodiments of that tired old cliché about men thinking with their dicks?'

'Who ever said it was a cliché?' asked Finn.

Before Charlotte could think of a suitable riposte, Alex's phone rang. 'Hey, babe,' he said, and from the sexy smile on his face, Charlotte guessed that it was Thea on the other end. 'Yeah. I'm looking at it right now. It's a great pic. OK – it's a *sensational* pic.'

There was a 'blip blip blah blah blah' as Thea jabbered over the line.

'Next weekend?' said Alex. 'I'll run it by him – he's here beside me … No, I'm in

Charlotte's … Yeah. Give me five minutes and I'll ring you back.'

Alex put his phone back in his pocket. 'That was Thea,' he said unnecessarily. 'She's been asked to participate in a television slot called *Birthday Bonanza*, or some such crap. She says she'd love to be filmed celebrating the occasion at Cholyngham.'

'Sorry?' said Finn. 'Are you telling me she wants to descend on Cholyngham with a film crew?'

'That's the general idea. How do you feel about that?'

Finn shrugged. 'I guess how I feel isn't important. It's really up to Mum and Dad. When *is* her birthday?'

'Next Sunday.'

'Jesus. That soon? How can they pull a stunt like that at such short notice?'

'They'd lined up some *Big Brother* bimbo, but apparently she broke her shoulder jet-skiing. Don't mention that to Thea, by the way. She wouldn't like people to know that she was second choice to a Z-lister.'

'So how *does* she intend celebrating her birthday?' asked Charlotte, pretending to examine her fingernails and trying not to sound piqued. Thea didn't *belong* in Cholyngham!

Cholyngham belonged to Finn – and to her, and to Anna and Vivien and Alex. Thea wasn't part of their gang – she was an arrant interloper.

'Oh, strolling round the grounds,' replied Alex. 'Feeding the animals in the model farm, enjoying a glass of champagne by the fire – that kind of shit. Maybe cutting the cake baked for her by the Cholyngham chef.'

'It's a pity about the hunting ban. She could have got footage of herself riding to hounds with Finn's parents,' said Charlotte. 'That would have been good for a laugh.'

Alex ignored her. 'Why don't you run it by Lavinia?' he asked Finn. 'I'm sure she'd be glad of the publicity.'

'I daresay she would.'

'After all,' said Charlotte, 'they say there's no such thing as bad publicity.'

'Well, that's something you should know all about,' retorted Alex, 'since bad publicity's how you earn your living.'

'I beg your pardon?'

'Pantoufle, anyone?'

'Children, children,' said Finn. 'Cut it out and let me put in a call to Cholyngham.'

Charlotte helped herself to another bagel and ignored Alex by leafing through the

Sunday supplements while Finn spoke to his mother. Her horoscope read: 'What's going on, Capricorn? It's not so hard to choose as you might think between being a blinkered carthorse or a gallivanting goat.' (*Ha ha*, thought Charlotte. Why was horoscope humour always so pun-heavy?) 'The weekend promises to be entertaining. Good food and good company in the form of old friends. And don't forget to book those airline tickets!' Well, she wasn't going to book them. The bloody Pantoufle people could take care of that.

'Here's your horoscope, Alex,' she said. 'Listen up. "You've been spending too much money on a particular individual,"' she read out loud. '"Your munificence may not be appreciated." Oo-er. Maybe Thea won't be wearing her "Little Miss Trouble" T-shirt for you on her birthday after all.'

'I doubt that. But if I got her bra size wrong, she might elect not to wear it. And if that happens, Charlotte Cholewczyk, it's your fault for not affording me an accurate assessment.'

She dismissed him with a look and returned her attention to the magazine. '"Travel is on the agenda,"' she resumed.

'Well, they got that right. I'm off to Paris soon to interview Ciarán Hinds.'

'Ciarán Hinds? Really? Lucky you. "On Wednesday you will give someone with the initials 'C.C.' a lovely, lovely present such as a Lulu Guinness handbag, and on Thursday you will make an utter prat of yourself by falling down a manhole slap in the middle of Piccadilly Circus."'

'Well, the oracle got that one wrong,' said Alex. 'There is no manhole slap in the middle of Piccadilly Circus. And I'm not so sure about giving the "C.C." individual a Lulu Guinness handbag, either.'

'Why not?' asked Charlotte.

'Because I don't believe she deserves it.'

Finn hung up the phone. 'That's cool with Lavinia,' he said. 'Ring the birthday girl back, Alex, and tell her Cholyngham's all hers.'

Charlotte felt very miffed indeed at the thought of Cholyngham being 'all Thea's'. Make-believe mistress of Cholyngham was *her* game!

'Thanks, pal,' said Alex. 'I owe you one. I'll phone her back now with the tidings of great joy.' He pressed speed-dial, and then Charlotte heard Thea's voice on the line going 'blip blip blah blah blah' again for what seemed like forever.

'Yeah,' said Alex, finally getting a word in

edgeways. 'Yeah. Well, I'll ask them … No, Anna's in France with Vivien … No, darling, I don't think they'd come back specially. Yeah, yeah. Leave it to me.' He put the phone down with a heavy sigh. 'Thea,' he said, 'has requested that I organise a few people to give the documentary a kind of "house party" vibe.'

'What do you mean?' asked a mystified Finn.

'She wants it to look as if she's part of a set who frequent Cholyngham on such a regular basis that they're looked upon as virtual family. She wants us all to be part of it.'

'She wants *us* to appear in the documentary?' Finn looked doubtful.

'In a word, yes.'

'And pretend to be her friends?' The look Alex gave her made Charlotte add: 'Oops! Sorry. Of course we *are* her friends.'

'Jesus, Alex!' said Finn. 'Talk about media manipulation.'

Alex made an ambiguous gesture. 'Her rationale is that if she doesn't manipulate them, they'll manipulate her. She has a point.'

Charlotte looked down at the photograph of sultry Thea gazing out at her from the glossy mag and decided that, actually, manipulating a dame like her could *never* be an easy feat. For some reason she felt as sullen as she had when she'd lost at Cluedo to Alex when she was a kid. The last thing Charlotte wanted to do was be part of Thea's cunning plan for world domination – but, on the other hand, the thought of the Birthday Girl prancing around Cholyngham pretending it was practically hers and being the centre of attention made her feel more than a little sick. Anna and Vivien would hate the idea, too, but being stuck in France, there was little they could do about it.

'So. Whaddaya say, pals? Are you up for another Cholyngham weekend?'

'I guess,' said Finn, picking up his phone. 'Let me check with Lavinia what kind of accommodation's available.'

'Will that be a problem?'

'I doubt it. There's often a dip in bookings after the Easter weekend. Presumably the documentary people will pick up the tab?'

'Damn right. Thea says it'll be on an all-inclusive basis.'

'Free liquor?' asked Finn.

'Free liquor,' said Alex.

That decided it. If she was to be treated to a weekend at Cholyngham with free liquor,

Charlotte was definitely up for it – even if she had to smarm up to Snootypants Thea.

'Charlotte?' Alex raised an interrogative eyebrow at her.

'Count me in,' she said.

And for some reason the image came back to her of her dream that morning, where she'd been all dolled up in Coco de Mer lingerie, standing in the drawing room at Cholyngham. She looked back down at the photograph of gorgeous Thea gazing right back at her through her peekaboo hair, and imagined how the Divine One might look in baby-blue ruffled silk, and she felt a stab of jealousy. Snootypants didn't deserve such a fabulous present!

'Thanks, Mum,' Finn was saying on the phone. 'That's great news. See you Saturday, then.' He slid his phone into his pocket and turned to Alex. 'You're a lucky man, Thornton,' he said. 'You and your lady friend are booked into the Boudoir.'

Noooo! The Boudoir was Charlotte's!

'Hey! The one with the four-poster, right?'

'Right.'

'Cool.'

Charlotte didn't need to look at Alex to know that they were thinking the same thing.

In front of her mind's eye gleamed the elegant silver handcuffs that she'd picked out for his and Thea's delectation yesterday.

'Looks like I could be in for an interesting weekend,' said Alex.

nine

'I'll pick you up at eight o'clock—'

'Eight o'*clock*? On a Saturday morning? That's inhu*mane*, Alex!'

'Eight o'clock *sharp* outside your front door. And if you're not there, we're going without you.'

Charlotte made a face at him down the phone, but he was gone without even the courtesy of a goodbye. She put the phone down and aimed the remote at the telly to turn up the volume. What was the point? It was yet another reality show peopled by insufferable thugs and egomaniacs. One of the ego-maniacs, a bootylicious brunette with a mouth like an exotic flower, reminded Charlotte of Thea, and she found herself wondering what Thea would choose to wear for the television cameras this weekend. The thought of Thea swanning round Cholyngham in designer threads made Charlotte veer into her bedroom to check out the contents of her wardrobe.

Could she compete? Probably not, but she'd give it a go. For travelling: Keds, Levi's and a plain white shirt. For dinner tomorrow night? Hmm. How about that vintage dress, the black velvet one with the Peter Pan collar? It looked great teamed with white petticoats and plain black stilettos. And for Sunday, when she'd have to play the part of Thea's pal? Well, there was no point in even trying to upstage the Divine One. She'd *love* to wear her flouncy little polka-dot number (the only good thing to come out of Paris), but she suspected that it might make her look as if she was trying too hard. She'd keep it simple in jeans and a plaid shirt and the walking boots that reminded her of Rupert Bear's.

She packed her suiter with more than usual care. The skirt of the black velvet frock was constructed from yards and yards of fabric and stowing it proved problematic, but she was determined to make it work. By the time she'd finished, Sky News was announcing its midnight headlines. And she'd have to set her Saturday-morning alarm for seven o'clock! Damn and blast Alex and his megalomaniac plans for avoiding the early-morning traffic.

She went to bed and had awful problems falling asleep. When she finally did, she was visited by a nightmare in which Thea and she were having lunch in some posh Parisian bistro where the waitresses all sneered at her black velvet dress, and Thea was confiding in her about the sex games she got up to with Alex. The alarm clock woke her just as Thea was about to share with her an ode that she'd written in praise of Alex's penis.

* * *

Charlotte landed on her front doorstep just in time. Alex's beat-up Saab convertible was rounding the corner, with Thea lounging like a leopardess in the passenger seat and Finn in the back. Thea clearly fancied herself as Gina Lollobrigida, because she was wearing big sunglasses and an Hermès scarf tied round her head 50s-film-star fashion. She exuded effortless glamour, and Charlotte felt like

Little Miss Hicksville in her Keds and Levi's and simple white shirt.

Finn, always the gentleman, helped her stow her suiter in the boot, and together they got into the car and made faces at the back of Thea's head.

'*Hiiiii!*' said Thea in her husky drawl. 'So glad you could join us at Cholyngham for the weekend, Charlotte.'

Jesus! From the way she said it, you'd have thought Cholyngham was her very own des res. Charlotte was just about to make another face at the back of Thea's head when Thea turned round and hit Charlotte with the full-on beam of her gaze – which the sunglasses did little to diminish. Charlotte tried to turn her expression into a kind of contemplative one, and beside her she heard Finn snigger.

'How was the Caribbean?' Charlotte enquired politely.

'The Caribbean was … blue.' Thea gave her a smile that the Sphinx might have envied, and nodded a little pensively. 'Yes. *Blue* is the word.'

Charlotte refrained from asking about the movie Thea had been shooting there, in case that turned out to be blue too. Instead she said, 'So. I understand it's your birthday tomorrow.'

'Yes.' Thea smiled at her, then turned to Alex and ran an index finger along the line of his jaw. '"Because the birthday of my life is come, my love is come to me,"' she said.

'Come again?' said Charlotte.

'Christina Rossetti. It's from her poem "A Birthday".' Thea cleared her throat and recited in full declamatory mode:

'My heart is like a singing bird
Whose nest is in a watered shoot;
My heart is like an apple-tree
Whose boughs are bent with thickset fruit;
My heart is like a rainbow shell
That paddles in a halcyon sea;
My heart is gladder than all these
Because my love is come to me.'

'Very nice,' said Charlotte inadequately. *Oh, God,* she thought. *This journey is going to be longer than Odysseus's.*

* * *

She was right. By the time they got to Cholyngham, Thea had treated them to enough quotes and aphorisms to make the *Iliad* and *Odyssey* combined seem like novelettes. She'd recited reams more Rossetti and whole speeches from Shakespeare and pithy *pensées* from Proust. The final one came as they finally, *finally* rolled up the drive to Cholyngham, where a gardener was strimming the verges. "'Let us be thankful to those who gladden our hearts,'" murmured Thea, swivelling herself out of the passenger seat, "'those delightful gardeners who make our spirits bloom.'"

'Proust?' asked Finn, stifling a yawn.

'Proust,' confirmed Thea.

They watched as Thea sashayed up the front steps of Cholyngham, and so did the delightful gardener, who was so mesmerised by Thea's *derrière* in the skin-tight black capri pants she was sporting that he very nearly strimmed his foot off.

'Let us be thankful to those who gladden our hearts,' muttered Finn as Roger the porter came to claim Thea's Louis Vuitton, 'those delightful porters who lead Thea up to the tower room and lock her in before throwing away the key. How the fuck does Alex stick her? All I can say is, she must give excellent head.'

'Let's set the Gruff Gang on her,' said Charlotte. 'Her *haute couture* gear would tickle their taste buds more effectively than my chain-store threads could. Hermès scarf,

Vuitton luggage – I ask you. *Haute cuisine* indeed for goats.' Charlotte kicked the gravel with a scuffed Ked. 'And I bet those loafers are Gucci. And you should get a load of the underwear she's getting for her birthday tomorrow.'

'You helped Alex choose it?'

'Yeah. I wish I'd bum-steered him and advised him to get her tacky red satin stuff instead.'

'Charlotte?' Finn was watching her curiously.

'Yeah?'

'Are you jealous?'

'Jealous? Of who?'

'Thea.'

'Thea? Why should I be jealous of Thea?'

'I dunno. It's just the way you were kicking the gravel.'

'Don't be daft, Finn. She just makes me mad, with her showy-off quotes and her husky voice and her swingy hair.'

'I prefer your hair,' said Finn loyally. 'It's lovely and wild and natural-looking.'

'Wild is right,' said Charlotte gloomily. 'It's as untameable as the Cholyngham goats.'

'Come on,' said Finn, mock-punching her shoulder. 'Let's go and have a drink to cheer ourselves up.'

In reception, Alex and Thea had just finished signing the visitors' book and were on their way upstairs, clearly with every intention of bonking each other's brains out, since Alex's hand was lingering on Thea's fabulous arse.

'Well,' said Finn, 'let's not hold our breaths until their re-emergence from the Boudoir.'

Charlotte made one last childish face at Thea's retreating bum before following Finn across the lobby. As she passed the reception desk, she snuck a look at the Divine One's film-starrish signature. It was in shimmering emerald-green ink, with the dramatic 'T' practically taking up half the page, and below it she'd written: 'Cholyngham. Where the heart is.'

'Get me that drink now, Finn,' said Charlotte.

* * *

Later, after she'd finished dressing for dinner, Charlotte went for a stroll around the grounds. She'd stowed her Swiss Army knife in her handbag in the event of meeting up with the Gruff Gang, but there was no sign of them.

It was a beautiful evening. The air was balmy and heavy with the scent of jasmine and rambling roses, and monkey-puzzles cast long, intriguing shadows across the manicured lawns. Charlotte wished that she'd chosen to wear something a little lighter than her black velvet dress. Its sleeves with their dinky white cuffs were quite tight, and she suspected she'd have sweat-stains under her arms before long. But as she walked, the skirts made a satisfying swishing motion, which had the effect of circulating the air around her thighs. She couldn't walk far – her stilettos were not designed for strolling – so she sat down in the shade of one of the rustic gazebos that had been so thoughtfully provided by the delightful Cholyngham gardeners.

On the other side of the gazebo, a couple were conversing in tones so infuriatingly low that Charlotte had to strain to eavesdrop. Once she'd adjusted her ears to the decibel level, she realised that she was eavesdropping on Alex and Thea.

She debated. Thea was fair game, but there was something not quite ethical about eavesdropping on one of her oldest friends. She was just about to creep away when she heard her name being mentioned.

'Charlotte's a lot more sophisticated than you think,' Alex was saying. 'You don't survive long in the advertising business if you don't develop a reasonably tough carapace.'

'She's a little hoydenish, isn't she? Not terribly in touch with her inner goddess.'

'I dunno,' said Alex. 'She usually manages to scrub up quite well.'

'I just hope she won't let down the tone of the documentary. This is Cholyngham, after all, and I'm sorry, Alex, but jeans and sneakers just don't fit the bill.'

'Go easy, Thea. We can't all afford designer labels, and Charlotte's style is very much her own.'

'That being?'

'Um. Quirky, I guess. Maybe you could call it boho.'

'Boho?' Thea gave a throaty laugh. 'That quirky thrift-shop-meets-Zara look is about as common as they come. Speaking of which …'

Charlotte's face went puce. How *dare* Thea diss her like this? She was just about to make her presence felt, with a withering retort that had taken her some moments to dream up, when Thea spoke again.

'You came like a train earlier, darling,

didn't you?' she purred. 'You love it when I do this, don't you? Hmm? Shall we try it again al fresco?'

Charlotte heard Alex give a groan.

'Let me whisper dirty nothings in your ear, darling, while I make you a little more comfortable ...'

Charlotte heard the sound of a zipper being unfastened, a low laugh from Thea, the susurration of clothing being discarded. Oh God, oh God. Alex and Thea were going to make out on the other side of the gazebo. She *couldn't* eavesdrop on them any longer – she'd have to get out of there.

She rose to her feet and took a cautious step across the wooden floor. But in high heels, the step wasn't cautious enough: the creak of the floorboard sounded deafening in the meaningful silence that had descended on the gazebo. Maybe she should take her shoes off? Charlotte bent down to slip off her right stiletto, then realised that the heel had got stuck in a knothole. She tugged and tugged at it, but it was too firmly wedged to dislodge without making a noise. There was nothing for it – she'd just have to leave it behind and come back for it later. She slid her left foot out of its shoe, crept down the steps of the gazebo and fled across the lawn like Cinderella fleeing from the ball.

Negotiating the gravel of the driveway was painful on her feet and did nothing for the soles of her black Wolford stay-ups. As she teetered along on tiptoe, she became aware of Finn standing in the bay of the drawing room, watching her. He opened the French window and came to meet her.

'What on earth are you doing, perambulating in stockinged feet?' he said.

She explained.

'How will you know when the coast's clear?' he asked.

'I guess I'll have to wait until they come in for cocktails. I'll scoot back down to the gazebo and retrieve my shoe then.'

'In the meantime,' Finn said, 'I've ordered you a drink. It's waiting for you in the drawing room.'

'Am I allowed to go in with bare feet?'

'Absolutely,' said Finn. 'Just curl them up under you on the couch and you'll look perfectly at home.'

She followed him back through the French windows and did as he'd instructed her, covering her feet with the folds of her voluminous velvet skirt.

'So,' said Finn, sitting down opposite her, 'Alex and Thea were making out in the garden? I hope the goats don't happen upon them.'

'I hope they do,' said Charlotte. 'Especially after the things she said about me. She's a perfect bitch. I shall never, *never* understand what Anna saw in her. What perverse impulse prompted her to include Thea in that SHEF evening?'

'Which one was that?'

'The one where she bagged Alex.'

'You make him sound like a trophy.'

'He's not. He's a gullible git for falling for that – that – Circe.'

'Circe?'

'You know, the goddess in the Greek myths who turns all the men into pigs. Huh. She's certainly succeeded with Alex.'

'The reason Anna invited her,' said Finn, 'is because she's quite naïve.'

'*Thea* is?'

'No. Anna. She tends to see the nice side of everyone.'

'Thea doesn't *have* a nice side. She's incorrigibly nasty. Ooh, look. Here she comes now, strolling over the greensward with her bloody swain in tow. That must have been something of a quickie. Maybe they *were* interrupted by the Gruff Gang after all.'

As the glamorous couple reached the French window, Charlotte heard Finn say, 'Uh-oh.'

'What's wrong?'

'Thea's found your shoe. See? She's carrying it.'

'Shit!' Charlotte froze, then sprang into action, grabbing her other stiletto and thrusting it under a cushion.

'What are you doing?' asked Finn.

'I can't let her know they're my shoes,' Charlotte told him in an urgent whisper. 'She'll guess I was on the other side of the gazebo while they were doing it. Hi!' She greeted Alex and Thea with such effusion that Alex immediately looked suspicious. 'Join us for a drink, why don't you? What's that you've got there, Thea?'

'It's a shoe,' said Thea, stating the obvious as if Charlotte were an infant learning to talk. 'We came across it while we were strolling in the garden. Is there someone who takes care of lost property, Finn?'

'Yes,' said Finn. 'I can leave it with Roger, the porter.'

He reached out a hand for the offending item, but Thea said, 'I'll give it to him.'

'No. No – that's my job as, you know, Cholyngham host-type person,' said Finn.

Thea looked a tad surprised. 'It's no problem, Finn. I'm on my way up to the Boudoir to change for dinner, and I'll pass by reception. I'd be glad of a chat with Roger and his amusing accent. Although' – she looked at the object in her hand with an expression of plangent incomprehension – 'why anyone should want this hideous thing returned to them is beyond me.'

And off Thea went, swinging Charlotte's right shoe by the heel.

'Let me get you a drink, Alex,' said Finn.

'No!' said Charlotte. 'Let Alex get his own drink.'

'What?' Finn looked at her in surprise. 'Why shouldn't I get Alex a drink?'

'Because.'

'Because why?'

'Because' – Charlotte directed a meaningful look at the cushion under which she'd stowed the other shoe, trying to make Finn aware of her predicament – 'he owes you one.'

'That's cool with me,' said Alex. 'Although how you know I owe Finn a drink is beyond me, Charlotte.' And off he strolled in the direction of the honesty bar.

'What was that all about?' asked Finn.

'Don't you see? I can't let Alex see the matching shoe. He'd put two and two together at once. Oh, *bugger*! Why didn't I just tell her it was mine, and that you were just about to go off and unstick it for me? She'd never have imagined that I was eavesdropping on them. And even if she had, she wouldn't have cared less. She'd probably have got some kind of perverse thrill out of it.'

'You really don't like her, do you?' said Finn, giving her a look of borderline admiration. 'I'd hate to be struck off your Christmas-card list, Charlotte.'

'Thea was never on it.' She looked over her shoulder at where Alex was standing by the bar. 'I'm going to have to leg it up to my room before Alex comes back and sees my shoe. Hell's *teeth*! What'll I do about dress shoes for this evening?'

'Don't you have another pair?'

'No.'

'What size are you?'

'Five. Yikes – I'd better make tracks. Alex is on his way back.' Charlotte grabbed the discarded stiletto from under the cushion and fled.

The room she'd been assigned this time wasn't as luxurious as the Boudoir, but it did boast a rather ornate cheval glass. Charlotte stood in front of it, forlorn in her stockinged feet, and regarded her reflection. The look she'd contrived was completely compromised without her shoes. Hell and death. She could hardly go down to dinner in her Keds or her Rupert Bear walking boots, and the only alternative was the complimentary Cholyngham towelling slippers. What was she to do? She'd have to feign illness and have dinner in her room. But the idea of Thea sitting in the dining room with Alex and Finn on either side of her like a pair of gallants filled Charlotte with murderous rage. No!

Charlotte sank onto the bed. Although she thought and thought and thought, she could come up with no solution to her problem. Unless she went to Thea? She could invent some sob story about forgetting to pack her shoes, and ask Thea to lend her a pair ... But Thea was no fool. She'd put two and two together and work out that the black stiletto she'd found in the gazebo was a perfect match for Charlotte's black velvet dress.

A knock came at the door. 'Who is it?' Charlotte asked.

'It's Lavinia,' said Finn's mother's voice. 'Finn tells me you have a problem.'

Charlotte ran to the door. Lavinia was standing there holding a carrier bag. 'Can I come in?' she asked.

'Of course.' Charlotte held the door open.

'I understand you forgot to pack dress shoes,' Lavinia said. 'I'd be happy to lend you a pair, but my feet are the wrong size. And then I remembered that a guest left a pair behind recently. They're a bit vulgar, but they're the right size, and they're better than nothing.' Lavinia reached into the carrier bag and produced a pair of shoes.

Oh, God. The shoes had clear plastic heels and platforms in which were suspended artificial flowers in a Dyno-Rod shade of orange. The ankle-straps were of silver plastic, as was the vamp. They were categorically the most hideous shoes Charlotte had ever seen.

But she didn't have a choice. She took the shoes from Lavinia and regarded them with trepidation. 'Thank you, Lavinia,' she said.

'You're welcome,' said Lavinia. 'Enjoy dinner.'

She left Charlotte standing in front of the cheval glass, gingerly holding the shoes by their straps. Charlotte turned her back to the mirror and sat down on the bed again. She slid her feet onto the clear plastic soles and fastened the straps without looking. She couldn't bear to see her feet sporting these – these *travesties* that had the presumption to call themselves dress shoes.

She stood up and moved to the door, feeling like the Little Mermaid must have done when she learned how to walk, and then she proceeded to negotiate the corridors and stairs that led down to the reception rooms. As she crossed the lobby, she saw a couple struggling to suppress astonished looks as they stared at her feet, and a teenaged girl had the temerity to burst out laughing. Charlotte stomped manfully on, holding her head high in an attempt to look elegant, but the further she progressed, the more dumbfounded the reactions she provoked from the Cholyngham guests.

Finally she reached the drawing room, where Alex and Finn had been joined by Thea, who was looking glorious in what had to be Roberto Cavalli silk chiffon. Finn took one look at Charlotte, then jumped to his feet and moved to the window. She could see his shoulders shaking. Charlotte bypassed

Alex and Thea, who were apparently mesmerised by her feet, and moved to join him.

'OK, OK – I know they're hideous, but what else could I do? I could hardly come down to dinner in my slippers, could I?'

'Actually,' said Finn, 'slippers might have been less outré than those.'

'I know they're a bit flashy—'

'A *bit*?' said Finn with a guffaw.

'And your meaning is?' she said with a hauteur she was far from feeling.

'Well – they're *literally* flashy.'

Charlotte looked at him without comprehension.

'They *flash* when you walk, Charlotte. Didn't you know?'

She clamped her hands to her face and gave Finn a stricken look. 'No!' she said.

''Fraid so.'

She looked down and took a cautious step forward. *Bling*! went the sole of her shoe, lighting up like a firework.

'Oh! Oh!' whimpered Charlotte. 'Oh, no! This is the worst moment of my life. What am I going to do?'

'Grin and wear 'em,' said Finn. 'There's nothing else you *can* do. Glass of wine?'

'A large one,' she said, and Finn moved off to procure her alcohol.

Charlotte remained standing by the window, pretending to admire the view, putting off the dread moment when she would have to walk back to where Alex and the Queen of the Universe were sitting. She finally screwed her courage to the sticking point and went for it.

Bling bling bling! went her shoes as she crossed the thick pile carpet.

'Hey, Flash Gordon. How's it going?' said Alex, inviting her to grind glass in his face.

Thea was regarding Charlotte's shoes with a contemplative expression. Her silence was many times more eloquent than any words she could have uttered.

Charlotte lunged for the menu so that she could use it as a shield for her glowing face. She scanned it unseeingly, humming a little tune, all the while conscious of her shoes like blocks of lead on her feet, not wanting to move them in case they lit up. *Please, please can we go into the dining room soon?* she prayed. *At least in there I can hide them away under the table.*

Finn came back with her wine. 'Shall we go in?' he said.

'Yes!' Charlotte arose with such haste that

her shoes sprang to life and blinged all over the place.

'Ladies first,' said Alex, standing back to allow Charlotte and Thea to precede him into the dining room.

Charlotte would have legged it in there, but she felt she had to match her pace to that of Thea, who moved maddeningly slowly, in a kind of undulating fashion. Their progress was followed by the eyes of all the diners, and it was hard to tell whether it was Thea's beauty they were feasting on, or Charlotte's shoes. Behind her, she could hear Alex and Finn sniggering like schoolboys.

At last, the maître d' rolled up to show them to their table. He bowed at Thea in an irritatingly ingratiating manner as he pulled her chair out for her. Charlotte didn't bother waiting for him to pull hers out. She wanted those shoes out of sight ASAP. She grappled with her seat in such an ungainly fashion that she set the crystal ringing and the stem vase in the centre of the table toppling. There was a mortifying silence in the room as all the diners looked round. Then everyone started talking over-animatedly to compensate, which made Charlotte feel even more conspicuous.

'Do not concern yourself, madam,' said

the maître d', who was still waiting for Thea to assume her throne. 'I shall send for a waiter to mop up the spillage.'

Thea gave the maître d' a gracious nod as she took her seat in a waft of chiffon. She looked cool as Cristal, and Charlotte was even more conscious of the sweat-marks that she knew were beginning to spread under her armpits.

The stem vase had contained a single tiger-lily. Thea took a waxy petal between her thumb and forefinger and murmured: '"Tiger! Tiger! Burning bright in the forests of the night …"'

And Alex said, 'But not as bright as Charlotte's shoes.'

Oh, God. If Alex was going to wisecrack his way through dinner, it was going to be a long evening.

***

It was. Between Smart-Alexisms from Alex and lofty literary quotes from Thea, the evening stretched on and on until Charlotte felt like the dormouse in *Alice in Wonderland*. 'I think I'll go to bed now,' she said.

'What?' said Finn. 'It's only half past nine. And you haven't had pudding yet.'

'Half past nine? I thought it was around midnight.' It certainly felt like it.

'I think I'll skip pudding,' said Thea. 'All those naughty calories! And I'd better get an early night – that is, if you allow me my beauty sleep, lover.' She gave Alex a meaningful look. 'Don't forget I have to be in front of the cameras bright and early in the morning.'

Don't forget! They couldn't have forgotten even if they'd tried their damnedest to. During the course of dinner, Thea had made myriad references to her starring role in the documentary that was being filmed the next day.

'Well, I'm having pudding,' said Alex.

'And so am I,' said Finn.

'And so am I,' said Charlotte, feeling mutinous in the face of Thea's calorie-consciousness. 'I'm having profiteroles.' She glared back at the pitying look on Thea's face and added, 'With cream *and* ice-cream.'

Just then, the teenage girl who had laughed at Charlotte's shoes sidled up to the table. 'Miss de Havilland?' she said, proffering an autograph book. 'I'm sorry to disturb you, but may I ask you to sign this?'

'Of course you may, child,' said Thea, reaching into her little beaded evening clutch and extracting her shimmery green pen. 'What is your name?'

'Juliet.'

'"It is the east, and Juliet is the sun."'

'I beg your pardon?'

'"Arise, fair sun, and kill the envious moon, who is already sick and pale with grief that thou her maid art far more fair than she." Shakespeare. *Romeo and Juliet*. Act two, scene two.'

'I see,' said the girl, clearly not seeing at all.

Thea signed the book with a flourish and handed it back to the girl with a gracious smile.

'I'm a great fan of yours,' said Juliet. 'I've seen everything you've ever done. I even saw you in that children's programme you did ages ago, before you got famous. *Spotty Cat and the Furball*. You were brilliant as Furball.'

'I? Some mistake, I think. Goodbye, little Juliet.'

'No,' persisted Juliet. 'You were fantastic. I never missed an episode. That furball costume was—'

'Run along, Juliet. Children aren't welcome in the dining room after nine o'clock.'

'I'm not a child. I'm sixteen. Do you remember the episode where Spotty Cat mistook Furball for a—'

Thea rose to her feet with alacrity. 'Excuse me, please. I've just remembered an urgent phone call I need to make to the documentary people.'

She picked up her beaded bag and skedaddled towards the dining-room door so fast she forgot to undulate.

Juliet looked at the signature in her autograph book and smiled. 'She really was brilliant as Furball,' she said.

* * *

Later, a weary Charlotte wended her way across the Cholyngham lobby, feet flashing sluggishly as she trailed behind Thea and Alex. Finn linked her arm.

'By the way,' he told her, 'Mum said to tell you that she didn't realise the shoes flashed. She'd never have offered them to you if she'd known. But she's glad she knows now. She's going to order a pair from the internet so that she can be zany in them.'

'Well, at least something good's come out of them.'

'Finn!' Lavinia called from behind the reception desk. Tonight she was wearing a tiara, an apron with a picture of one of the Cholyngham goats, and a pair of carpet slippers. 'Can you come here for a minute? I need to tap your legal brain for some advice on litigation. There's only so much those bastards can get away with.'

'Oh, God. Not again,' muttered Finn.

Charlotte didn't ask. Instead she said, 'Good night, darling Finn,' and kissed him on the cheek.

Up the stairs she trudged, wishing she hadn't demolished all her profiteroles. She felt at least a stone heavier than she'd been when she'd gone in to dinner, and the shoes on her feet were more leaden than ever. Finally she reached her door and swiped it unsuccessfully with her key.

'Are you going to leave your shoes out for the shoe-shine boy?' Alex threw over his shoulder at her as he and Thea proceeded Boudoir-wards. 'Or maybe they're shiny enough. They certainly lit up my life tonight.'

Charlotte didn't deign to respond. As she swiped viciously a second time, wishing the key were a razor and the lock Alex's cheek, she heard Thea say, 'What was it T.S. Eliot said, in "Rhapsody on a Windy Night"? About putting your shoes at the door and preparing for life?'

'Prepare for your television appearance,

more like,' said Alex. 'You're going to need your eight hours tonight, darling.'

'Ah. But will I get them?' said Thea, and her smoky laugh drifted down the corridor.

Charlotte shut her door on it. And then she did the thing she'd been longing to do all evening. She kicked off her shoes.

But the Evening of Doom was not yet over. One of the shoes hit a Dresden shepherdess on the mantelshelf and sent her flying. She landed decapitated on the carpet, a reproachful look on her face.

'Don't look at me like that,' said Charlotte. She picked up the figurine and tried to set its head on again, but the shepherdess was having none of it.

Charlotte could feel pent-up stress beginning to take the form of a constricting steel band around her temples. It had been a *wretched* evening. No wonder she was suffering from neuralgia.

The shepherdess was still regarding her accusingly. 'At least you'll never have to worry about headaches again, doll,' Charlotte told her, turning her to face the wall.

And then she shuffled into the bathroom to fetch Panadol.

ten

The next morning, Charlotte was beyond relieved to dump the flashy shoes back in their carrier bag and get into her walking boots. She wanted to race straight out into the blue-sky day that was waving to her from beyond the windowpanes. But first she had to 'fess up to decapitating the shepherdess.

She found Lavinia in the drawing room, sitting at the grand piano, wearing a sunhat and sunglasses and playing a Beethoven sonata. 'No worries,' she said when Charlotte showed her the headless ornament.

'I'll pay for it, of course,' Charlotte told her. 'I do hope it wasn't irreplaceable.'

'Irreplaceable? Not at all. I got a job lot of them in B&Q. And it looks like the head can be glued back on, anyway.'

'That's a relief. Is there anything I can do to make up for it?'

'Yes, actually. You could go and lend Finn a hand in the model farm. He's painting some fences. We need all the help we can get today, with that film crew descending on us.'

'What time are they due?'

'Half past ten. They're doing a tour of the house and grounds – and the farm, of course. And then they want me to set up champagne and a birthday cake for Thea.'

'Has she come down yet?'

'No. She's doing her make-up. But Alex is in the dining room having breakfast. Have you eaten?'

'I'm not hungry,' lied Charlotte. She couldn't face any more of Alex's insufferable jokes about last night's shoes. 'I'll wander on down and find Finn.'

As she let herself out of the French windows, she heard an American accent say, 'Hey, Lavinia! You should be playing "The Sun Has Got His Hat On"!' Lavinia responded with a merry peal of laughter. *Poor Lavinia,* thought Charlotte. *It really must be bloody hard work pretending to be eccentric.*

Outside, the sun really *was* coming out to play. Charlotte slid her shades on and walked down the path that led to the Cholyngham model farm, enjoying the satisfying thud-thud-thud of her walking boots on the packed earth.

Finn was hunkered down by the rabbit pen with a paintbrush in his hand, talking to a little girl who was cuddling a fluffy black-and-white bunny. He flattened the rabbit's ears back against its head and said something that made the child bubble with laughter. *He's going to make a fantastic father,* thought Charlotte. *And I hope that he and Anna will ask me to be godmother.* And then she remembered that being a godmother meant being responsible for a child's spiritual education, and she thought that, actually, maybe she wasn't the best person in the world to undertake such a monumental task.

Finn got to his feet when he saw her.

'Hi,' said Charlotte. 'Lavinia suggested I come down and lend you a hand.'

'Wouldn't you prefer to take it easy? You're meant to be on a weekend break, after all.'

'No. I'd rather do something constructive. And I'm aiming to stay out of the way of the Queen of the Universe. She did my head in big-time last night. It was like sitting opposite an audiobook version of the *Dictionary of Quotations*. What can I do here?'

'Um, not sure. Ask David. He's the manager. You'll find him in the barn.'

Charlotte set off to the barn, which had been converted to an indoor play-area for rainy days. David was a fit bloke with crinkly blue eyes and Hugh Grant hair. Charlotte automatically found herself segueing into flirt mode as she asked him what she could do to help.

'Well, you could feed the silkies.'

'Are they those adorable little chickens?' she said, dimpling up at him.

'They're not chickens. They're bantams. You'll find a sack of pellets in the shed. Sling some into a bucket and get going, farm girl.'

As Charlotte followed David's instructions, she remembered how Alex had called Chucky 'farm girl', and she wondered if Chucky had carried out her threat and uploaded that compromising photograph of her and Alex and Finn to the internet.

The silkies came running when they saw the bucket. Charlotte loved them, with their cute little topknots and their adorable fluffy legs that looked as if they were sporting trousers designed by Lainey Keogh. Around her, children were petting piglets and lambs and cuddling gerbils and rabbits. A llama ruminated in a grassy enclosure, and goats gambolled in a pen.

After she'd fed the silkies, David showed her how to groom the goats, who were shedding their winter coats. These were civilised little goats that bore only a passing resemblance to their relations, the Gruff Gang. 'I could get used to this,' she told him as she combed a kid's flank. 'It's kind of compulsive.'

'It's a bonding process,' David told her. 'Goats love it. Some breeders spend hours grooming their goats.'

And indeed, Charlotte spent nearly a whole hour combing out undercoats. The goats looked great when she'd finished, but her hands stank something awful. She'd just put the finishing touch to a little white kid by placing a daisy-chain circlet on its head when she heard a voice from behind her say, 'Hey, Capricorn. Found a new best friend?'

It was Alex.

'Yes.' Charlotte adjusted the circlet to a more becoming angle. 'I've been bonding with them. Now, darling,' she said to the kid, 'you can run along and play. How pretty you look!' And the little goat jumped onto a wooden cable-spool to show off its new look. 'I could be the Trinny and Susannah of goats,' said Charlotte, admiring her handiwork. She turned to Alex. 'How's the birthday girl?'

'Entertaining the film crew. She's on her way down here now.'

'How did she like her presents?'

'She hasn't opened them yet. She wants to do it in front of the camera.'

'Jesus, Alex! She can't do that!'

'She's taken to chanting the mantra beloved of Max Clifford – the "no publicity is bad publicity" one. I did warn her that the gift wrap concealed items of an, er, intimate nature, but she laughed and said, "All the better to bait them with."'

Charlotte pictured Thea holding up the diaphanous baby-doll nightie for the delectation of the camera and the titillation of the viewer, and she wished more than ever that she'd gone for the tacky option.

'What's she going to *do* down here on the farm, anyway? Ooh and ah over the gerbil?'

'I guess. She wants to sit on a horse, as well.'

'But she can't ride!'

'She just wants one shot, for effect, of her being led around the stable yard.'

'Oo-er.'

'What's wrong?'

'Here she comes.'

Thea was striding along the path, accompanied by a guy with a boom, a guy with a Steadicam, and a woman who was clearly the director of the programme. The director was a skinny, glamorous type with long nails and stripy hair, and she was very busy bonding with Thea, chatting away nineteen to the dozen and laughing loudly at the starlet's aphorisms. Or maybe she was laughing loudly at Thea's outfit.

Thea was wearing a swashbuckling shirt, a black bolero, and a pair of wide black culottes that skimmed gleaming black cowboy boots. She also had a hat-strap slung around her neck, the gaucho hat to which it was attached bouncing becomingly off her shoulder-blades. The look was very Rita Hayworth in *Blood and Sand*.

'Jesus,' breathed Charlotte. 'And she had the gall to criticise *my* dress sense.'

'When did she do that?' asked Alex sharply, and Charlotte felt her face suffuse with colour – because it had, of course, been the previous evening, when Charlotte had been eavesdropping in the gazebo.

'Well, she didn't *exactly* criticise. It was just the way she looked at the shoes I was wearing last night.'

'Well, they *were* seriously weird shoes, Charlotte. What on earth made you choose them?'

'I thought they were ... witty. I was trying to make an anti-fashion statement.'

'It struck me as more of a proclamation than a statement.'

'*Hiiiii*!'

Thea rolled up and threw herself at Alex, while the Steadicam man filmed stoically and the director smiled a big, white, shark-toothed smile. Then Thea proceeded to disport herself for the camera, running hither and yon, revelling in the wonders of nature afforded by the Cholyngham menagerie. 'Oh! Look at the divine little goat with the daisy-chain crown! Oh, look at the baa-lambs! Oh, look at those funny little furry chickens. Oh!

Give me a go of the bunny rabbit!' The only thing she steered clear of was the llama, who had a thick string of saliva dangling from its rubber-lipped mouth.

The cinematic triumvirate dutifully recorded Thea cuddling a piglet, and then they went into a rugby scrum and jabbered for a bit in arcane filmmaker talk.

'Thea?' said the director, who had introduced herself as Janine Benedict. 'I think we've got enough of you in the menagerie. We'd like to move on.'

'Oh? Shame,' said Thea, finally breaking eye contact with the piglet she'd been cooing over. Charlotte had been praying that the pig would poo on Thea, but it seemed that her prayers were being roundly ignored latterly. 'Will someone take the little piggie away from me?' said Thea in a baby-girl voice.

Hunky David obliged, clearly delighted to be able to do anything for the bewitching siren.

'We'd like to see you on a horse now,' said Janine, sounding businesslike.

'Certainly, Janine.'

'Could you maybe jump a fence for us or something?'

Thea looked genuinely contrite. 'Sorry, Janine. No can do. The most strenuous activity I can engage in would be a gentle walk. I'm afraid these culottes aren't designed for riding – they could easily flap about and spook the animal.'

Jesus, the woman was clever!

'Pity,' said David, wiping pig hairs off Thea's black bolero. 'I'd say you have a terrific seat.'

'Which way to the stables?' asked Janine.

'Follow me,' said Finn.

And down to the stables they all dutifully trundled, and up Thea got on a handsome bay, and Finn led her around the manege and Thea looked *magnificent* on horseback. Really bloody magnificent. The outfit had been inspired, Charlotte realised as Thea paraded past. She remembered how a character in one of her favourite books had pretended to know how to ride and had come a cropper, and a horrible mean vengeful voice in her head *so* wanted Thea to come a cropper too.

But no such luck. After her display of 'horsemanship', Thea dismounted gracefully with Finn's help and kissed the bay's face (Charlotte saw her surreptitiously rubbing her mouth with a tissue afterwards), and then Janine announced that it was time to go up to the main house for champagne and birthday cake and presents.

Thea and Alex linked arms cosily, and the cameraman followed their progress back up the path, Thea pausing here and there to admire a tree or sniff at a bloom, all the while swinging her Pantene hair around ostentatiously and reciting great chunks of Gerard Manley Hopkins in her actressy voice.

'What has made you so miserable, little Charlotte?' Finn asked as they trailed in Thea's wake.

'Am I miserable?'

'Yes. There's an air of mournfulness about you these days, that you wear when you think no one's looking.'

Charlotte sighed. 'I don't really know what's wrong with me, Finn,' she said. 'Everywhere I look there seem to be couples, and it's a long time since I've been part of a couple, and I kind of miss it. I suppose it's that time of the year, isn't it, when the sap's rising and birds are nesting and lambs and foals and calves are popping up all over the place? I'm probably just hormonal – and maybe a bit broody, too, since you told me the news about you and Anna. And I'll be perfectly honest and say that I miss having sex.'

'But you've got lots of other things going for you, honey child! Look on the positive side. Don't you get masses of satisfaction from your job?'

'I used to, but I'm enjoying it less and less. I don't want to be a career girl forever, Finn. And I get scared when I see all the young Turks who have been invading our workplace recently. Advertising's becoming more and more Pot Noodle, and it's in*sane*ly stressful. I think I'd rather like to meet some gorgeous man and settle down and have a baby.'

'Charlotte! You're not even thirty, for God's sake. You've loads of time to think about settling down and having babies.'

'At the risk of coming on like the Queen of the Universe, may I quote John Donne to you? "But at my back I always hear Time's wingèd chariot drawing near." I'm not really getting anywhere career-wise, Finn – I'm treading water. And I feel like an awful charlatan sometimes, trying to persuade people to buy crap they don't need. Consumers are terribly insecure, you know. Especially women.'

'How so?'

'Well, take the beauty business. It's the most ruthless of them all. I'm paid to convince women that forking out hundreds of pounds for face creams is going to make them look younger and more desirable.'

'And don't they work?'

'Of course they don't. Ageing isn't optional. But women are prepared to pay the price because they're desperate. Like me.'

'Oh, sweetheart!' Finn slung an arm round her and pulled her close. 'Are things really so bad?'

Charlotte shrugged.

'Maybe you should go on a retreat or something? I read an article recently about how more and more people are taking time out to get in touch with their spiritual side.'

'That's funny. I was just thinking earlier that I don't *have* a spiritual side.'

'Everybody does.'

Charlotte smiled at him. 'Even Thea?'

'Even Thea.'

The production team had gone into one of their rugby scrums outside the main entrance to the house, conferring again, and Thea was sitting on the steps with her head on Alex's shoulder.

'OK, Thea,' Janine called out. 'How about champagne and cake in the drawing room?'

'Absolutely!' said Thea with enthusiasm. 'Just allow me to change first.'

'Oh, God. I wonder what she'll pull out of the dressing-up box next,' said Charlotte.

'A crown, probably. And maybe an orb and a sceptre to boot.'

Finn and Charlotte moseyed into the drawing room, where champagne was waiting in an ice bucket and a birthday cake bore the legend 'Happy Birthday, Thea' in strawberry icing.

'Ha!' said Charlotte. 'I bet there's millions of calories in that cake. And she'll *have* to eat it.'

'Fancy some champagne?' asked Finn.

'We can't really help ourselves until Thea descends from heaven, can we?'

'We'll go into the library. There's a bottle in the fridge in there.'

'Great. I really, really feel like getting pissed.'

In the library, Janine the director was sitting in front of a laptop. She gave Finn and Charlotte a bright fake smile as they came in. 'Well,' she said. 'Thea is clearly a great animal lover. She was in her element in your manege, Finn. And in your menagerie, for that matter! We got some great footage.'

'Good,' said Finn, moving to the fridge that was concealed in a satinwood pedestal desk. 'Were you happy with the interior shots?'

'Oh, yes. One of the guests played the piano while Thea lay on top like Michelle Pfeiffer in *The Fabulous Baker Boys*. And we shot Thea standing by the portrait of your grandmother, mimicking her pose.'

It was then that it struck Charlotte that the programme really wasn't about Cholyngham at all. It was all about Thea. *You shot her the wrong way, you idiots,* she thought. *You should have used a rifle.*

'By the way, your wi-fi's a bit erratic,' Janine told Finn. 'I got cut off from the internet earlier.'

'Sorry about that. You can send e-mail from reception if it's urgent.'

'Oh, no. There's nothing urgent. I'm just having a random Google while I'm waiting for Thea. It passes the time.'

Charlotte knew that if Thea had been there, she would indubitably have come out with the famous quote from *Waiting for Godot* about how time would have passed in any case.

Just then Alex strolled into the library, swinging Coco de Mer carrier bags by their silken handles. Janine clocked the logo and raised an eyebrow in enquiry.

'Presents for the birthday girl,' explained Alex.

Janine looked doubtful. 'But Coco de Mer is a – is a *sex* shop, isn't it?'

'It's a very *upmarket* sex shop,' Alex corrected her.

'I'm sorry. I shall have to ask if there are sex toys in there.'

'Yep. And there's some pretty classy underwear, too.'

Janine looked horrified. 'But – you don't expect Thea to open such gifts in front of the camera, do you?'

'*She* doesn't seem to have a problem with it,' said Alex. 'She's quite an exhibitionist, is my missus. Oh, good,' he added as Finn popped the champagne cork.

'I really don't think we can have Thea receiving presents wrapped in Coco de Mer paper,' said Janine, sounding rattled. 'It's got – male organs all over it, and this show goes out way before the watershed. It's a family show.'

'Well, they're the only presents she has.'

'Couldn't we mock up some presents for her? We could wrap up some – some …' Janine cast her eyes wildly around the library. 'Some old books or something. Maybe one of those Dresden shepherdesses.'

'I think you'll find,' said Alex, 'that Thea's thespian skills will be severely taxed if she unwraps a parcel containing a pile of old books and shepherdesses.'

'Well, then,' said Janine snittily, 'we shall just have to leave the presents out of the picture and stick to cake and champagne. I must say, I think it's extremely unprofessional of you to buy her presents from a sex shop when you knew she was going to have to open them in front of a camera.'

'Hey,' said Alex, spreading his hands. 'Less of the "unprofessional", please. You can't hold me responsible for this glitch. Charlotte and I bought those presents before we knew Thea was going to be appearing on *Birthday* bloody *Bonanza.*'

'Some of the presents are from *you*, Charlotte?' asked Janine, sounding shocked.

'No, no,' protested Charlotte. 'I just helped Alex choose them.'

The look Janine gave her made Charlotte feel as if she'd been implicated in some kinky sex act. The presenter pursed her lips together and returned her attention to the screen of her laptop, fingers flying over the keys like stick insects.

'Here you go.' Finn passed round three

flutes of champagne (Charlotte was glad that he hadn't offered Janine one), and they raised them. 'What'll we toast to?' he asked.

'To many more gang bangs with the Cholyngham goats,' said Alex urbanely, directing a wicked sideways glance towards where Janine was sitting, looking even more like there were a poker up her bum.

'To gang bangs,' chorused Finn and Charlotte.

Unfortunately, Thea chose that moment to make her entrance. All eyes went to the doorway, where she was framed against the light that flooded into the library from the hall. She was clad in a cloud of ruffled, shredded silk taffeta, the hem of which grazed the floor at the back and rose to the very tops of her thighs at the front. She was wearing wedge sandals so high that she was almost as tall as Alex. She looked statuesque – a goddess, a terrestrial Aphrodite – and Charlotte in her plaid shirt and jeans and Rupert Bear boots had never felt punier.

'*Hiiiii!*' drawled Thea. 'What's all this talk about gang bangs?'

'Nothing,' Alex assured her. 'It's just a joke.'

Suddenly a cry came from the corner of the room, where Janine's tip-tapping had come to an abrupt standstill. 'Ohmigod,' she said. 'Oh. My. God.' And then she looked at Finn and Alex and Charlotte where they stood nursing their champagne flutes in the centre of the room.

'Well,' she said in a steely voice. 'Thanks to *you* three, Thea's *Birthday Bonanza* has just been officially axed.'

'What?' gasped Thea. 'What are you talking about?'

'Your birthday,' said Janine, 'has been scuppered by your boyfriend.'

'But I don't understand! The highlight's still to come. The champagne, the presents!'

'No champagne,' said Janine in an authoritative voice. 'And *categorically* no presents.'

'I don't believe you! What's gone wrong?'

'Sorry, Ms de Havilland. I just performed a search for the Cholyngham menagerie. And this is what came up.' Janine turned her computer screen around to face the room. The image displayed on it was of three surprised-looking people who had quite clearly been caught *in flagrante delicto* under cover of a sally bush. And they were unmistakably recognisable as Charlotte, Alex and Finn.

Thea moved across the floor like a

somnambulist, her gaze fixed on Janine's computer screen.

'I'm sorry,' Janine said again. 'But this is like some sick joke. If our younger viewers were to be confronted with this image when they entered those two words into a search engine, the integrity of our television programme could be seriously compromised. I'm afraid my crew and I shall have to pack up and leave.'

'But – but—' spluttered Thea. 'You can't! You'll have no *Birthday Bonanza* for next week's slot if you do that!'

'We'll just have to substitute a rerun,' said an implacable Janine, shutting down her computer. She gave the miscreants in the centre of the room the kind of icy look a headmistress might reserve for her most troublesome pupils. 'You,' she said, 'are indubitably three of the most depraved people it has ever been my misfortune to meet.' She shook her head. 'Sex toys, troilism, gang bangs with goats …'

'Gang bangs with *goats*?' echoed Thea, who was looking less and less like a Greek goddess and more and more like the Green one.

'My advice to you, Ms de Havilland,' said Janine, sliding her laptop into its case, 'is to extricate yourself ASAP from your current relationship and find a man who's worthy of you.'

And Janine Benedict picked up her phone and her computer case and strode from the room.

* * *

Half an hour later, Charlotte watched through the library window as Thea slung her Louis Vuitton bags unceremoniously into the back of a taxi. 'Nor hath hell any fury ...' she murmured.

Finn joined her. 'Alex clearly wasn't able to talk himself out of that one,' he said. 'I'm not surprised. I had another look at Chucky's online pic. Whatever angle she took it from really makes the three of us look as if we were up to something pretty kinky.'

'Have you told your mother about it?'

'Yeah.'

'How did she take it?'

'She found it hilarious. She's converted it into a screen-saver.'

'Really? She doesn't think it'll be bad for business?'

'Nah. You have to do quite a detailed search before that image comes up. And most people looking for Cholyngham aren't going to type in the word "menagerie". It was just bad luck that Janine happened on it.' Finn laughed. '"Cholyngham Menagerie at Troy"! Talk about Chucky's revenge.'

'But isn't Lavinia gutted that Cholyngham won't be appearing on *Birthday Bonanza*?'

'Actually, I think she's rather relieved. She found the idea of Thea sprawled across the grand piano rather cringe-making. Not *quite* the image of Cholyngham she's keen to promote.'

The taxi containing Thea took off down the drive, and Finn and Charlotte stood side by side at the French windows, waving good-bye and smiling broadly. They wiped the smiles off their faces when Alex walked into the room.

He moved towards the glass of champagne that he'd left on the pedestal desk, and raised it. 'Well,' he said. 'What can I say but good riddance to God's gift.'

'Good riddance?' echoed Charlotte.

'She behaved like a harpy up there,' he told them. 'She made Angelina Jolie in *Mr & Mrs Smith* look like the Singing Nun.'

'She actually got violent?' asked Finn.

Alex pulled up the sleeve of his T-shirt to reveal a nasty scratch on his bicep.

'Wow. Did she have a knife?' asked Charlotte.

'No. She used her nails.'

'You should get a tetanus shot, man,' remarked Finn.

'Yes, yes, you really should,' agreed Charlotte, nodding enthusiastically. She knew that Alex's aversion to needles bordered on the pathological.

'Didn't you try and explain the situation to her?' asked Finn. 'About the goats eating Charlotte's clothes?'

'Of course I did. But, somewhat un-surprisingly, she didn't believe me.'

Finn started to laugh. 'So she really thought that the three of us were doing it in the sally bush?'

'Yeah. But her real bone of contention wasn't even that I'd been unfaithful. It was all to do with the fact that she's been dropped from *Birthday Bonanza*.'

'So,' said Charlotte, 'does that mean that you are now no longer a couple?'

'Damn right,' Alex said with feeling. 'As of today, I have officially reverted to bachelor status.' He drained his glass and set it down, and then his eyes lit on the Coco de Mer carrier bags. 'At least she didn't abscond with her presents.'

'Did you keep the receipt?' asked Charlotte.

'Probably not.'

'So you can't get your money back.'

'Do I *want* it back? Can you imagine the looks of pity I'd provoke if I went back to that shop and asked for a refund? I'd look like the ultimate loser.'

'Why?'

'Mr Sad returns his sex aids because he hasn't managed to score.'

'You could always exchange them.'

Alex gave her a 'Doh!' look. 'For what? Lingerie in my size?'

'Oh. I guess you have a point.'

Finn refilled their glasses, and they sipped in silence for some moments before Alex turned to Charlotte and said, 'You have them.'

'What?'

'You take Thea's presents.'

'Alex, don't be daft! I – I *couldn't* do that!'

'Why not? You handpicked the stuff, ergo you should have it.'

'But—'

'But me no buts, little Charlotte. It would actually afford me great glee to know that you were deriving pleasure from your selected items. A kind of revenge on Thea for being such a narcissistic bitch.' He struck his forehead with the heel of his hand. 'Sweet Jehovah! How did I not see it before?'

Finn and Charlotte slid looks at each other and stayed schtum.

'I guess I did do a lot of thinking with my dick,' continued Alex a little morosely. 'She had a way with her mouth that would bring tears to a man's eyes.' He strolled across the room and picked up the carrier bags, and then he moved to Charlotte and forced her to wind reluctant fingers around the silken handles.

'They're all yours, sweetheart,' he said.

eleven

Back in her flat that evening, Charlotte poured herself a large glass of chilled Sauvignon Blanc. She was tired – the journey back from Cholyngham had taken forever because Alex's car had got a flat, and then they'd discovered that the spare was flat too and the AA had had to be called. But she knew she had reached that level of tiredness where sleep is somehow maddeningly elusive, and she also knew that if she went to bed now she'd be tossing and turning for hours.

In the bedroom, she set her wine glass down on the bedside table and exchanged her street clothes for her winceyette sleep-suit.

Then she unpacked her suiter and hung her Cholyngham threads back in the wardrobe. To her annoyance, she realised that she'd forgotten to rescue her black stiletto from Lost Property after Thea had whisked it away the previous evening. Had a mere twenty-four hours elapsed since the Evening of Doom? It seemed like a lifetime ago. Charlotte set the companion stiletto on her shoe rack, then changed her mind and slung it in the wastepaper basket. She wouldn't be back in Cholyngham for God knows how long, and there was no point in hanging on to a single shoe. They were only cheap old things anyway – she could afford to buy another pair.

She stowed the suiter in the bottom of her wardrobe, then turned to face the room. The glossy Coco de Mer carrier bags lay on the bed, beseeching her to open them. Charlotte regarded them for several moments, then moved to the bed, sat down and reached for one at random. The first item her hand made contact with was the artfully shaped ceramic dildo, wrapped in tissue paper. She unwrapped it, then set it on the bedside table beside her wine glass so that she could admire it. Next out was the bra-and-panty set, followed by the marabou-pompomed mules and the silk chiffon baby-doll nightie. Item after item was divested of layers of tissue and strewn on the bed. What treasure trove was here! But how very, very sad that there was no one to share it with …

Still, she might as well see how the lingerie fitted her. She discarded her sleep-suit, stepped into the ruffled blue panties and pulled them up. Oh! They were perfect! The way they were cut made her ass look more voluptuous and her legs look longer – especially when she slid her feet into the high, be-pompomed mules. The bra was a work of genius too – it enhanced her cleavage beautifully, giving her more oomph than Eva Herzigova. And as for the little marabou-trimmed baby-doll nightie … it was the sweetest thing she'd ever worn! It wafted round her like gossamer petals as she twirled and pirouetted and struck poses in front of the mirror, piling her hair up on her head one minute, then shaking it out and letting it fall round her shoulders the next, dancing to the rhythm of an imaginary samba band.

After she'd admired her cover-girl look to her satisfaction, she returned to the bed and continued the ransacking of her treasure trove. The final jewel in the Coco de Mer crown was a book of short stories – Anaïs Nin's *Little Birds*. Charlotte opened it and found herself confronted with the following:

> He felt his power coming back to him, his usual power and deftness. He knew by each move she made where she wanted to be touched. When she pressed against him, he covered her little round buttocks with his warm hands, and his finger touched the orifice. She leaped under his touch but made no sound ...

And half an hour later, Charlotte was lying on the treasure-strewn bed, fast asleep, with a dreamy smile on her face.

* * *

The next day at work was depressingly Monday-morningish. Hilary, Charlotte's immediate superior, was in awful form, still clearly miffed by the fact that Charlotte was the one who was to check out the hotel that featured in the Paris weekend break.

'How was your weekend?' Charlotte asked her by the water-cooler. 'Eventful?'

'On the contrary,' said Hilary. 'It was event-less. How was yours?'

'I spent it at Cholyngham.'

'*Again*? Well, we are moving in illustrious circles these days, aren't we? How can you afford to stay there so often?'

'It was a freebie.'

This information did nothing to improve Hilary's mood. She just called Charlotte a 'jammy bitch' and moved away.

Charlotte sighed, then went back to her desk to bone up on Paris. On the other side of her partition, a colleague was accepting delivery of a dozen birthday roses from her boyfriend. Charlotte glued a big smile to her face and said, 'Happy birthday.'

She checked her e-mail. To her astonishment, there was an unopened envelope icon from Thea de Havilland. The subject line read: 'Rightfully Mine'.

Dear Charlotte,
I imagine you are more than a little surprised to hear from me after your perfidious behaviour – the image of you half naked in the bushes with Finn and my ex (whose name I cannot bring myself to utter, even in an e-mail) is one

that I shall not easily forget. But the fact remains that I left something behind at Cholyngham, and I want it back. I phoned that bumpkin who is in charge of lost property about the bags in question, but he informed me that he loaded them into my ex's car along with your luggage, so I can only assume that they are now in your possession. I imagine that you can guess to what I am referring? The contents of the Coco de Mer bags were intended for me. For obvious reasons, I have no intention of importuning my ex for said contents, so I am asking – nay, demanding – that you let me have them back. It is the least you can do after betraying me with you-know-who.

I look forward to hearing from you on this matter.

Yours,

Thea de Havilland

Sweet Jesus! She *couldn't* let Thea have the Coco de Mer stuff back! What was she to do? What was she to *do*? It was all bloody Alex's fault – he'd landed her in it again. She reached for her phone and pressed speed-dial.

'Alex Thornton,' came his lazy drawl over the earpiece.

'Alex? It's Charlotte. Something's come up – something kinda urgent.'

'Fill me in.'

'I – I can't. Not on the phone.'

'E-mail me, then.'

'No. I couldn't trust you not to pass the e-mail on.'

'You clearly have a very high opinion of my moral integrity, sweetheart.'

'Can we meet? After work?'

'Today?'

'Yes.'

'That urgent, huh?'

'Yes!'

'Just let me check …' A couple of beats while Alex checked out his agenda. 'You're in luck. I have, as they say, a window.'

'The tapas bar? Seven o'clock?'

'I'll be there.'

She looked at her computer screen with an agonised expression, and then, resisting the impulse to send the message pirouetting back into the ether, she clicked on the printer icon with a reluctant finger and printed out Thea's e-mail.

* * *

At seven o'clock on the dot, she was sitting in the tapas bar with the printout in an envelope in her handbag, drumming her fingernails on the tabletop. There was a glass of red wine in front of her, and a Budvar for Alex.

He rolled up ten minutes late, unapologetic. 'What's the problem?' he asked.

'I received an e-mail in work today.'

'Popular girl.'

'Don't be smart, Alex. It was from Thea.' Charlotte reached into her bag and pulled out the envelope, then slid it across the table to him.

'You look like some shifty Cold War spy,' he said. 'Am I supposed to open this?'

'Yes.'

'And then I suppose I'll have to tear it into tiny bits and eat it?'

'Just read it, Alex.'

He scanned the letter, then skidded it back across the table to her. 'Well, what can I say? She's rapacious as a raptor, but she quite clearly feels that she was the injured party. It's really up to you, Charlotte, whether you let her have the stuff. Personally, I'd tell her to go fuck herself, but I imagine that Thea crossed is an enemy for life, and I know you like to keep people sweet.'

Charlotte looked down at the paper napkin she was twisting.

'You may think you're in a quandary, sweetheart,' he continued, 'but, as I see it, it's a pretty clear-cut choice. You either keep the goodies for yourself or you FedEx 'em to Polly Pot.'

'It's not so clear-cut as you might think,' said Charlotte, still looking down at her napkin.

'Why not?'

'Because I – because they're – um – *second-hand* goods now.' She finally made herself look up at him.

'What do you mean, they're second hand—' Realisation dawned, and Alex's glass of Budvar, which had been halfway to his mouth, hit the table with a thunk. 'You mean – they're *used*?'

'Yes,' she said, in a very small voice.

Alex sucked in his breath, and when he let it out again, it was in a crow of laughter. 'Whoa! Res*pect*!' he said. 'Little Charlotte Cholewczyk, you have just soared a million miles skywards in my estimation.'

Charlotte maintained a dignified silence.

Alex leaned back in his chair with one arm over the back and gave her a look that a demon might have envied.

'Stop it,' she told him.

'Stop what?'

'Stop thinking like that.'

'How do you know what I'm thinking?'

'I just do.'

'Then,' said Alex, 'it's useless asking me to stop. You should know. Remember the crotchless-red-panties theory?'

Charlotte looked down at her napkin again. It was looking very tatty.

'Well,' said Alex, 'were they any good?'

'Were what any good?'

'Your new playthings.'

'I think what a girl gets up to in the privacy of her own bedroom is her business and no one else's.'

'Oh, come *on*, Charlotte. You might allow me just a glimpse into the enigma that is the female psyche. I was the one who *gave* you the, er, items in question. Don't you think I deserve a little insight? A mental picture that I can carry around in a portfolio in my head and take out for my viewing pleasure during an idle moment?'

'No.'

'Did you try the—'

'Shut up, Alex.'

He did shut up, but he didn't stop looking

at her with a maddeningly knowing expression.

'I wish I hadn't told you now,' she said. 'You're clearly not going to be any help to me at all.'

'On the contrary. I'm thinking very hard. *Very* hard indeed.'

'Some fucking friend you are.'

'And I think I may have found a solution to your problem. Have you still got the Coco de Mer carrier bags?'

'Yes. They're far too pretty to throw out.'

'They're covered in pictures of penises.'

'They're very pretty penises.'

'An oxymoron, I'd have thought.' Alex narrowed his eyes at her. 'Drink up, little Charlotte, and come with me. I want to take you shopping.'

'Shopping? Why?'

'Wait and see.' He drained his glass, then got to his feet. Charlotte did likewise, winding her chenille scarf around her neck and stuffing the printout back in her bag.

On the street, Alex took a left and started striding in the direction of Soho. Charlotte had to trot to keep up with him. 'Where are we going?' she asked.

'D'you know, I've often wondered about

that. According to Schopenhauer, our spiritual journey through life takes us …'

Charlotte stopped listening. There was no point.

Five minutes later, Alex stopped outside a shopfront which bore the legend 'Madame Erica's Erotik Emporium'. He held the door open for her.

'We're not going in *here*?' she said, looking at him incredulously.

'We most certainly are. I apologise in advance for the offence to your delicate sensibilities, Ms Cholewczyk.'

'Ew,' said Charlotte, stepping across the threshold. 'This has to be the tackiest joint I've ever been in.'

'I'm very glad to hear it.'

'Why?'

'Because this is where I bought Thea's birthday presents.'

Charlotte looked at him, completely baffled. 'What are you on about, Alex? You know very well you didn't. *We* bought them, in Coco de Mer.'

'That's what Thea thinks. Actually, I bought them here, peeled the labels off and *pretended* I'd bought them in Coco de Mer.'

Charlotte looked at him, and a broad

smile began to spread across her face as she copped on. 'You *clever* person!' she said, clapping her hands. 'Oh, Alex – you are *evil*!'

'I know,' he said complacently.

'Yay! Where shall we start?' Charlotte grabbed a wire basket and looked around Madame Erica's Erotik Emporium with unbridled enthusiasm. 'Here! Get a load of these outfits. Oh – they're brilliant! Naughty Nurse or French Maid?'

'How about Pussy Cat?' said Alex, directing her towards a confection that married black acrylic fur with fishnet.

'"Stroke My Little Pussy,"' Charlotte read out loud. 'Yes! I can just picture Thea in those ears. And what are those?'

'Pulsating Panties.'

'Why? Oh – there's a secret compartment for a vibrating device. How clever!'

'Very cunning indeed. Want a pair?'

She gave him a withering look before remembering that her withering looks never worked on Alex. 'No, I do not want a pair. But I'm pretty sure Thea does. Into the basket they go.'

They moved on. '*Ew*!' said Charlotte as they found themselves confronted by a shelf of multicoloured vibrators in all shapes and sizes, ranging from 'Biggus Dickus' to 'Behemoth'.

'I'll leave it up to you to choose,' said Charlotte, 'since you know what she's used to.'

'Very well,' said Alex, reaching for 'Behemoth' and tossing it into the shopping basket.

Charlotte hummed *The Ride of the Valkyries* as she prowled the length of the shelf, helping herself to an assortment of tack. 'What on earth,' she said, picking up a weirdly shaped rubber thing with a curious attachment, 'is *this* supposed to do for a girl?'

'Not a lot, sweetheart. It's for a bloke.'

'Oh. You mean ...' She gave him a look of enquiry.

'Yep.'

She examined the attachment. 'What's that for?'

'It's for suction.'

'Does it work?'

'Dunno. I've never tried it. I prefer the real thing myself.'

Together they wandered around Erica's Emporium, picking some items up only to discard them as being too good for Thea, alighting upon others with glee. 'Chocolate willies! Excellent,' said Charlotte. 'These'll have loads of calories.'

'She won't touch anything that isn't fat-free,' said Alex.

'They don't have a fat-free option,' said Charlotte happily. 'She'll just have to gain a few pounds. Now. Reading material.' She picked up a magazine. '*Dog Lovers' Quarterly*? Holy shomoley. I don't think any of *these* canines would win prizes for good behaviour at Crufts. *Lola Loves It*?' She opened the magazine, then promptly shut it again. 'She certainly does. *Cream Buns*? Hm. Reads like no recipe *I've* ever tried.'

'How about a DVD?' suggested Alex.

'Definitely. *Slutty Secretaries' Office Party*? Or *Spanking Nancy*?'

'Neither. How about this one?'

'What's it called?'

'*Two Into One.*'

'Any particular reason?'

'Let's just say it might remind her of the Cholyngham Menagerie at Troy. Uh-oh.'

'What's wrong?'

'She's in it.'

'What?'

'Thea's in it.'

'Ha ha.' Charlotte returned her attention to the DVD rack.

'I'm not joking,' Alex said. 'She used to pull that stunt on me.'

The hint of nostalgia in his voice made her turn back to him. He was looking at the DVD upside down.

'No! You're serious, Alex? Show me!' Charlotte snatched the DVD from him. 'Starring Cha-Cha Fox, Studs Lonnergan and Rock O'Toole,' she read out loud. 'I can't see any Thea de Havilland here.'

'I know. She's Cha-Cha Fox.'

'Cha-Cha Fox? I don't believe you!'

'Turn it over,' he told her, and Charlotte did. 'See? There she is on the front with Studs and Rock.'

'Oo-er,' said Charlotte. 'Oooo-er! And she thought Chucky's pic of you and me and Finn was dodgy? Hee hee! We're positively *prim* in comparison!' She turned shining eyes on him. 'Oh, Alex – did you *know*?'

'I, er, *intuited*.'

'Oh – this is brilliant! I can't wait to tell Anna and Vivien!' She turned the picture upside down and squinted at it. 'I wonder how she managed *that*.'

'She's very bendy.'

'No wonder you were besotted. Shall we add it to our shopping cart?'

'She probably already has it.'

Charlotte held the DVD at arm's length and squinted at it again. 'And no wonder her star is in the ascendant. From Furball to porn star to fully fledged film star. It's like a fairytale.'

'A fairytale for grown-ups,' Alex corrected her.

'Do you want to buy it to remember her by?'

'I think not. My own home videos are memento enough.'

Charlotte said nothing. She didn't want Alex to think she was remotely interested in his sex life.

'Are we done?' he asked.

'I guess so. All I need to do now is buy some fresh tissue paper to wrap the goodies in, and then they're all Thea's. Thank you, Alex, for this excellent strategy.'

'You're welcome, ma'am.'

Charlotte started rooting in her bag for her wallet.

'What are you doing?' Alex asked her when he saw her credit card. 'I should be footing the bill for this.'

'No, you shouldn't. I got the good stuff, ergo I should fork out for the tack.'

He shrugged. 'What's the damage likely to be?'

Charlotte did some rough mental arithmetic. 'A bargain compared to the Coco de Mer damage.'

'OK. You can pick up the tab this time.'

'*This* time? I think it's highly unlikely that there'll be a *next* time.'

'You never know. If I ever need to go shopping for girly birthday presents in the future, I might ask you to come along. You've proved to be something of a revelation, Ms Cholewczyk.'

They looked at each other for a moment without saying anything, then came the sound of Alex's ring tone. 'Excuse me while I take this.' He slid his phone out of his pocket, and as he moved off Charlotte heard him segue into flirt mode: 'Darlin'! Yeah, sorry about that – something came up.' A low laugh. 'Your pleasure is my pleasure. I couldn't ask for a nicer girl to have telephone sex with.' Well! He flirted exceptionally well for an idiot. 'Let's make it tomorrow – same time, same place.'

And as she made her way past a display of surprised-eyed blow-up dolls towards the checkout, she found herself wondering who 'darlin" was. Alex was such an incorrigible womaniser, he must have found a substitute for Thea already.

The woman behind the cash register was a blowsy, stripy-haired blonde with footballers'-wives nails and penis-shaped earrings. She clocked up the items, chewing gum vigorously as she did so, then passed the credit slip to Charlotte to sign.

'You're a lucky girl,' she told Charlotte as she passed the bag of sex toys over the counter.

'They're not for me,' said Charlotte hastily.

The woman gave her a fat wink. 'That's what all the girls say,' she said.

* * *

At home later that evening, Charlotte chose to get into her new bra-and-panty set and her baby-doll nightie instead of her winceyette comfies. There was something about the lingerie that made her feel quintessentially feminine – even though there wasn't much point in feeling quintessentially feminine when there was no one around to appreciate it.

She was pottering about in her pompoms, heating up baked beans and buttering toast, when the doorbell rang. 'Who could that be?'

she found herself saying out loud as she clip-clopped across the sitting-room carpet to pick up the entrance phone.

But it was only someone looking for a different flat.

* * *

Charlotte was back at school. It was exam time, and she was desperately trying to remember a Christina Rossetti poem. For ages she struggled and struggled with the first sentence – 'My heart is like a tum-ti-tum …' – until suddenly it all came rushing back to her.

'Time's up. Time's up,' came the voice of the English teacher. 'Hand in your papers now, please.' The teacher started walking down the aisles between the desks, and Charlotte knew she was going to blow it. She could hear his footsteps coming closer and closer, and faster and faster she scribbled.

And then, to her horror, she realised that she'd got it all wrong. Oh, God, oh, God. She'd got it all wrong – she'd answered the wrong question. She'd have to scribble it all out and go back to the beginning. 'My heart is like—' she wrote as the footsteps drew nearer and nearer. And then she heard the familiar voice of the English teacher saying, 'Time's up, Ms Cholewczyk. I must ask you to hand over your paper.'

'Just one more minute, please,' she begged him. 'I can get it right – I know I can.'

'Time's up,' he repeated, and just as she looked up at him with desperate eyes, her alarm went off.

Charlotte reached out a hand to silence it, then peered groggily at the display. Why had she set it for so early? And then she remembered: she wanted to drop off the Coco de Mer bags at Thea's apartment on her way to work.

She showered and dressed and knocked back some coffee, trying to remember her strange dream. It was vestigial already, but she couldn't forget the panicky feeling of trying to finish that exam paper. People dreamed of exams when they were stressed, she knew – and she really was stressed, with the prospect of Paris looming large on her horizon. But the weird thing was that all her teachers at school had been women. And what was that poem she'd been trying to remember? She'd heard someone recite it recently. Where?

And then it came back to her. It was the Rossetti piece that Thea had recited on the way to Cholyngham, the one about having a glad heart.

As Charlotte let herself out of the flat, she found herself wondering how glad Thea's heart would be once she'd unwrapped the contents of the Coco de Mer carrier bags.

* * *

At lunchtime she phoned Alex.

'The deed is done,' she told him. 'Thea is now the proud owner of Madame Erica's finest.'

'Did you send them via FedEx?'

'No. I didn't want to run into yet more expense. I delivered them myself.'

'I salute your courage, comrade.'

'I'm not *that* brave, Alex. Or that stupid. After seeing the damage she inflicted on you, I had no intention of being on the receiving end of the harpy's claws. I left the bags with the concierge. I'd love to be a fly on the wall when she opens them.'

She registered the smile in Alex's voice. 'What a coincidence. So would I,' he said.

twelve

We're back!' It was Friday morning, and Anna was on the phone.

'Yay!' said Charlotte. 'What time did you arrive?'

'Midday. Can you talk?'

'Yep. I'm on my lunch break.' Charlotte had spent most of her lunch break consulting the Dorling Kindersley *Eyewitness Travel Guide to Paris*, concentrating on the Montmartre area, which was where her hotel was located. (The guide had told her that the hill of Montmartre was called the Butte, which seemed somehow fitting. 'I'm sure it'll be the Butte of many jokes,' she'd told Hilary earlier, but Hilary hadn't laughed.) 'Did you have a fantastic time?' she asked Anna.

'No. We had an *über*-fantastic time. And it's all down to you. Thank you so very much, Charlotte Cholewczyk.'

'*De nada*. Did you get many pics?'

'Loads and loads.'

'When are you going to bore me with them?'

'Tonight. We're having a SHEF evening.'

'This evening? Oh, Anna, I don't think I can be there. I've an early start tomorrow.'

'But tomorrow's Saturday.'

'I know. But I've to go on a business trip.'

'Oh. Poor you. Where to?'

'Paris.'

'*Paris*! I don't believe you.'

'It's true. I've to recce a hotel for the Pantoufle weekend breaks.' Charlotte filled Anna in on the account they'd won.

'What time's your flight?'

'Ten o'clock. I'll have to set my alarm for six-thirty.'

'Jeepers. That *is* an early start for a Saturday. But couldn't you come over just for an hour or so? Please? Your Jimmy Choos are just dying to meet their new owner.'

Charlotte debated. It would be a truly fine thing to sport genuine Jimmy Choos in Paris, instead of her crappy fakes. 'No,' she said finally. 'I really need to get my beauty sleep tonight.'

There was a disappointed silence on the other end of the phone, and then Anna said, 'Please come, Charlotte. You don't have to stay too late, and I'll get Finn to run you home. It's just that – we have some good news. And we really want all our nearest and dearest together when we announce it.'

Of course! Anna wanted to tell everyone about the baby. That swung it. Charlotte *couldn't* not go this evening. She performed a swift U-turn. 'OK, Anna. I'll come. I'd love to. But I really can't stay long.'

'No worries, no worries. Oh, I'm *delighted* you're coming. We'll have a full house.'

'Too many for poker?'

'Sadly, yes. But you can look at Viv's and my photographs instead – and don't worry, there aren't too many of them. We culled them on the flight home and lost all the drunken, incriminating ones.'

'Talking of incriminating photos—'

'Oh, Finn showed me! You mean the one of you and him and Alex in the sally bush at Cholyngham? That story's too hilarious, Charlotte!'

'I'm glad you can see the funny side of it. Did he tell you about Thea flouncing off?'

'Yes, isn't it brilliant? Thanks be to God we don't have to put up with *her* any more.'

'There's more,' said Charlotte. She was just about to launch into the Coco de Mer story when something made her stop. For some reason, she didn't want to say too much about her and Alex's shenanigans in sex shops. There was something kind of *personal* about it.

'There's more what?'

'There's more to her than meets the eye,' said Charlotte.

'What do you mean?'

'Somebody told me that she was a porn star in a former life.'

'You're not serious!'

'I am. She called herself Cha-Cha Fox.'

Anna crowed. 'Cha-Cha Fox? I bet she jolly well does. How on earth did you find out?'

'Um … it's a long story. I'll tell you all about it when I see you.'

'I can't wait. Cha-Cha Fox! How OTT – even for a porn star. Hey, you know the porn-star name game?'

'The one where you combine the first name of your childhood pet with your mother's maiden name?' asked Charlotte.

'Yeah. Well, it certainly doesn't work for me. If I were a porn star, I'd be called Dorcas Burke.'

'You had a childhood pet called Dorcas?'

'Yes. It was a Jack Russell.'

'What a weird name.'

'Jack Russell or Dorcas?'

'Dorcas.'

'I chose it because it means "fawnlike".'

'A fawnlike Jack Russell? That's one hell of an oxymoron, Anna. My porn-star name would be Pussy Willow.'

'Pussy Willow? Oh, how fabulous! I'm going to start calling you that all the time now. Oops – I'd better go. There's the doorbell. See you around eight?'

'You bet. Bye, Anna.'

'Bye, Pussy.'

As Charlotte put her phone away, she remembered the acrylic cat outfit that she'd bought for Thea – the one with 'Stroke My Little Pussy' on it – and wondered if she shouldn't have kept it for herself.

* * *

Before she set off for Anna and Finn's, Charlotte went home to change. She could have worn the Whistles ensemble she'd worn to work, but she wanted to freshen up. She showered, rubbed in her Chanel No. 5 body lotion, retouched her make-up and deliberated over her wardrobe. She finally decided on the white ensemble that she'd worn to dinner in Cholyngham the weekend before last. Alex and Finn might have seen it before, but that didn't matter, because they were just boys and wouldn't notice. And Alex had been wrong about it: it wasn't sexy. It was only a tiny bit see-through. OK, you might discern that her underwear was of a baby-blue hue, but only if your gaze lingered longer than necessary. And nobody would be looking at her tonight, anyway – all eyes would be on Anna.

Vivien and Russ and Toad and Angus and two longtime friends of Anna's, Marian and Cathy, were already there when Charlotte arrived. There was no sign of Alex.

'Have a drink,' said Anna, pouring wine into a glass, 'so we can toast your Jimmy Choos. Just let me run and get them.'

She dashed into the bedroom, and emerged holding the shoebox as reverently as if it were a votive offering. Charlotte accepted it and lifted the lid. There, snuggled in a nest of tissue paper, were the most beautiful shoes she had ever seen. They were a confection of glossy biscuit-coloured leather and multicoloured beads. They boasted four-inch heels and soft leather straps. Jimmy Choo's name was writ large on a white satin label on the instep.

'Oh, Anna, Vivien – thank you!' She gave each of them a kiss on the cheek, and then she kissed the shoes. I'd *much* rather these than that poxy trip to Paris – no offence; I know you two enjoyed it. But I reckon I *definitely* made the right decision. I win. Yay!'

'We knew you'd love them,' said Vivien. 'They're called "Erica".'

Erica! These shoes were at the other end of the spectrum from the last Erica Charlotte had had dealings with. 'Did they talk to you?' she asked Vivien.

'*Bien sûr!*'

'In French?'

'*Mais oui!*'

'What did they say?'

'They said, "Please take us home to Charlotte Cholewczyk. She was destined from the moment of our birth to be our mistress, but a wicked witch substituted fake Choos. Have pity on us! Help us to live the life we were destined to live, under the fair feet of Charlotte Cholewzyck!"'

'The poor shoes. Come to me, oh beauteous ones.' Charlotte kicked off her LK Bennetts and slid her feet into the Choos. The leather against the soles of her feet felt like a caress, the straps clung around her ankles in a tender embrace, the label beneath her instep seemed to invest her with a kind of authority. 'Little Choos, happy at last,' she said, sliding one foot forward in the kind of pose favoured by Sarah Jessica Parker.

'They're smiling,' said Marian.

'Beatifically,' said Cathy.

'To Jimmy Choo!' said Vivien. She raised her glass and they all joined in – even the men.

'May I propose another toast?' said Finn rather shyly, after the health of the Choos had been toasted. 'This one is to the woman I am proud and honoured to call my future wife. To my darling Anna.'

Little oohs of surprise scooted round the room. 'You're getting married?' squealed Russ.

'We are,' said Finn. 'And we hope that you will all join us at Cholyngham later in the year for the ceremony. But the real reason we asked you all here tonight is to celebrate the fact that Anna's pregnant.'

The oohs turned into cheers and the cheers turned into tears as everyone in the room fell upon Finn and Anna and congratulated them roundly. Even though she already knew the good news, Charlotte liked to think she looked passably surprised as she kissed the happy couple, and she was thrilled when Anna whispered in her ear, 'I'm going to ask you and Vivien to be joint godmothers.'

But there was one little thing niggling at Charlotte. Once the brouhaha had died down and more drinks had been poured and plates of food handed around, she managed to get Anna to herself in the bathroom, where they had both retired to repair the lipstick that had been ruined by all the kissing.

The lippy done, Charlotte sat down for a pee. 'Anna,' she ventured, 'you said something earlier about wanting all your nearest and dearest here for the announcement.'

'And here they all are.'

'Um ... what about Alex?'

'Oh – he phoned just before you arrived to say that he wasn't going to be able to make it after all.'

'Did he say why?'

'No. He just said something urgent had cropped up.' Anna smiled at her. 'A new girl, knowing Alex.'

For some reason, Charlotte had difficulty returning the smile. The image came back to her of Alex in Madame Erica's Emporium, talking on his mobile phone to someone he'd called 'darlin''. That was probably who he was seeing tonight. She flushed the loo, then pulled up her panties.

'Oh, Charlotte!' said Anna. 'What fabulous knicks. Show me!' Charlotte obliged, raising her skirt so that Anna could have a good look. 'They are the most divine things I have ever seen!'

'There's a bra to match,' said Charlotte absently.

'Oh, you lucky girl! I'd kill to be able to wear stuff like that. But now I'm three months gone, there's not a lot of point in forking out money for scanty stuff. I'll be wearing mumsy bras and big pants from now on. Where did you get them?'

'Coco de Mer.'

'Were they wildly expensive? They certainly look it.'

'I didn't look at the price.'

'Finn's got me stuff from there, from time

to time,' said Anna. 'Come to think of it, I was wearing something from Coco de Mer on the night the baby was conceived. Their clothes have to be the ultimate aphrodisiac, don't you think?'

I wouldn't know, thought Charlotte. *But I'd love to find out ...*

* * *

Later, when she got home, she decided to pack, even though she was feeling tired. Magazines like Condé Nast's *Traveller* always advocated packing the night before.

Charlotte had wasted many hours of her life hanging around baggage carousels because she had never learned the art of packing light. She envied those women in *Traveller* who gave advice on how to pack so as to avoid having to carry anything heavier than one of those dinky little cabin bags on wheels. She was always reading articles that told her to carry Evian water to spritz on your face and cashmere socks because they were far preferable to the synthetic ones handed out by the airlines, and she knew she was meant only to pack only pure silk clothes because you could simply roll them up and ping!, the minute you arrived in your hotel they'd be creaseless, so there was no need even for the butler to iron them. (The butler? Charlotte thought when she read this class of article. What kind of joints did these gals stay in?) One stylish woman's solution was to pack her Boudicca, Veronique Branquinho and Alexander McQueen suits in a hanging suiter to take as hand luggage. Well, bully for her!

But, unfortunately for Charlotte, she suffered big-time from 'What If' syndrome. *What if it gets really cold and I've nothing warm to wear? What if it rains and I've nothing waterproof? What if I get asked out somewhere posh and I've nothing classy? And if I bring those shoes I'll have to bring that handbag, and if I bring that handbag I'll have to bring those earrings ...* And so on and on, through permutation after permutation.

She decided against packing her sleep-suit on this occasion. If she was to stay perforce in a posh Paris hotel, she might as well make like a Parisienne and sport the kind of clothes that were *de rigeur* for fancy five-star living, and winceyette jim-jams just didn't fit the bill. So she packed underwear and casual stuff and her floaty Ghost number and the Donna Karan cashmere she'd picked up for very little cash in a sale. Then she slipped items of underwear into her brand-new shoes (as recommended by Condé Nast's *Traveller*), which she then wrapped in layers of tissue paper. She slid the Beauteous Ones into her case, with as much care as she might have put babies to bed, before going to bed herself.

As she settled back against her pillows, Charlotte wondered what she might dream about tonight. She'd been having a lot of weird dreams recently.

Some time later, as she slid into sleep, she found herself winging her way to Paris courtesy of Air France. All was perfectly normal. The only weird thing was that the passenger sitting beside her was a goat.

thirteen

The next morning, Charlotte was up bright and early to get the bus out to London City Airport. But despite having packed the night before, she was running late. She'd dropped her cafetière and had had to spend ten valuable minutes clearing shards of glass and coffee grounds off her kitchen floor. Although she'd managed to do her hair, there simply hadn't been time for her face. There was nothing for it but to do her make-up in the airside loo, because there was no *way* she was going to arrive in the style capital of the world barefaced. Once she hit airside, she hastily applied *maquillage,* spritzed herself with scent, then legged it to the gate, one of the final passengers to board.

As she negotiated the aisle of the aircraft, she heard a familiar laugh. There, sitting beside a stunningly gorgeous redhead in row 18, was Alex. Death and hell!

Charlotte thought fast. She would have to pass him – she was in row 21 – but she didn't want him to see her, didn't want him to get a load of her flushed face and panicky eyes and the sweat-stains that she could feel starting under her armpits. She held her handbag up to the side of her face as she proceeded down the aisle, feeling very thankful indeed that she was sitting behind the happy couple and not in their direct view.

The man beside her was one of those people who insist on talking to you so that they can tell you all about themselves. Mr Lynch was his name, and he was pleased to meet her. He was an estate agent, he told her, and wasn't that the game to be in these days, especially in Dublin, which was where he lived? Hadn't he only last week sold a house in some place called Ballsbridge for millions of euros (he called them yoyos)? He was coining it, so he was, and he'd just spent a week in London at the Dorchester – a fabulous hotel, he could highly recommend it – and had she seen *Billy Elliot* and wasn't it just marvellous, especially when viewed from a box? And now he was off to meet the wife in Paris because he wanted to treat her to a shopping spree, and wasn't that the way to live your life, getting and spending like there's no tomorrow? Sure, we could all be dead as dodos tomorrow.

Charlotte found herself wishing that she were dead as a dodo now, so that she wouldn't have to listen any longer to this big florid man who had hogged the armrest for the entire journey so far. Last night's dream about sitting beside a bleating goat had clearly been prophetic, and she wished that she'd had the cop-on to pay heed to it. If she had, she would have pretended to be deaf and dumb when she'd boarded the plane. Instead, she found herself making the mistake of saying, 'If you're so rich, how come you're not travelling in business class?'

'Ah, there's a story to be told about that,' said the man, and Charlotte thought, *Oh, no!* 'It's something I've learned on my travels around the world,' he informed her. 'It's always more advisable to fly ordinary class – if you're not on a long-haul, of course; that goes without saying – because it is a *fact* that you always meet the most interesting people in ordinary class.'

How would you know they're interesting, Charlotte wanted to ask him, if you never allow them to open their mouths? Hell's teeth! This man could talk for the Olympics. He was suffering from the worst verbal diarrhoea she'd ever heard – and working in advertising meant that she'd heard a *lot*. There was a word for his condition, she knew – what was it? Logorrhoea. That was it. And he was steeped in it. On and on and *on* Loggy Lynch droned, while Charlotte nodded like a rear-window toy dog, all the while aware that, three rows up, Alex and the redhead were getting on like a house on fire. Their body language was almost indecently eloquent.

At last she could take it no longer. If she couldn't die, she could at least *faint*, and that would mean that he'd *have* to shut up. But then she realised that, if she fainted, the steward would be called to administer first aid, and *that* would be bound to attract the attention of all the passengers, including Alex and his new lady friend. Or, worse still, Alex might be called upon, in his capacity as

Emergency First Responder, to minister to her. Oh, God! This was what it must be like in purgatory – being forced to listen against your will to an overweight estate agent from Dublin rattling on about his children, and weren't they just brilliant, with honours in the Leaving Cert, whatever that was. Charlotte just couldn't help it. She started to cry.

'What's the matter?' said the man.

'I'm dying,' she said. It wasn't a lie. Wasn't everyone on this plane dying? *We're all dying from the minute we're born,* Charlotte told herself. After all, hadn't Sam Beckett once famously said that we give birth astride the grave?

They were the two most effective words she had ever uttered in her entire life. 'I'm sorry for your trouble,' mumbled the man, and then he unfolded his red-top and didn't say another word to her for the rest of the journey.

When they landed, Charlotte remained in her seat until the plane was empty. She watched Alex and the redhead swing their cabin luggage out of the overhead lockers and waltz down the aisle together. She hoped that hand luggage was all they had, because she didn't want to run into them by the baggage carousel.

She finally knew she could sit in the sanctuary of the aeroplane no longer when the cabin staff started to give her 'would you please get the fuck out of here so that we can go home' looks. She hauled herself to her feet and prepared to meet Parisians.

At the luggage carousel, there was no sign of Alex and his flame-haired temptress. The estate agent was avoiding Charlotte ostentatiously, but as luck would have it, theirs were the last two bags to emerge onto the conveyor belt.

'I'm very sorry for your trouble,' he told her again as he loaded his Samsonite onto his trolley, tch-ing when he saw that one of the bags had got scratched.

Together they trundled out past Customs into the abode of the damned that was Charles de Gaulle airport. As an Anna Wintour lookalike revved past, clipping Charlotte's suiter with her wheelie Vuitton, Charlotte Cholewczyk found herself agreeing with Loggy Lynch for the very first time. *That*, she thought, *makes two of us who are very sorry for me.*

* * *

Charlotte strap-hung all the way into Paris, her face inches away from a fellow straphanger's armpit, tinny tunes from other people's iPods rattling in her head. It was raining outside, as she'd guessed it would be. Paris had it in for her again. She emerged in the Gare de Lyon feeling fraught, then took a taxi north to Montmartre. The clock on the tower of the station told her the time was one o'clock.

The taxi driver pointed out places of interest as he drove, but Charlotte really wasn't interested. She wished she'd packed her eye mask in her handbag rather than in her suitcase, so that she could put it on now. The words of Marianne Faithfull's 'Ballad of Lucy Jordan' came back to her, and she envied tragic Lucy, who had *never* got to drive through Paris with the wind in her hair.

Her hotel, the Relais Geneviève, was located not far from the red-brick St-Jean l'Evangéliste, under the shadow of the Sacré Coeur. Charlotte paid off the driver and climbed the steps, hefting her suiter and wishing she'd taken the travel mags' advice and opted for something lighter. The suiter was a thing of beauty to behold, but being crafted from cowhide, it weighed a ton.

'*Madame*! *Permettez-moi*.' A fiendishly good-looking young porter immediately came forward to claim her bag, and when a grateful Charlotte relinquished it and said, 'Oh, thank you so much,' he segued at once into effortless English. She knew that really she should make the effort to speak French, but she was tired and cross and couldn't be arsed.

The porter led her to the reception desk, where Geneviève Villiers, the owner of the hotel, was ready to receive her. She was thirty-something, friendly and elegant in a slim eau-de-Nil skirt and matching French-cuffed shirt. Geneviève instructed the porter to carry Charlotte's baggage to the Burgundy Room; then she said, in flawlessly accented RP English, 'Fancy a glass of champagne? Courtesy of the hotel, of course.'

It was the first time Charlotte had felt glad that they'd won the Pantoufle account. 'I'd murder one, thanks,' she said. 'That journey was pretty stressful.'

'You can relax now,' said Geneviève. 'Come on down to the salon. You don't mind if I call you Charlotte, do you?'

They small-talked their way down a corridor whose walls were hung with original paintings, to a room furnished with squashy linen-covered couches and low tables piled with the kind of big, glossy picture books you yearn to leaf through.

'This is lovely,' said Charlotte. 'It's so unpretentious and comfortable-looking.'

'That's what we're aiming for,' said Geneviève, moving to the bar. 'We want to make our guests feel at home here. As you know, Pantoufle city breaks aim to please. You must promise to let me know if we can do anything to help. If you want theatre or museum tickets, or if you need to book a restaurant, just ask our concierge.'

'Is there no restaurant here in the hotel?'

'There is, but I'm afraid it's being refurbished, so we're currently serving breakfast only. I'll let you have a menu to take home with you, to give you an idea of the *cuisine* on offer, and I'm proud to be able to tell you that we headhunted our chef from a Michelin-starred establishment.' Geneviève popped the cork on the champagne and poured. 'Cheers,' she said.

'*Santé!*' said Charlotte.

As she sipped, she realised that she'd never drunk so much champagne in her life as she had over the course of the past few weeks, and she decided that since she couldn't afford a champagne lifestyle, she'd better not get too used to it. There'd been champagne in Cholyngham, champagne *chez* Anna and Finn, and champagne with Alex in Joe Allen's … She wondered what had brought Alex to Paris, and then remembered that he'd said something about travelling over to interview the actor Ciarán Hinds for his newspaper. How fortunate for him that his new inamorata had been available to come along for the ride!

'You'll probably want to take in a little sightseeing in the vicinity?' Geneviève asked. 'I can recommend a nearby cemetery – the Cimetière St-Vincent, where Utrillo is buried. Because it's small, it's often overlooked by tourists, who are more interested in the Cimetière Montmartre.'

'That sounds like my kind of place. I've always found old cemeteries fascinating.'

'And the Musée d'Erotisme is well worth a visit.'

Charlotte raised an eyebrow. 'Really?'

'Yes. Don't be put off by the title – it's quite fascinating, and not remotely salacious.'

'I'm glad you told me. I left my guide to Paris behind, working on the assumption that

I could learn more from the people who actually live here. Of course, the whole Pantoufle principle is …'

Between sips of champagne, Charlotte and Geneviève discussed the Creative Rationale behind the Pantoufle marketing campaign. Finally, champagne quaffed, Charlotte was shown upstairs to her room.

Oh! It was easily as pretty as the Boudoir in Cholyngham, but in a very different way.

A carved wooden cupid suspended from the ceiling gazed beatifically down upon the patchwork quilt draped over the king-sized bed. A rocking chair piled with faded tapestry cushions had been positioned next to the window, in which was framed a postcard-perfect view of Montmartre. On the burgundy-coloured wall, a framed sampler bore the legend: 'He is the happiest, be he king or peasant, who finds peace in his home.'

'Oh, Geneviève – it's perfect! It really is like a homecoming.'

'That's exactly how it's meant to feel,' said Geneviève with a smile. 'It's a retreat from real life. I'll leave you to make the most of it.' She backed out of the bedroom, and the door shut with a gentle click.

Charlotte immediately set about exploring

the room, which had numerous little surprises tucked away – lavender sachets in the drawers of the walk-in wardrobe, nubbly hand-made writing paper on the escritoire, a burgundy-coloured pashmina with the initials 'RG' embroidered on one corner. She was also glad – even though mini-bars were considered by some to be very déclassé – to find one tucked away discreetly in a unit that also housed the entertainment system. Charlotte preferred to help herself to her nightcap of choice rather than have some hapless night porter trail up to her bedroom. She valued her privacy – especially when she was wearing winceyette jim-jams and had Vitamin E cream all over her face.

After she'd done exploring, Charlotte dived into the shower in her en suite bathroom to wash away the grubby feeling she always got from navigating airports and railway stations. Then, fortified by champagne and Bulgari bath products (my word, how they bubbled!) she set off for the Cimetière St-Vincent.

The Butte proved to be quite a steep climb. Diverging from the beaten track, Charlotte found herself walking up towards the Basilica du Sacré Coeur, through a park dripping with cherry blossom and bursting with birdsong – but surprisingly bereft of tourists. The rain had stopped, and a bleary sun was trying to shine. Yes! This at last was the Paris evoked by all those songs! As she climbed to the top, she dreamed of nursing a beer on the *terrasse* of some small café where Monet and his mates might once have been regulars, and indulged in an *Il Postino*-esque fantasy where she had the village of Montmartre practically all to herself. Maybe she would be able to go back to London and tell Hilary, 'Oh, I discovered this wonderful little café where the proprietor took such a shine to me that he gave me a cassis on the house,' or 'I came across a totally unspoiled little square surrounded by plane trees and ended up being invited to play boules with the locals,' or 'I bought some olive oil in an amazing little boulangerie where nothing has changed since the fifties …'

Cue ominous music. If Charlotte had gone by the regular route, she might have been forewarned of imminent chaos by the tour buses parked bumper to bumper. As it was, she emerged onto the summit of Montmartre into a square milling with tourists and with artists, who were all trying to grab the tourists and force them to sit for their portraits. A couple of local residents slunk by; Charlotte could tell they were residents by the fact that they were carrying bags bulging with store-cupboard staples as opposed to souvenirs, and by their general air of deep despondency. An elderly lady stared from behind a lace curtain at her beleaguered village with the stoical expression of someone who was once again resigning herself to a season in hell and solitary confinement. Charlotte sent the old lady a look of sympathy, and the woman curled her lip at her as if she were mad. And why shouldn't she curl her lip? Charlotte was, after all, just another tourist.

She wanted off that Butte ASAP! She decided to retrace her steps and find the Musée d'Erotisme.

The Musée was an oasis of civilised calm in Pigalle – the armpit of Paris. The interior was classy, all marble floors and brass banisters, and the erotic vibe was evident from the moment you went through the entry turnstile, where vintage silent films were being projected onto a screen in all their recently restored black-and-white glory. There was nothing terribly subtle about the films, but they were sexy in a kind of boisterous, uninhibited way. As Charlotte moved from floor to floor, admiring fertility icons and erotica that had been amassed from all around the world, and sex aids that could have been designed by Heath Robinson, she had the impression that she was privy to a quite unique fusion of sex, history and art.

She also had the impression that she was being watched. It had happened before in art galleries that she had *intuited* that she was being observed. The last time she'd had a similar experience had been at an exhibition of nude photographic portraits in an upmarket gallery in London. She'd been convinced, as she negotiated the interconnecting rooms, that her progress was being monitored, and a couple of oblique glances had confirmed that she was being eyed up by a ravishingly beautiful boy in a leather jacket. They'd kept up a silent flirtation for the half-hour or so they'd lingered in the gallery, and had left at the same time, with knowing smiles and meaningful backward glances at each other. But on this occasion, although the feeling intensified as she climbed the stairs to the top floor of the museum, she couldn't work out who amongst the punters was sending the interested vibe in her direction.

Amongst the intriguing items on display on the top floor was a chair that had been commissioned by Edward, Prince of Wales, before he had become monarch. It was a cunningly constructed wooden affair, with tiers of seats that could easily accommodate more than one derrière, and the kind of stirrups that Charlotte was always reluctant to put her feet into when she visited her gynaecologist. She was just trying to work out exactly how it configured when a voice from behind her said, in French, 'Fancy giving it a go?'

She turned, outrage writ large on her face, to give out to the geezer who'd had the audacity to proposition her. It was Alex.

He laughed out loud when he saw her expression. 'It's all right, Charlotte. I know we've had some fun in sex shops, but I really don't expect you to be *that* obliging.'

'What the hell are *you* doing here?' she asked him.

'Pretty much the same as you, I imagine. Taking in a little art, a little culture.' Alex nodded at King Edward's contraption. 'It's like something Tracey Emin might dream up,' he said, smiling down at her. There was a beat, and then: 'Fancy a beer?' he asked.

'Um. Do I fancy a beer?' Charlotte echoed stupidly. She was still quite gobsmacked by the encounter.

'It's an invitation, Cholewczyk, not a subject for metaphysical speculation.'

She shrugged. 'Yeah. OK. You can buy me a beer.'

They walked downstairs in silence. It was weird. For the first time ever with Alex, Charlotte felt uneasy to be surrounded by such overtly sexual stuff. She hadn't been remotely fazed in either Coco de Mer or Madame Erica's Emporium – what was with her now? She tried to keep her gaze fixed straight ahead as they descended the stairs, but all around her arcane sex objects kept going, 'Cooee,' the way the bubblegum-pink bag had that day in Harvey Nicks, and she was glad when they finally emerged from the building and hit the street.

They took a left, away from Pigalle and its purveyors of tack, and found a little café bar where they could enjoy their beer on a *terrasse* shaded by plane trees – a bit like the one Charlotte had fantasised about finding in Montmartre. The waiter brought them two *demis* of Stella.

'What brings you to Paris?' Alex asked.

'Pantoufle. You?' She knew he was there to interview Ciarán Hinds, but she was finding small talk uncharacteristically difficult.

'Ciarán Hinds. I've to interview him for the rag.'

'When are you heading back to London?'

'Monday morning. I flew over this morning, from London City.'

'Me too.'

'Really? We must have been on the same flight.'

'We were. You were sitting up ahead of me.'

'Why didn't you come and say hello?'

'I didn't want to cramp your style with your new girlfriend.'

'What new girlfriend?'

'The one you enjoy telephone sex with.'

'Telephone sex?'

'I heard you talking to her about telephone sex, that time we were in Madame Erica's Erotic Emporium.'

Alex crowed. 'That wasn't a girlfriend. That was a work colleague.'

'Are you trying to tell me that you routinely have telephone sex with work colleagues?'

'No, I don't. But to put you out of your

nosey-parkerish misery, I will enlighten you. Lauren and I were working together on a scam to do with phone-sex lines.'

'Oh. And the redhead you were sitting beside on the plane wasn't a new girlfriend, either?'

Alex gave her a look of incomprehension. 'What on earth made you think she was?'

'The way you were flirting with her.'

'Darling, she was a married woman.'

'She didn't look married.'

'What makes a woman look married?'

'I dunno. What made you flirt with her?'

'I flirt with all beautiful women, married or single, young or old. It's mandatory to flirt on journeys when you find yourself sitting next to a babe. It's one of the greatest pleasures life can afford.'

'Oh.' Charlotte suddenly felt incredibly stupid, and because she hated being made to feel stupid, she decided to change the subject.

'Anna and Finn are getting married,' she told him. 'They're having a baby.'

'No *shit*! That's fantastic news. When did they tell you?'

'Just last night. Although I've known about it for ages – since that Cholyngham weekend when you accused me of fancying Finn. They made an announcement and we all had champagne. Apart from Anna, of course.'

'I'm sorry I couldn't be there.'

'Anna told me you'd phoned to say something urgent had come up?'

'Yeah. I had to go look after my mother. She was having one of her panic attacks.'

'Oh, Alex – I'm sorry to hear that.' Alex's mother had become prone to panic attacks since his father had died, and Alex was periodically required to go do some hand-holding, to lead her away from the dark place she went to. 'Is she better now?'

'A little. You know her – she always rallies eventually. Sarah's staying with her for the weekend.' Sarah was Alex's sister.

There was silence for a moment, and then: 'What made you decide to visit the Erotic Museum?' Alex asked.

'I ran screaming from Montmartre.'

'What did you expect from Montmartre? Artists sitting around under awnings drinking pastis and talking about Modigliani and Matisse?'

'No,' Charlotte lied. 'But I *was* hoping to find peace and quiet in the Cimetière St-Vincent.'

'Peace and quiet? That's a valuable

commodity, especially in a city like Paris. Which guidebook are you using?'

'I checked out Dorling Kindersley, but I left it behind deliberately. I'm relying on the know-how of people who live here – like the staff of my hotel.'

Alex gave her an interested look. 'You could be on to something by not carrying a guide. I once visited a café in Florence that the Lonely Planet described as being "far from the tourist hordes".'

'Wasn't it any good?'

'I never made it as far as the menu. When I got there, it was crowded with Americans who were all clutching dog-eared copies of the Lonely Planet guide to Florence. It seems you can't go anywhere in the world now without Lonely Planet and Rough Guide readers descending, lemming-like, upon the latest unspoiled beauty spot or quaint taverna.'

'I suppose every place on earth is a tourist magnet now. A bit like everybody being famous for fifteen minutes.'

Alex wasn't listening to her. He was eyeing up a Brigitte Bardot lookalike who was sitting on the other side of the terrace. To Charlotte's annoyance, Brigitte Bardot was returning the compliment. The cheek of her!

For all she knew, Alex and Charlotte could be a devoted married couple.

The meaningful eye contact came to an abrupt end when Bardot's boyfriend rolled up.

'I could show you around tomorrow, if you like,' said Alex, returning his attention to Charlotte. 'I know Paris quite well.'

'But I hate Paris!'

'You might as well give it a second chance, Charlotte.'

She looked mulish, and then thought better of it. It might be more fun to be a tourist in Paris if you had a friend in tow. 'Where are you staying?' she asked him.

'In a hotel in the ninth *arondissement*.'

'Is it a Relais & Château hotel?'

'I wouldn't have a clue. It's a hotel. Why don't you call by tomorrow and we'll do stuff? There's a fantastic food shop on the Place de la Madeleine. Or we could visit Harry's Bar, where Hemingway and Fitzgerald hung out.'

'Sounds good.'

Charlotte took a sip of cold beer, and suddenly she felt herself beginning to relax a little. Since she'd stepped onto the airport bus that morning, she had been aware of knots of tension in her shoulders. Now she felt them begin to unravel.

'You're into cemeteries, aren't you, Charlotte?' said Alex. 'You should give Père Lachaise a go sometime.'

'Where Oscar Wilde is buried?'

'Among others.'

'Who else is there?'

'Only Jim Morrison and Simone Signoret and Yves Montand and Edith Piaf and Chopin and Sarah Bernhardt and Proust and Molière.'

'Show-off. What about Ciarán Hinds?'

'He's not dead yet.'

'That's not what I meant, stand-up. Don't you have to meet up with him tomorrow?'

'No. I'm taking him out to dinner tonight.'

'OK,' said Charlotte. 'It's a deal. Shall I call round to you in the morning? At, say, eleven o'clock?'

'Make it midday.'

'Cool. Give me directions. Which Metro should I take?'

'You shouldn't. You should take a taxi. I know you and your crappy sense of direction. If you take the Metro, you'll end up getting completely lost.' He handed her a card with the hotel pictured on the front, and its address underneath. It looked like quite a classy joint, Charlotte decided. It might be worth a recce to see how it compared with the Relais Geneviève.

Alex shot a look at his watch, then drained his glass. 'I'd better make tracks. How are you planning on spending your evening? Taking in some culture?'

'No,' she said. 'I'm going to eat out and read my book.'

'That,' he said, 'sounds like a much better idea.'

* * *

It *was* a much better idea.

Geneviève directed Charlotte to a small restaurant on one of the quieter side-streets of Montmartre, where the locals ate. She enjoyed *escargots* and *oeufs en cocotte* and *tarte tatin*, and had a *pichet* of wine with her meal. And occasionally she raised her eyes from the latest Harry Potter and exchanged flirtatious looks with the waiter, who bore an uncanny resemblance to Johnny Depp. Maybe it *was* Johnny Depp, she conjectured, getting into character for his next film role as a sexy waiter.

Charlotte strolled back down the Butte to her hotel after dinner, feeling comfortably replete and a little heady from good red wine. She said good night to Geneviève and declined her invitation to join her for a night-cap; even though Geneviève was the nicest Parisienne she had ever met, Charlotte was way too jaded to shoot any more breeze today with anyone.

As she let herself into her room, she found herself wondering what she should wear for her guided tour of Paris the next day. Because she always over-packed, there were many, many options. She opened her wardrobe door and gazed longingly at her beautiful Jimmy Choos. And then she pictured Alex's expression if she rolled up at his hotel wearing four-inch heels, and she knew she'd be asking for trouble. In the end she selected jeans, a T-shirt and a pair of trainers.

The last thing she did before she went to bed was hand-wash her Coco de Mer underwear and hang it on the towel rail to dry.

fourteen

Charlotte was back at school. It was exam time, and she was desperately trying to remember a Christina Rossetti poem. For ages she struggled and struggled with the first sentence – 'My heart is like a tum-ti-tum ...' – until suddenly it all came rushing back to her.

'Time's up. Time's up,' came the voice of the English teacher. 'Hand in your papers now, please.' The teacher started walking down the aisles between the desks, and Charlotte knew she was going to blow it. She could hear his footsteps coming closer and closer, and faster and faster she scribbled:

'My heart is like a singing bird
Whose nest is in a watered shoot;
My heart is like an apple-tree
Whose boughs are bent with thickset
     fruit;
My heart is like a rainbow shell
That paddles in a halcyon sea;
My heart is gladder than all these
Because my love is come to me.'

And then, to her horror, she realised that she'd got it all wrong. Oh, God, oh, God. She'd got it all *wrong*! She'd have to scribble it out and go back to the beginning. 'My heart is—' she wrote as the footsteps drew nearer and nearer. 'Just one more minute, please,' she begged him, continuing to scribble frantically. 'I can get it right – I know I can.'

And then she heard the familiar voice of the English teacher saying, 'Very well, Ms Cholewczyk. I'll allow you one more chance to get it right.'

'Thank you, sir,' she said, not raising her eyes from the paper. And this is what she wrote:

'My heart is like a ladybird
Beneath the heel of someone's boot;

My heart is like an unripe Brie
And rawer than a new recruit;
My heart is like a cracked church bell
Chiming a doomy liturgy;
My heart is sadder than all these
Because my love comes not to me.'

'Thank you, Ms Cholewczyk,' said the English teacher.

'Thank *you*, sir, for allowing me to finish.' Charlotte looked up at him with a grateful smile. But it wasn't her English teacher. It was Alex.

Her alarm went off.

Charlotte reached out a hand to silence it, then peered groggily at the display. Why had she set it at all? And then she remembered that she was meeting Alex this morning, so that he could give her his guided tour of Paris.

* * *

Alex's hotel in the Opéra Quarter was pretty stunning. The exterior was vast and imposingly traditional, but inside it had been gutted and refurbished to twenty-first-century standards.

Charlotte asked the receptionist to put her through to Monsieur Thornton's room.

'Alex?' she said when he picked up. 'It's Charlotte.'

'Charlotte! Sweetheart. I am so sorry. I've been on the phone for the past half-hour, and I'm running late.'

'OK. No worries. D'you mind if I come up to the room? I'd love to have a peek and see how it compares with the Relais Geneviève.'

The receptionist shot her a disapproving look, and Charlotte wasn't sure whether it was because she didn't approve of Charlotte going up to a resident's room or because she didn't approve of Charlotte making comparisons with another hotel. Whichever it was, the snooty look took her by surprise. Since meeting gorgeous Geneviève Villiers, she'd forgotten how small some Parisiennes could make her feel.

'Feel free to compare away to your heart's content,' said Alex. 'I'm in room 369.'

Charlotte shot the receptionist a mutinous look and went on up.

An unshaven Alex answered the door wearing a pair of loose cotton pyjama bottoms. 'Sorry about this,' he told her. 'I'll be as fast as I can. But I had to take that call – it was from Sarah.'

'Is everything all right?'

'It is now. She couldn't find my mother's repeat prescription anywhere, so I had to talk to Mum while Sarah searched the house from top to bottom. She found it in the end, thank God.' Alex glanced at his watch. 'Gimme ten minutes to shave and grab a shower,' he said, ducking into the bathroom. Over the sound of running water she heard him add, 'Help yourself to whatever you want from the mini-bar.'

'Thanks.'

Charlotte moseyed over to the mini-bar and checked out the contents. There were the usual suspects, including chocolate-covered amaretti, which Charlotte thought were rather a nice touch. But since she'd demolished an entire bread-basket of croissants at breakfast that morning, she decided to resist the temptation and helped herself instead to a bottle of Evian. She tossed the cap into the wastepaper basket and took a swig, then she started to wander round the room, making mental notes. An X-Box, a discreet plasma screen, a single blue iris in a stem vase. Cool!

Alex had set up his laptop on a desk by the window, beside the folder containing the list of hotel services. Charlotte opened the folder at the room service page, but just as she was about to scan the menu, something caught her eye. Alex's computer had gone into stand-by mode. What Charlotte saw when his screen-saver shimmered into view made her go all wobbly. It was a photograph of her.

The photograph had evidently been taken on the afternoon at Cholyngham when she and Finn and Alex had taken the picnic off into the woods. Charlotte was on one of the Cholyngham bicycles, freewheeling downhill with both her legs stretched out, feet off the pedals. One hand was on the handlebars, the other was clutching her straw sunhat. Her cheesecloth skirt was fluttering up around her bare brown thighs, and she was laughing.

Charlotte tried to think, but it was as if her brain had shut down. No thoughts, no ideas, no explanations came to her. However, cerebrally challenged as she was, she did know one thing. She couldn't allow Alex to know that she had seen the image.

She backed away from the computer and set the bottle of Evian down on top of the mini-bar.

'Alex?' she called into the bathroom. 'I really fancy a cup of coffee. I'm going to go back downstairs and order one.'

'Have you done all the spying you need to do?'

'Yes.'

'OK. I'll see you downstairs.'

Charlotte let herself out of Alex's hotel room, feeling more confused than she had ever felt before in her life.

* * *

He took her to Fauchon, the millionaire's supermarket, where she bought a tiny box of truffles. He took her to Les Passages, where she oohed and ahed over window displays, and he took her to Harry's Bar, where she spilled red wine all down the front of her T-shirt.

'Shame,' said Alex. 'I was going to take you out for dinner later. I can't take you anywhere now. You look like a wino.'

'Why don't I take *you* out to dinner, then? I'll get changed back in the hotel and take you up to Montmartre. Geneviève told me about a great place – the Coq d'Or, where I had dinner last night. The food was fantastic. It's where all the locals eat, apparently.'

Alex considered. 'Well, if the locals hang out there, it must be good. All right. I'll allow you to buy me dinner.'

They took the Metro back to the Place des Abbesses and headed to her hotel. Alex went down to the salon for a drink, while Charlotte legged it upstairs to change out of her stained T-shirt. She cracked the complimentary half-bottle of champagne that Geneviève had thoughtfully left on ice for her, and sipped as she consulted her wardrobe, on the horns of a dilemma.

What to wear, what to wear, what to wear? If she wore her wafty Ghost dress, she'd be able to wear her Coco de Mer undies. But if she wore her Ghost dress, she wouldn't be able to wear her Jimmy Choos, because they were the wrong colour. She could wear the sandals if she wore her clingy camel cashmere, but if she wore *that*, she wouldn't be able to wear her ruffly undies because they'd ruin the line. Charlotte couldn't decide. Choos or undies? Undies or Choos?

In the end, she had to choose the shoes, because she knew she couldn't pass over an opportunity of wearing such fabulous footwear in the fashion capital of the world. She also thought the shoes might cry if she didn't allow them out to be admired.

And admired they were.

When she went back downstairs, Geneviève Villiers was standing by Alex's table, deep in conversation with him.

'Jimmy Choo!' she exclaimed the minute Charlotte walked into the salon.

'Yes,' said Charlotte, feeling smug that the provenance of her shoes was so very self-evident.

Alex tore his eyes away from Geneviève with difficulty. 'What can I get you to drink, Charlotte?' he asked.

'I'd love a glass of champagne,' she said, wanting to toast the first outing of her Choos in style. 'Thanks so much for the bottle in my room, Geneviève. It was lovely to have a glass while I dressed.'

'You are most welcome.'

'What brand was it?' asked Alex.

'Veuve Clicquot.'

'Veuve Clicquot coming up,' said Alex, ambling off in the direction of the bar.

'It's the first time I've worn them,' Charlotte confessed to Geneviève.

'They're stunning. And so is your boyfriend.'

Charlotte looked so taken aback that Geneviève apologised immediately. 'I'm sorry,' she said. 'It was indiscreet of me to make such a personal remark. And I hope you didn't mind the fact that I was talking to him when you came down. I was just trying to be friendly.'

'No, no. I didn't mind at all. It's just that he's not my boyfriend.'

Geneviève looked surprised. '*Vraiment?*' she said, in a very French purr. She slid an interested look across at where Alex was standing at the bar, and suddenly Charlotte didn't like Geneviève as much as she had before.

'He's my oldest friend,' she said in a proprietorial way. And then, to her own surprise, she found herself adding, 'He's my best friend.'

Geneviève raised an approving eyebrow. 'Well,' she said, 'you are one lucky lady. I wouldn't mind being escorted out to dinner by *un beau mec* like him. Enjoy your evening.' She gave Charlotte the benefit of her great smile, and went about her business.

Alex came back to the table. 'Oh. She's gone, is she? Shame.'

He sounded so disproportionately disappointed that Charlotte felt miffed. What was so great about Geneviève, anyway?

Alex sat down opposite her and slid a

champagne flute across the table. 'A glass of fizz for an airhead,' he said.

'You're the airhead, mate,' she told him. 'Wasn't it rather blonde of you to have to call the AA on account of your flat spare tyre?'

'Looks like we'll have to call the AA again,' Alex told her, 'what with all the liquor you've put back today, Cholewczyk. Cheers.'

* * *

In the restaurant, Charlotte was sorry to see that the Johnny Depp lookalike had been replaced by a very attractive gypsy-esque waitress, whose name, according to the pin on her not inconsiderable bosom, was Maria. Dammit. Charlotte had hoped that Alex might notice the lookalike looking at her appreciatively, the way he had last night, and now she was clearly going to have to put up with Alex ogling Maria all evening.

Charlotte ordered Coquilles Saint-Jacques with a green salad, and Alex ordered Andouillettes à la Lyonnaise.

'What's that?' she asked him.

'Sausages. They're made from pigs' intestines.'

'Thank you for sharing that with me, Alex,' she told him crisply.

'That's nothing. I've eaten pigs' feet and *cibreo* in Italy.'

'What's *cibreo*?'

'It's a classic Tuscan dish made of cock's combs – you know, the wattly stuff on roosters' heads – and ducks testicles.'

Charlotte yawned. 'Why do men deem it necessary to boast about the macho stuff they eat?'

'Because it reminds us of the good old days, when we went out and killed wild boar and sabre-toothed tigers with our bare hands before dragging them back to the cave where our lily-livered wives were waiting for us like good girls. That's why.'

Maria arrived with their wine. Alex had ordered a *pichet* of house red, Charlotte a *pichet* of house white. Maria poured, then turned to the next table to take another order. Alex's eyes went to the waitress's fabulous derrière. 'Bottoms up, Charlotte,' he said, 'and tell me this. Are you any more enamoured of Paris this time round?'

'I guess I am. But I still prefer Rome.'

'Why's that?'

'I dunno. It's something to do with the fact that it's such a laid-back city. And the fact that Italian men love women. There's none of that godawful British political correctness about them. I just adore watching the boys and girls flirting at junctions on their Vespas. And the language is the sexiest in the world.'

'*Credi? Veramente?*' asked Alex.

'What?'

'*Credi veramente che l'italiano sia la lingua la più erotica del mondo?*'

'Alex, I may think it's sexy, but I don't understand it. I haven't a clue what you're trying to say to me.'

'*Ti attizza? Perché guardarti mi attizza. Ce l'ho duro, Carlotta.*'

'Oh, shut up, Alex. If you're going to spout Italian, I'm going to hum.'

'*Dio, quanto sei bella in quel vestito.*'

'Three, six, nine,' sang Charlotte.

'*Che c'hai sotto?*'

'The goose drank wine …' She took a sip from her glass, and saw Alex smile. 'I am *not* the goose,' she told him. 'You are utterly insufferable, do you know that?'

'*Vorrei mettere la mia mano sotto la tua gonna e farla salire su per la tua gamba fino alla pelle morbida, morbida in alto sulla tua coscia.*'

'The monkey chewed tobacco on the streetcar line—'

'*Vorrei spogliarti molto, molto lentamente.*'

'*Molto molto* yourself. The line broke, the monkey got choked—'

'*E poi …e poi vorrei fare l'amore con te.*'

'And they all went to heaven in a little rowboat. That's that.'

'*Perchè ti ho sempre amato, sciocchina. Fino ad ora, non me n'ero reso conto.*'

'Thank you,' said Charlotte as Maria turned back to them to refill their water glasses.

'Thank you,' echoed Alex.

As Charlotte watched him smile at Maria's retreating rear, she wondered what on earth he'd been saying to her.

* * *

'Excuse me,' said Alex some time later. 'I hate to interrupt this riveting conversation about why *Footballers' Wives* makes better television than *Desperate Housewives*, but I have to pay a visit to the little boys' room.'

'You're excused.'

Charlotte put her knife and fork together and watched as Alex strolled across the restaurant. She wasn't the only one watching him, she realised. Most of the women in the restaurant were doing likewise – including gypsy-looking Maria, who came sashaying over once she realised that Charlotte had finished eating.

'Thank you,' said Charlotte, crossing her legs ostentatiously so that the girl would notice her shoes. She wasn't disappointed.

'Oh! Jimmy Choos?' said Maria, looking down at Charlotte's feet with undisguised envy. 'What a lucky, lucky woman you are.'

'They were a present,' Charlotte confessed. For some reason she didn't want the girl to think that she was the kind of rich bitch who could afford to splash out on designer leather. Charlotte had spent many months waitressing in her student days, and she knew how hard it was to subsist on a minimum wage and tips. As a legacy, she felt an abiding solidarity with waitresses.

'Did your lover buy them for you?' asked Maria.

'My lover?' asked Charlotte. 'I don't have a …' And then the penny dropped for the second time that evening. 'He's not my lover,' she explained. 'He's just a friend.'

Maria gave her a sceptical look. 'That's some way for a friend to talk,' she said.

'What do you mean?'

The girl laughed. 'You obviously don't understand Italian.'

'No, I don't.'

Maria said nothing. She just shrugged and picked up the plates with a maddeningly enigmatic expression.

'What *did* he say?' asked Charlotte, suddenly curious.

'I don't know if I can repeat it.'

'What? Why not?'

'Well ...' Maria looked over her shoulder to make sure that Alex wasn't on his way back from the jakes, and then she sat down in his seat. 'He was making love to you.'

'*What*? What do you mean?'

'He was speaking the language of love.'

'The language of *love*?' Charlotte was completely flummoxed. 'In Italian?'

'*Sì*. I understood perfectly. I am from San Gimignano.'

'But – but it's impossible that Alex would talk to me that way!' said Charlotte, shaking her head. 'You must have misheard.'

'I misheard nothing.'

Charlotte was curious now, as well as flummoxed. 'What – what did he say?'

'Well, he started off by asking you if you really thought Italian was the sexiest language in the world. And then he speculated as to whether you were getting turned on listening to him speak it, because he was getting turned on watching you.'

'Are you *serious*?'

'Yes. He was also wondering about what you were wearing under your dress. He was very complimentary about the way you look, incidentally. He, erm, said he had a hard-on.'

'Oh! How – how very rude of him.' Charlotte took a sip of her wine, and then she took up her napkin and started pleating it. 'What was that stuff about "*coscia*"?' she asked.

'*Coscia*? Oh, yes – "*in alto sulla tua coscia*" means "at the top of your thigh". He wanted to touch you there. He said it in the nicest possible way.'

Charlotte couldn't help it. She had to know more. 'What else did he say? What was that "*molto molto*" stuff?'

'*Molto, molto lentamente*? It means "very, very slowly". That's how he wants to undress you.'

Oh, God! Alex couldn't possibly want to undress her! Was this waitress having her on?

Maria smiled at her. 'You're a very lucky girl.' People were always saying that to her when Alex was part of the equation. 'You heard the word "*amore*", didn't you?'

'No. I must have been singing too loud.'

'"*Fare amore*" means "to make love".'

'Alex wants to make love to me?'

'He certainly does.'

Charlotte thought hard, then shook her head again. 'He was obviously trying to send me up,' she said.

'I don't think so,' said Maria. 'Unless he is a *very* good actor. The last thing he said was the most beautiful of all.'

'What was it?'

'He said—'

'*Shhh*! Here he comes.'

Maria stood up to allow Alex to resume his seat. 'Can I get you anything else?' she asked them.

'I don't think so,' said Alex. 'Are you ready to leave, Charlotte?'

'Yes, thanks. Can you bring me the bill, Maria?'

'At once,' said Maria. And there was the hint of a smile on her beautiful mouth as she turned with a switch of her hip.

'Beautiful girl,' observed Alex. 'I wonder what nationality she is. I'm pretty sure she's not French.'

'No. She's – Norwegian.'

'*Norwegian*? How do you know? She certainly doesn't look it.'

'I asked her.' Charlotte knocked back the rest of the wine in an effort to quash the fluttery feeling that was going on big-time inside her. She couldn't look Alex in the eye.

'Enjoy the rest of your evening.' Maria was back with the bill.

'Thanks,' said Charlotte. She signed the slip, then added twenty per cent.

'Service is included,' Alex warned her.

'I know. But I know what it's like to be a waitress. Half the time they don't get to see any of the service charge, and tips make all the difference.'

Alex shrugged. 'It's your bill,' he said.

As they left the restaurant, Maria gave Charlotte a meaningful smile.

'*Tusen takk og god natt,*' Alex said urbanely, and Maria looked baffled.

'What did you say to her?' asked Charlotte.

'I said, "Thank you and good night" in Norwegian.'

Charlotte resisted the impulse to snigger. 'You speak Norwegian too?'

'A smattering.'

Well! Alex was proving to be chock-a-block full of surprises.

'You two must have got very cosy when I was in the jakes,' said Alex as they hit the footpath. 'She looked at you as if you were her long-lost best friend.'

'Maybe she's a lesbian,' improvised Charlotte. 'I understand loads of Norwegians are.'

They walked on in silence. The silence was rattling Charlotte badly, but Alex didn't appear to have a problem with it. He was humming something under his breath, a song that Charlotte identified at last as 'La Vie en Rose'. *He may speak honey-tongued Italian, but he's crap at holding a tune,* she thought abstractedly.

On the Rue St Pierre, she steeled herself to bid him good night.

'Are you mad?' he said. 'I'm not going to allow you to walk back to your hotel on your own. Someone might mistake you for a prostitute.'

'Thanks, Alex.'

'I don't mean the way you're dressed, sweetheart. I'm referring to the fact that the most notorious red-light district in Paris is a mere stone's throw away.' He took her arm, and Charlotte stiffened. 'What's wrong?' he asked her.

'Nothing,' she lied. She was actually extremely fazed by the unexpected physical contact.

They walked in an increasingly unsettling silence until they reached the door of the hotel, Charlotte acutely conscious all the time of Alex's hand on her arm. Oh, God, oh, God. What was happening? This wasn't right, this feeling that she was experiencing in the pit of her stomach. It felt as if some long-dormant animal in there was waking up and stretching, and the animal had no business doing that. *Bad dog*, she told it crossly. *Stop stretching at once.*

But if it was a dog, it was a very disobedient one. The nearer they got to the hotel, the more aroused the beast became. 'Do you want to come in for a drink?' Charlotte asked Alex as they drew level with the front door.

He shot a look at his watch. 'Why not?' he said. 'I don't have to be at Charles de Gaulle until midday tomorrow.'

'Me too,' she told him. 'We must be on the same flight again.'

'How serendipitous. After you.' Alex stepped back to allow her to precede him into the hotel.

She went through the door and took a right. 'The bar's that way,' said Alex, indicating left.

'I know. But there's an open bottle of champagne in my room, and I don't want to waste it.'

'OK,' said Alex.

They got into the lift together, and in the confined space, Charlotte was sure that Alex must be able to hear her heartbeat. It felt as if Meg White of White Stripes fame were performing a solo behind the cage of her ribs. In order to drown out the drumming, she started singing.

'Three, six, nine, the goose drank wine, the monkey chewed tobacco on the streetcar line … I wonder why that song's been stuck in my head all day?'

'It's the number of my hotel room,' said Alex.

'What is?'

'Three six nine.'

'Oh.' Charlotte shut up.

'Incidentally,' he told her, 'it's not "that's that" at the end of that song. It's "clap clap". That's why it's called "The Clapping Song".'

The lift door opened. 'This way!' she sang, walking down the corridor. When she went to swipe the lock, her fingers were so clumsy that she failed three times running.

'I'll do it,' said Alex, taking the card from

her. When his hand made contact with hers, she jumped as if she'd been electrocuted.

'What's up?' Alex asked her.

'Electric shock. The carpet must be synthetic.'

'It doesn't look synthetic,' he remarked.

'You can get some bloody good fake wool these days,' Charlotte told him knowledgeably. 'It's nearly as expensive as the real thing. Well, here we are.'

They were in the room.

Charlotte teetered towards the mini-bar. 'What'll you have?'

'A beer would be good.'

'Sit down! Sit down! Make yourself at home. Behold the motto on the wall. "He is the happiest, be he king or peasant, who finds peace in his home."' Oh, God. What was she twittering on about?

Alex sat down on the rocking chair and stretched his legs, crossing them at the ankle. Then he folded his arms up behind his head.

Don't do *that*! Charlotte wanted to tell him, but didn't. Instead, she busied herself with organising drinks.

'Mango?'

'What?'

'There's chocolate-covered mango in the fridge. D'you want some?'

'No, thanks.'

She handed him his beer, and then she sat on the bed, kicked off her beautiful shoes and tucked her feet underneath her.

'D'you mind?' Alex picked up the remote control.

'Do I mind what?'

'There's a match on.'

Oh, *shit*!

'No, no – fire away,' she said breezily. Oh – this was *useless*!

It was the ad break. One of those ads with a girl sucking on an outsize ice-cream was on. 'Those ads shouldn't be allowed,' said Alex.

'Why not?'

'Because they give men hard-ons.'

OK. This showed promise.

'Do they?'

'Er, yes.'

'What else gives men hard-ons?' Charlotte asked provocatively.

'Oh, you know – the usual suspects. Bare flesh, lingerie, dirty talk. We men are complete suckers.'

'If I talked dirty to you now, would it give you a hard-on?'

Alex looked as if she'd slapped him across the face. '*You*, Charlotte?'

'Yes.'

'I – I can't imagine you talking dirty.'

'Why not?'

'I've known you since I was a kid. You're a well-brought-up girl.'

'I'm also full of surprises. I surprised you that time in Coco de Mer, didn't I?'

There was something guarded about the way he was looking at her. 'Yes,' he agreed. 'You certainly did.'

'Would you like me to surprise you now, Alex?'

'I'm not sure,' he said carefully. Her eyes went to his crotch. His jeans looked suspiciously tight. She tore her eyes away with difficulty.

They looked at each other, then looked away again immediately. *Go away*! Charlotte told the syrupy sensation that was stirring in the pit of her stomach. *Don't dilate*, she commanded the pupils of her eyes. *Whatever you do, don't dilate*! But when she snuck a look, she could see that Alex's narrowed eyes had gone a much darker shade of green.

Oh, God. She was weak, now, from wanting him. She wanted to taste him, she wanted to inhale him, she wanted to feel his skin against hers. What could she do to make him want her too? Whisper dirty nothings in his ear, the way Thea had in the gazebo at Cholyngham? She tried to remember some of the lines she'd read in the *Black Lace Book of Women's Sexual Fantasies*, and realised that she had started to blush. Oh, Jesus. She couldn't talk dirty to Alex – she just *couldn't*.

The sexual tension that stretched between them was bowstring-tight. They were regarding each other with a kind of hungry desperation, and Charlotte was reminded of the way the brother and sister had looked at each other in the arthouse flick *'Tis Pity She's a Whore*, when they had realised the depth of the incestuous passion they felt for each other. Making love with Alex would be like committing incest. But what a sweet, sweet way to break a taboo!

She had to do *something*.

Charlotte slid off the bed and reached for the remote. She aimed it at the television and the screen went blank. 'I know sex isn't love, Alex,' she told him. 'But it's such an attractive facsimile.'

'Charlotte.'

'What?'

'Charlotte – if you're going to do what I think you might be going to do, I'm not sure—'

She put a finger on his mouth. 'Shh. Don't say anything, Alex. Just wait. Wait there.'

Alex put his head in his hands as she moved away, and she could hear his breath coming fast. In the walk-in wardrobe, her baby-blue baby-doll nightie hung on a padded hanger. She whisked it off, shot a meaningful backward glance at Alex, then went through the bathroom door and locked it behind her. *Oh, God – oh, God,* she thought, as she had a quick pee. Was she really going to do this? Was she really going to seduce her best friend? Yes, she was.

She flushed the loo, washed her hands and took a deep breath. Then – quickly, quickly, before she could change her mind – Charlotte stripped off her skin-tight cashmere, her bra and her knicks. Her lace-tops could stay. She stepped into the ruffly silk panties and pulled them up, and then she hooked herself into the matching bra, shimmied into the diaphanous chiffon and turned to face the mirror. Her skin was flushed and dewy. Her parted lips were plump and peony-pink, ripe for kissing. She loosened her hair and shook it out. It looked wild, but she had no time to do anything about that now.

Charlotte took a deep breath, then turned to the door. She twisted the key in the lock and pulled.

Nothing happened. She pulled again. Still nothing. She rattled the handle and tugged and tugged, exerting all her strength, but the door was obdurate. After several more moments of futile struggle, she gave up and sank down on the tiled floor.

'Charlotte?' came Alex's voice through the bathroom door. 'Are you all right?'

'No,' she called back in a plaintive wail. 'I'm not all right at all. I've locked myself in.'

Feeling as if she were in a bad dream, she watched the handle move to and fro. Alex was trying to open the door from the other side.

'It's not going to happen,' she heard him say. 'One of the pins must have jammed. I'll have to get the concierge.'

'OK,' said Charlotte morosely. She was still slumped on the floor, feeling like a deflated blow-up doll.

There was a beat or two of silence, then Alex's voice again. '*Bonsoir*,' she heard him say into the phone. 'I'm calling on behalf of Ms Cholewczyk. I'm afraid Madame has locked herself into her bathroom.' There was a pause, then: 'Thank you,' said Alex.

A knock came on the bathroom door. 'Charlotte?'

'Yes?'

'He'll be up as soon as he's located the spare key.'

'Great.'

Charlotte lay there feeling flaked out for several minutes, and then –

Shit!

She leapt up, only to be confronted by her image in the mirror again.

Sweet Jehovah! She couldn't allow the concierge to see her dressed like this. Quickly she discarded the incriminating lingerie and stuffed it into a Relais Geneviève laundry bag, then got back into her clothes, smoothing the cashmere over her hips just in time. The concierge was calling to her through the door.

'Madame?' he said. 'Please withdraw the key from the lock, and allow me to try from this side.'

Charlotte did as he asked. There was a smooth click, and the door swung open. Alex and the concierge were standing on the other side like Tweedledum and Tweedledee.

'I must apologise most profusely,' said the concierge. 'That is the second time this has happened in the last fortnight. I will ensure that the lock on this door is replaced.'

'That's all right,' said Charlotte. 'It's just as well my – brother was here to alert you.' She congratulated herself on her quick thinking. She didn't want word getting back to Geneviève Villiers that Ms Cholewczyk had been entertaining men in her hotel bedroom.

She caught Alex's eye. The toad! He was laughing at her.

'Well, thank you,' Charlotte told the concierge, willing him to go.

He took his cue, bowed and turned. Alex did likewise, winking at her over his shoulder as he ambled towards the door. 'Night, sis,' he said. 'Maybe I'll see you at the airport tomorrow.'

'Good night, Ms Cholewczyk,' said the concierge. 'And many apologies again for the faulty lock.'

'Good night.'

And as idiot Alex left the room followed by the concierge, Charlotte resisted the impulse to slam the door shut behind them.

Apologies for the faulty lock? Thank you, *thank* you, God, for the faulty lock! If she hadn't locked herself in the bathroom, she'd have ended up in bed with Alex Thornton, and she would never have been able to look him in the eye again. The thought made her shudder. Imagine sitting across the poker table from him, with him knowing what she got up to in the sack, and what her little peccadilloes were ... What had she been *thinking* when she'd set out to seduce him? One of the first rules of friendship etiquette was that you never *ever* sleep with your mates because it only leads to serious complications. She would evidently have to stop drinking so much – she was developing a serious case of beer goggles.

Oh, God, oh, God – what an *idiot* she'd made of herself! She remembered what Alex had said to her before she'd gone charging into the bathroom to dress up for him: *If you're going to do what I think you might be going to do, I'm not sure ...*

She finished the sentence for him. *I'm not sure I want you to? I'm not sure you won't make a complete arse of yourself? I'm not sure I'm going to be able to get it up for you, because I don't find you remotely sexually attractive ...*

Oh *God*, how humiliating. And as for all that Italian sex talk in the restaurant earlier? That was like a scenario straight out of a nasty Neil LaBute film. He'd clearly been sending her up rotten.

Her champagne flute was still sitting on the bedside table; Alex's beer was on the floor by his chair. Charlotte took the glasses into the bathroom and poured the contents down the loo. Then she started to take off her eye make-up. She would have to invest in a new brand of remover, she thought as she rubbed at her eyes with a cotton-wool pad. This stuff stung like fuck.

fifteen

The next morning found Charlotte strap-hanging again, on the train back to the airport. After lugging her suiter to the check-in, she ran the gamut of unsmiling French security and made her way to the departure gate.

There was bloody Alex, lolling in a bucket seat, talking on his phone. She pretended not to see him, but she was too late. He raised a relaxed right hand at her, and she moved across the departure lounge and sat down beside him on the seat he'd indicated.

'What time's the flight?' he was saying. 'OK. Book me in somewhere central, will you? … No – there's not a lot of point in going home and travelling all the way out to the airport again. I'll just have to buy a fresh set of underwear.' A low laugh, then, 'Yeah. You never know. Talk later, mate. Oh – organise a car to meet me at the airport in Dublin, will you? Thanks.'

Alex was clearly flying off again today.

'What's up?' asked Charlotte when he ended the call, glad to have something to small-talk about. 'Are you off to Ireland?'

'Yep. They want me to cover a rock festival in the Phoenix Park.'

'Cool. That's pretty short notice, though.'

'Lauren was to do it, but she's off sick.'

'Lauren's the one you collaborated with on the, er …' Oh, shit!

'On the sex-line scam, yeah.' Alex yawned and stretched.

Oh, God! What was the word to describe how he looked? Was it rangy? Or raunchy? The cotton of his T-shirt was like a second skin, his legs in bad-boy black were endless, the gap at his waistband showed a fine arrow of dark hair that pointed invitingly downwards.

'I wonder if I can pick up underwear at London City airport,' he mused. 'I can't remember—'

'Oh, *shit!*'

'What's the matter?'

'I've just remembered that I left my underwear behind in a laundry bag in the Relais Geneviève.'

He gave her a surprised look. 'Underwear's not irreplaceable, Charlotte,' he pointed out.

'This stuff pretty well is,' she said glumly. 'At least, *I* can't afford to replace it.'

'Oh.' Alex's phone started ringing. He looked down at it and turned it off. 'Was it that stuff from Coco de Mer, by any chance?'

'Yes.' She looked away from him.

'Charlotte?'

'What?'

'Charlotte, about last night—' he began, but thankfully he got no further, because an elegant woman slid into the seat on his left.

'Alex – hello! What fun,' she purred. 'We're on the same flight back.'

It was the redhead who had spent many air miles flirting with him on the Air France flight last Friday.

Charlotte couldn't hack witnessing more of the same behaviour. She got to her feet, said, 'Excuse me,' made her way to the loo and waited there until her flight was announced.

* * *

It was a working week from hell. After filing her Pantoufle copy, Charlotte learned that her next assignment was a campaign to revamp the image of Tastispudz, a food manufacturer that specialised in bar snacks. For years they'd gone with a caring, hand-picked, hand-cooked image, but the powers that be had decreed that what wasn't broken needed to be fixed.

'We want more street cred,' the middle-aged Tastispudz marketing manager told her over the phone. 'We want the Spudz to be wick-*ed* – know what I mean? We want the Spudz to be the bar snack of choice for the coolest kids in town. Forget all that "down on the farm" crap – most kidz' (Charlotte could have sworn that he'd actually said it with a 'z') 'these days don't even know what a potato is, anyway. Our spudz need to *rock*! Think Pot Noodle, think that cool kid grabbing the girl by the neck to get at her last Rolo, think me me me. That's your brief, girl. Now go get it.'

Charlotte put the phone down and hit her head off her desk, and then she put her head in her hands and did some thinking. And it wasn't Tastispudz she was thinking about. It was Alex.

She hadn't seen him since the fabulous redhead had commandeered him at Charles de Gaulle. In order to avoid him at London City, she'd whizzed her baggage trolley across the concourse like Eddie Irvine. Thank God Alex had taken himself off to Dublin and put the Irish Sea between them. She wondered how long his assignment might take. The longer the better – every minute that went by meant that that appalling incident in the Relais Geneviève was being relegated to past history. Sometimes the memory of her narrowing her eyes at him and saying, 'I know sex isn't love, Alex, but it's such an attractive facsimile,' rose in front of her mind's eye, and it made her want to whimper with mortification. What a misled fucking *idiot* she'd been!

The only good thing about the week was that it was now Friday and Mr Tastispudz had taken himself off to the golf course, where he was presumably going to have a wick-*ed* time with his big-swinging-dick pals. Viv had phoned earlier to suggest meeting up in the tapas bar after work, but Charlotte was feeling too damn wretched. 'No, thanks,' she'd said. 'I'm suffering from serious *Weltschmerz*. I'm staying in with the movie equivalent of comfort food.'

'And that is?'

'*An Officer and a Gentleman.*'

'Hey! The most politically incorrect movie ever made. What's the betting that by the end of the evening it'll be *An Ossifer and a Gennelman?*'

'How so?'

'I challenge any gal alive to watch that film without consuming a bottle of wine, getting ossified drunk and weeping tears of pure joy. Enjoy, Charlotte!'

At home, Charlotte got into her winceyette comfies, made herself cheesy mash, opened a bottle of Sauvignon Blanc, slathered her face with Clinique's Skin Calming Moisture Mask and slid the DVD into the player.

She had just got to the crying bit when the doorbell went. What clown was ringing her doorbell just as she'd got to the best bit in the film? Apes on the street always did that for a lark on Friday nights. She wouldn't answer it.

Richard Gere was picking Debra Winger up in his arms and carrying her through the throngs of cheering factory workers when Charlotte's phone went. 'Shut up,' she told it. Why couldn't people leave her alone? She was just about to divert the call to voicemail when she got a load of the name lighting up in the display. It was Alex.

Oh, God. It was Alex. She picked up.

'What do you want?' she asked him.

'It's my birthday,' he said.

'Oh. Happy birthday.'

'I'm throwing an impromptu party,' he told her. 'Wanna come?'

'I don't have a present for you.'

'I took the precaution of buying something I really, really wanted, for you to give to me. I couldn't run the risk of you buying the wrong thing. You can pay me back on the never-never. I won't charge you interest.'

'That's big of you.'

'Well, what do you say, Charlotte? Are you ready to party?'

'Alex, I'm dead tired. I'm having a quiet night in.'

'Watching *An Officer and a Gentleman*.'

'How did you know that?'

'Viv told me. I ran into her in the tapas bar. You still haven't answered my question. Are you coming to my birthday party?'

'No. Thanks for the offer. But that would mean I'd have to get dressed and made up and get on the tube, and I've done that already today.'

'In that case, the party will have to come to you.'

'What do you mean?'

'I'm downstairs. Let me up.'

'Alex, what are you playing at?'

The doorbell rang again.

'Do you hear the doorbell?'

'Yes.'

'That's me. Beam me up.'

Charlotte didn't say anything.

'Please beam me up, Charlotte. It's cold outside and I so want to open the presents you got me.'

She moved like an automaton to the entry phone and pressed the release.

'You're in,' she said. Then she slung her phone onto the couch, grabbed the empty wine bottle, dumped it in the bin in the kitchen and prayed that she wasn't wearing her beer goggles.

Unfortunately for her, she *was* wearing them. When Alex walked into her sitting room, the badly behaved dog that had taken up residence in her stomach lunged forward on its chain.

'Why in the name of heaven,' she asked him – because she could think of nothing else to say – 'are you carrying a Maplin's Electronics bag?'

'It has my presents in,' he said. He shut the door, moved across the floor and dropped the bag on the couch where she was sitting. There was an awkward kiss on the cheek. Then Alex started moving around the room, picking things up and putting them down again.

'I gave you this, didn't I?' he asked, fiddling with a tiny antique porcelain monkey.

'Yes. To wish me luck in my finals.'

He moved to the bookcase, trailed a finger down a spine or two, took out a couple of volumes at random.

'Catullus, Rochester ... You're a well-read young lady, Cholewzyck. Ah. So *that's* where that came from!'

Alex had taken down a volume of erotic verse.

'What?'

'"A wanton young lady of Wimley,"' read Alex, '"reproached for not acting primly, answered: 'Heavens above! I know sex isn't love, but it's such an attractive facsimile.'"'

Charlotte ached to tell him to piss off, but she managed to hold on to her equilibrium by sitting up very straight with her hands in her lap.

'What age were you when this was taken?' Alex asked, putting the book down and picking up a framed photograph of Charlotte as a child.

'I dunno. About seven, I suppose.'

'I remember. That's when I started to allow you to play football with me and the lads.' He picked up another photograph. 'And what age were you here?'

'Fourteen or thereabouts.'

'I remember you then, too. That's when I stopped allowing you to play football with me and the lads.'

'You were a pig. Why did you stop letting me play? I was good at football.'

'You were *very* good at football. Unfortunately, you were also very distracting. The lads tended to keep their eye on you rather than on the ball.'

Alex put the photograph down, then turned and regarded Charlotte with an expression that she didn't recognise. 'Who'd have thought it?' he said, as if to himself. He moved to the couch and looked down at her, and then he reached out a hand and undid the very top button of her sleep-suit. The way his thumb grazed her collarbone made her feel as if her skin were singing. He stood looking down at her for a long time, and the longer he looked at her, the more erotically charged the atmosphere grew.

'I – I thought you wanted to unwrap your presents?' she said, just for something to drop into the silence. Her voice was all wobbly.

'They can wait,' Alex told her, running a finger along the dip under her collarbone. 'I would very much like to unwrap you first.'

'You would?' She lowered her eyes.

'Yes.' He undid another button. 'If that's all right with you?'

Wine had made her woozy. 'Um. I think it might be. All right with me, that is.'

'I need to know for certain, sweetheart. Do you want me to unwrap you?'

'Yes, please.'

And when she gathered the courage to meet Alex's eyes, that feeling started again – the feeling she'd had when she'd made up her mind to seduce him in Paris, that syrupy feeling that made her want to reach up and pull his face down to hers and kiss his beautiful mouth.

Alex pushed her hair back from her face, and she took his hand and held the palm to her mouth. He tasted just as she'd always imagined he would – of soap and salt.

'Why is your face all shiny?' he asked her.

'I'm wearing Clinique's Skin Calming Moisture Mask. I always wear it when I watch my favourite DVDs. And I always eat a bowl of cheesy mashed potato and have some wine. It's an arcane girl thing.'

'You, Charlotte Cholewczyk, are a riddle wrapped in a mystery inside an enigma.' Alex held out a hand and pulled her to her feet. Then he undid another button and slid his hand inside her sleep-suit.

'That's beautiful,' she said.

He caressed her breast, rubbed the nipple with a thumb. 'What I'm doing to you or what I just said?'

'Both. You have exceptionally clever fingers, Alex.'

He undid another button, parted the winceyette lapels. 'I've had a lot of practice,' he said casually.

She flinched. 'Ow. That hurt. Is this going to be another of your one-night stands?'

'I think not. I don't do one-night stands with my friends. I want you for keeps, Charlotte.'

'You want me for keeps?'

'Yes.' He bent his head and kissed first her left breast, then her right.

'Say it in Italian.'

'*Ti voglio per sempre.*'

'But how could you want me when I'm wearing the comfies that you once told me even a man who hadn't had sex for a century couldn't find alluring?'

'I think,' he told her, 'that this is the most alluring outfit I have ever seen in my life. But sadly' – he undid another two buttons – 'it will have to come off if I am to access all areas.'

Charlotte felt Alex's hand slide along her belly. He smiled down at her, narrowing his eyes as he crooked a finger between her legs.

'Unwrap more of me,' she told him.

He slid the brushed cotton down over her shoulders, then released it so that it settled at her feet. She stepped out of the garment, and Alex knelt down, the better to admire her.

'Sweet Jesus,' he murmured as he kissed her there. 'This feels so good.'

'How does it feel?' she asked, pulling him closer.

'It feels,' he said, 'like coming home.'

He is the happiest, be he king or peasant, who finds peace in his home, Charlotte thought, with a smile. And then she stopped thinking altogether.

* * *

Later, in her bedroom, they pillow-talked, lying in each other's arms.

'How has it taken so long,' Charlotte asked, 'for us to get our act together?'

Alex shrugged. 'I dunno. I didn't even realise I fancied you until I got so fucking jealous the night you started batting your mascara at Finn.'

'I didn't bat my mascara at Finn!'

'You could have batted for England, my little Yahoo. And as for the signals you were sending out over dinner that night in Cholyngham! Holy shit! Theda Bara might have envied you your body language.'

'Well, it wasn't for Finn's delectation.'

'For whose delectation was it, then?'

Charlotte thought about it. She'd been preening for Mr Tall, Dark and Handsome across the Cholyngham dining room – or so she'd imagined. But when she thought about it some more, she realised that it hadn't been for his delectation at all. She reached for Alex's hand. 'You, Alex. I was doing it for you,' she said.

'Why?'

'I guess I wanted to piss you off. Show you what you were missing.'

'I wish I'd known it. I could practically

smell the pheromones wafting off you. If I'd realised that you were sending them in my direction, I'd have dragged you up to the Boudoir and ridden the arse off you.'

'You're such a sweet-talker, Alex Thornton. You make Mr Tastispudz sound like Shakespeare.'

'Who's Mr Tastispudz?'

'He is the geezer who's been single-handedly responsible for wrecking my head all this week.'

'A client from hell?'

'Where's worse than hell?'

Alex considered. 'Fuengirola?'

'OK. We'll make him from there.'

Alex's other hand roved in the direction of her derrière.

'Hell's teeth, this feels positively indecent,' remarked Charlotte.

'What does?'

'Lying naked in bed with you. It's kinda incestuous.'

'I guess it has to feel a bit like incest when you go to bed with one of your oldest friends.'

'That struck me, the night I decided to seduce you. I kept thinking of Charlotte Rampling in 'Tis Pity She's a Whore. I think that's why I told the concierge that you were my brother.'

'That cracked me up. That's when I knew I had to get out of there.'

'I thought it was rather inspired,' she told him, feeling piqued.

'Darling, that "he's only my brother" trick is one of the oldest in the book. I was truly astonished that the concierge managed to keep a straight face. What a trouper he was!'

'I wonder, did he get a load of the erotic vibe?'

'The erotic vibe was stone-dead at that stage – especially since you'd spent ten minutes cooling your heels in the bathroom, and had presumably had time to deplore your impulsive behaviour.'

'I didn't deplore it until later.'

'I did,' Alex said.

'Deplore it?'

'Oh, yes.'

She was astonished. 'What? *Why?*'

'Because you hadn't thought it through, Charlotte. That's why I asked you if you were sure you wanted me to make love to you tonight.'

'I had thought it through,' Charlotte said stubbornly. 'And it took some nerve, I can tell you, to dress up in Coco de Mer underwear and set out to entice one of my best friends into bed.'

'You had *not* thought it through. It only occurred to you when I said that men found ladies' lingerie a turn-on. I did try to side-track you, you know, when you took off to the bathroom, but you wouldn't let me.'

'Wouldn't I?'

'No. You were too busy enjoying one of those movie moments.'

'What do you mean, movie moments?'

'You know, when the heroine goes all meaningful.'

'I didn't go all meaningful!'

'No? Try this for size.' Alex cleared his throat and put a finger to her lips. '"Shh. Don't say anything, Alex. Just wait. Wait there,"' he said, in a mean parody of Charlotte's voice.

'Shut up, you complete bastard!'

Alex looked at her and crowed. 'You look just like you used to when you lost at Cluedo.'

'Piss off, pal.'

'Hell, how I love to picture you locked in that bathroom. I bet you felt like a right tool when you knew the concierge was on his way up – having to change out of your frilly scanties and into that brown dress.'

'It's not brown. It's camel.'

'Yeah,' mused Alex, 'all that leaping around in the bathroom like a character in a bad French farce must have really given you the hump.'

'Oh, God. I'd forgotten you had such a jejune sense of humour. Why do you take such perverse pleasure in winding me up, Alex Thornton?'

'You'd better get used to being wound up if we're going to start hanging out together, sweetheart.'

'I bet you didn't wind up that bloody red-head in the airport. I bet you were *charming* to *her*.'

'What redhead?'

'The one you flirted with on the plane.'

'Roxanne?'

'She was *never* called Roxanne! That's nearly as bad as my porn-star name.'

'What *is* your porn-star name?'

'Pussy Willow.'

'Pussy *Will*ow?' Alex assessed, then gave a nod of approval. 'Very *nice*.'

'And she really was called Roxanne?'

'Oh, yes. Foxy Roxy was actually responsible for me missing you at London City.'

'What do you mean?'

'I was hanging around the arrivals hall, waiting for you to emerge from the baggage reclaim, when she twisted her ankle and fainted with the pain. It was my responsibility as an Emergency First Responder to go to her assistance, so I missed you when you came through. The last I saw of you was your forlorn little face looking out of the Liverpool Street coach window.'

'You were waiting for me?'

'Yes. I wanted to tell you that I'd be stuck in Ireland until today.'

'You might have phoned.'

'There are some things, Ms Cholewczyk, that are better said face to face – as you found out this evening.' He touched her, and she melted, spooning herself a little closer against him.

'Did you loosen Roxanne's clothing when she fainted?' she asked provocatively.

'A little.'

'Did you enjoy it?'

'Not as much as I enjoyed loosening your flannelette thingy earlier.'

'Don't remind me of that! If I'd known you were planning on seducing me, I'd have worn something a little more appropriate.'

Charlotte thought ruefully of the lingerie she'd stowed away in the Relais Geneviève laundry bag and hoped that Geneviève would make sure that it was posted on to her.

'That reminds me.' Alex suddenly swung his legs off the bed and crossed her bedroom floor in all his glorious nakedness.

'Where are you going?' she asked.

'To get my birthday presents. Now that I've unwrapped you, I may as well unwrap *them*.'

When he came back into the room, Charlotte was lying with her arms above her head, a cat-who-got-the-cream expression on her face.

'You look like Goya's Maja,' he told her, upending the Maplin's carrier bag. A load of gift-wrapped parcels fell onto the bed. 'Now, give me my presents, if you would be so kind.'

She picked up one of the parcels and handed it to him. 'There,' she said, not bothering to stifle a yawn.

'That might have been said with a little more graciousness.'

'The prospect of watching you unwrap stuff from Maplin's doesn't fill me to the brim with excitement. I'd never have taken you for a Maplin's geek, Alex.'

He shrugged and tore away gift-wrap. 'Who said anything about Maplin's? I'm nearly as full of surprises as you, Charlotte. Oh, look, what have we here? You silly girl, you must have made some mistake when you went shopping for my birthday. They're quite clearly the wrong size.'

The item he pulled out of gift-wrap wreckage was not a Maplin's gadget. It was a pair of the darlingest knickers Charlotte had ever seen, polka-dotted and trimmed on each hip with a miniature geyser of multicoloured ribbons.

'I suppose you'd better have them.' Alex tossed them towards her and started on the next parcel. Again, no Maplin's crap thing emerged from the gift-wrap. This time it was a bra in watered silk, with teeny bows on the straps and a rosebud for a clasp. Then came a pair of French *directoire* knickers in hummingbird hues, a butterfly's wing of a camisole, a wisp of a suspender belt, a pair of gossamer stockings.

'Oh, oh, oh!' cried Charlotte.

'Pah,' said Alex crossly. 'You are *useless* at buying presents, Charlotte. I can't wear any of this stuff. You'd better have it all. And,' he said, leaning in to kiss her, 'you'd better wear it well.'

'I promise.' She wound her arms around his neck and kissed him deeply, then broke the kiss and said, 'Would Monsieur like me to model them for him now?'

'Why not?' Alex made himself comfortable against the pillows, reclining like a pasha, and Charlotte sang a little song as she riffled through the ruffly stuff.

'What'll I put on first?' she asked.

'This thing.' He picked up the cobwebby suspender belt and dangled it between thumb and forefinger. 'With the stockings.'

'*Bien sûr, Monsieur!*' she said, sliding off the bed. 'Since you have been such a model of munificence, your wish is my command.'

She wrapped the belt around her waist, inserted a careful foot into one of the stockings and proceeded to slide the silk up her leg.

'You do that most elegantly,' said Alex, narrowing his eyes at her. 'I'm deriving almost as much pleasure from watching you get dressed as I shall from divesting you of the same gear in the very near future. Look at the effect it's having on me. Is my penis as pretty as the ones on the Coco de Mer carrier bags, incidentally?'

'Those penises,' Charlotte told him, 'could have been modelled on yours.'

'You can certainly talk the talk, Cholewczyk. Put this on next.'

Charlotte continued her striptease in reverse.

'Now that we're an item,' she said conversationally, 'we'd better start doing item-y stuff, hadn't we? Where'll we go on our first date?'

'I've put a great deal of thought into that,' said Alex, watching with fascination as Charlotte adjusted the cascades of ribbon on the sides of her panties. He was clearly becoming more aroused by the minute. 'Take a look in the envelope on the bedside table. It's the only one of your birthday presents that I haven't opened yet. But put your new bra on first. I want to make sure it fits.'

She hooked the rosebud clasp, then pirouetted for his viewing pleasure. 'How do I look?'

'How do you think you look?' he said, with a nod at his erection.

'*That* hot?'

He slid the envelope off the table, waved it at her and crooked a finger. 'Come here, sweetie-pie.'

Charlotte clambered – carefully – onto his lap, took the envelope from him and peeked in.

'Oh, Alex!' she said, withdrawing two airline tickets. 'How preposterously romantic. When are we going?'

'Tomorrow. Coming back on Monday.'

She looked doubtful. 'What about work?'

'The tube's holding a one-day all-out. Didn't you see the headlines? Nobody in their right mind will be showing up to work on Monday.'

He took the tickets from her and tossed them onto the floor. 'Now,' he said, 'let me just make *absolutely* sure that this absurd confection of satin and tat fits properly …'

As he set about his meticulous inspection, Charlotte thought that Black Lace fantasies with their cut-and-thrust raunch did absolutely nothing compared with what Alex did to her.

epliogue

Charlotte was back at school. It was exam time, and she was trying to remember a Christina Rossetti poem. Miraculously, it came back to her – no problem!

'My heart is like a pair of shoes
That dazzle when they strut their stuff;
My heart's as soft as chocolate cream
And fluffy as a powder puff;
My heart is bubblier than fizz
And madder than a spending spree;
My heart is gladder than all these
Because my love is come to me.'

'Time's up. Time's up,' came the dear, familiar voice of the English teacher. 'Hand in your papers now, please.' The teacher started walking down the aisles between the desks, and Charlotte put down her pen and sat there feeling smug. She could hear his footsteps coming closer and closer, and then she heard him say, 'Full marks, Ms Cholewczyk. You got it right at last.'

'Thank you, sir,' she said, looking up from the paper and registering the gleam in Alex's green eyes.

And then she was waking up, in the most delicious way imaginable, with Alex's mouth on hers and his hand on her breast.

* * *

A lot later, they were on their way to the airport. Alex had bought *La Repubblica* and was reading bits out loud to her. Charlotte hadn't a clue what he was saying, but it didn't matter. She'd told him to save the best bits for bedtime.

'By the way, Alex,' she said, as he scanned newsprint, 'remember that time in the restaurant in Montmartre when you talked Italian to me?'

'Yep.'

'What was the very last thing you said to me?'

'Why do you want to know?'

'Because the waitress said it was beautiful.'

'How did she know?'

'She understood Italian.'

'What? I thought she was Norwegian?'

'She was – um –studying to be a translator.'

Alex looked alarmed. 'Are you telling me that she eavesdropped on that entire conversation?'

'No,' lied Charlotte. She didn't want to run the risk of putting him off ever speaking Italian to her again. 'She only heard the last bit. Can you remember what you said?'

'Um. Let me think. Was it something like: "*Perché ti ho sempre amato, sciocchina. Fino ad ora, non me n'ero reso conto*"?'

'Don't ask me. What does that mean?'

'It means: "I've loved you forever, you daft bitch. I just didn't realise it until now."'

'Oh! Is that why you had a picture of me riding a bike on your screen-saver?'

Alex looked alarmed again. 'You saw that?'

'I couldn't help it. It came on, that day I was in your bedroom in Paris.'

'I guess. It's a lovely picture. It reminds me of you when you were a little girl.'

'Oh! I think I might cry.'

'If you cry on me, I'll stop reading to you.'

'Yikes! OK. No tears. Go on with the paper.'

'*Lunedì ci sarà—*'

Charlotte's phone went. 'Yo, Anna!' she said.

'Hello, darling,' said Anna. 'Fancy making up a poker seven tonight?'

'Sorry, Anna. No can do. I'm going away with—' Oops! She didn't want to tell Anna on the phone about Alex, she decided. She wanted to tell her and Viv the good news over a bottle of wine and a dish of tapas. 'I'm going away with – my lover.'

Alex looked at her and made an 'I'm going to be sick' face. She stuck her tongue out at him.

'You have a lover?' squeaked Anna. 'Tell, tell!'

'No. I'll talk to you when I get back, on Tuesday.'

'Where are you going?'

'Paris.'

'Paris? But you *hate* Paris!'

'Not any more,' said Charlotte. 'Paris is, as far as I'm concerned, the most romantic city in the world. Byee, Anna! Talk soon.'

She put her phone away and turned to Alex with a big smile on her face.

'What was all that guff about lovers?' he said.

'Well, we are. Aren't we?'

'I suppose so. It feels a bit weird. But I guess I'm going to have to get used to it.'

'Go on with the newspaper.'

'*Lunedì ci sarà sciopero a Londra nella Metropolitana,*' read Alex.

'Oh, God,' said Charlotte. 'It does it for me every time. I'm such a sucker.'

And as Alex continued to read from *La Repubblica* about the London Underground strike, Charlotte found herself humming a little tune.

'What's that song?' Alex asked. 'My mother used to sing it.'

'It's "I Love Paris in the Springtime",' said Charlotte. 'And do you know something? I think I really, really will.'

She stretched out her legs so that she could admire her feet in all their Jimmy-Choo-ed glory, and smiled down at them.

The shoes smiled right back up at her. 'We love Paris too,' they said.